As the late afternoon slowly turned to evening, she ate from her meager food supply. Her spirits plunged again. She would be all alone tonight. All alone forever. An empty, lonely future yawned before her.

She sat up with a little fire as long as she could. Her laundry of shirt and panties hung on sticks near the flames. She didn't want to go to bed too early, afraid she would wake in the middle of the night. Night noises surrounded her, clicking and chattering sounds. She heard a coyote yelp in the distance, then an answering howl. But she didn't fear the dark; she feared her thoughts.

She couldn't concentrate so tried recalling pleasant events from her childhood. There had been plenty of wonderful incidents, she knew, but her mind was such a tangled jungle she couldn't recall even one with clarity.

Finally, climbing into her sleeping bag, loneliness overwhelmed her. Oh God, I'm sorry. Please just let me die tonight. I've messed up so bad, there's no way anything can be right again. I could never go home and face Dad. Anyway, home won't be the same with *them* there. Please, please just let me die tonight.

*What Reviewers are saying about Rosemount...*

"...*Rosemount* is a fictional account of an all too common story...a teen running from home. *Rosemount* clearly demonstrates how a successful, happy teen can resort to extreme action when no other options seem available."

...Cindy Penn, Wordweaving

"The characters are as varied as the route Leslie follows on her trek for independence--old, young, generous, selfish, nurturing, threatening. The author handles them all with insight and skill..."

... Gloria MacKay, Radio commentator and author of The Bubbles Go Up

"*Rosemount* is a superbly written tale of one young woman's trip from childhood to maturity, set in the exquisite--and exquisitely described--farm and ranch country of the Pacific Northwest."

... Elizabeth K. Burton, Blue Iris Journal

"*Rosemount* is a wonderful novel about teenage angst, deftly portrayed by Ms. Trimble's skill and perception. She succeeds in expressing the many uncertainties and attitudes of today's teenagers in a way that will invite understanding and acceptance. Leslie's story is one of learning, of accepting disappointment, of growth, and meeting one's goals."

... Denise Clark, Amazing Authors Showcase Reviews

# Rosemount

By

Mary E. Trimble

Copyright © 2001 Mary E. Trimble

Manufactured in the United States of America

ISBN 1-4392-2052-2

Cover: Ariana Overton

## *ONE*

Tension charged the kitchen. Leslie stood her ground, determined to set this thing straight. It wasn't easy. Her father, equally determined, wore an almost visible shield of resistance.

"Dad, I don't want to go away to school." She swallowed as her father's sharp blue eyes narrowed. Raising her chin, she continued. "What have I done to deserve this?" She sprang from the kitchen chair.

John Cahill pointed to the chair. She slowly lowered herself back down. Her bottom felt as if it had sprouted springs.

The other two had cleared out as soon as this conversation started, even before finishing their ham and scrambled eggs. Wade, never one to skimp on a meal, had scooped up one giant bite, snatched another piece of toast, grabbed his hat off the rack and vanished. Maureen had splashed a little more coffee into her cup and disappeared into the office. The coffee maker hissed as a drip of coffee hit the warming plate.

"Leslie," her dad said evenly, "I've never said you've done something wrong. This isn't a punishment, it's a privilege."

"It isn't a privilege if I don't want to do it!" *Why couldn't he understand?* Dread crawled up her spine. She swiped at her eyes with the backs of her fingers. She took a deep breath. Tears wouldn't do any good--she'd tried that and all it did was anger her dad. How many times had they fought over this--five, six times? *It's got to work this time.* He simply won't stand for much more argument.

"Leslie," her father said, obviously fighting exasperation, "you act like I'm sending you to prison. Rosemount Academy is one of the finest schools in the state, if not the country. Give it a chance."

"Why can't I just go to Chewack? I like school, *that* school. I've almost finished my sophomore year! All I want is to go back there, Dad. My grades are good, I like the teachers, most of them. All my friends are there. Please, Dad." Her velvet brown eyes searched his, beseeching. She grasped the table so hard her hands ached; she could feel her face redden.

"As outgoing as you are, you'll have new friends the first day."

"My music. What about my music?" Leslie's music was almost as important to her dad as it was to her. Before she died, her mother had played the piano and, although her dad didn't have musical ability himself, Leslie knew he loved listening to her play. She had always thought it probably reminded him of her mother. "I've studied with Mr. Baxter for years. I'll never do as well with another piano teacher."

"You don't know that. Rosemount has a fine reputation for its music department. Mr. Baxter himself told me that. Besides, Les, you'll have so many other cultural advantages there, things that don't happen in Chewack."

"Dad...*why*?" Ever since her dad had dropped this bomb, she'd never really known why he wanted to send her away to a boarding school. A *girls* school.

"Leslie, we've gone over this a dozen times."

"No, we haven't. Nothing you've said has made any sense. None of the stu... reasons have anything to do with me." She caught herself just in time--saying her father's reasons were stupid wouldn't win her any points.

"They have everything to do with you. That's why you're going."

"Is it because of that rape? For Pete's sake, Dad, that can happen anywhere."

"That rape happened on school grounds, Leslie, after a school dance that you attended."

"So what? *I* didn't get raped. I don't go to those dances alone, I had a date."

She abruptly stood again, almost knocking the chair against the kitchen wall.

Her dad stood, too, deliberately clumping his riding boots to the floor as he walked to the counter. Leslie noticed his hands shake as he poured himself another cup of coffee.

"Is that why, because of that rape?"

"No, Leslie, and you know it." He returned to his chair at the head of the table.

"Then why else?"

His eyes blinked slowly, impatiently. "We've been through all this."

"Because I went to that party? Are you going to hold that against me for the rest of my life?"

Leslie stared at her father, biting her bottom lip. Going to a party without adults present had been a big mistake, but not the end of the world. Going to this stupid school would be the end of the world.

"Oh, Dad." She plopped back down onto the chair. "It was no big deal. Kip and I were there for about an hour, then left. Stuff didn't start happening until long after that."

"Still, you were there. When that girl's parents got home and found all the beds in the house messed up, their place almost destroyed --"

"It wasn't destroyed! The guys that stayed said there were a couple of cigarette burns on the coffee table and a broken window. The place wasn't that great to begin with!"

"That isn't the point. The point is, you're not to go to parties without adults present. I'd made that clear."

"I know. And I promised you it wouldn't happen again. Don't you believe me?"

Her father waved his hand in the air, erasing the conversation. "Leslie, this isn't getting us anywhere. It isn't any of these things. It's everything that's happening today. It's drugs, drinking, gangs, sex. I want you to go to a good school, get a good education and be *safe*. It's as simple as that."

Tears threatened again, "But I don't drink, do drugs, or have sex! The only *gang* I belong to are the kids I went to kindergarten with! I want to stay here at the ranch with you, with my family." She slumped disconsolately, lowering her head in her arms on the table. "Please don't send me away," she begged, her voice muffled.

"Honey," her father said softly, "you're making up your mind without even knowing what the school is like. When we visit Rosemount Academy next month you'll see what a great place it is. Don't judge it before you see it."

Leslie bolted upright and glared at her father. "I want to stay here. I don't have to see Rosemount to know that."

"You're going, Leslie." His voice, though quiet, was final.

"But Dad, none of the other girls are going. Why am I the only one?"

"Some are."

"Well sure, the dorky ones, but none of my friends."

"The other girls aren't any of my business, you are."

"*Whyyy*? Why are you sending me away? Don't you love me?"

John's large, open palm slapped the table. Breakfast dishes clattered. The butter knife leapt out of the butter dish and stuck to the table.

"Leslie! How can you even ask such a thing? It's *because* I love you! There's too much going on around here these days. I want you to be safe and to have a good education. That's it. That's the reason. Period."

"You didn't send Wade away."

"Stop saying I'm sending you away. I'm sending you to school--to one of the most expensive, finest schools in the state."

"So, why didn't you send Wade to an expensive school?"

Her father's eyebrows rose at her sing-songy, sarcastic voice. He leveled his index finger at her. "Like it or not, Leslie, life is different for a boy than it is for a girl. You have dangers that your brother never had. Besides, he's eleven years older. It's worse now than it was then."

"That isn't true. You can't tell me rape is a new thing-- rape's been happening since the beginning of time. Some of the drugs are new, but how about drinking? And you can't tell me that kids never used to have sex! That's what shotgun marriages were all about!" Leslie's voice ascended from above normal to almost shouting. Her throat hurt, her head throbbed.

"You will not talk to me in that tone." His voice was strained, his face dark. "We've talked about this enough, Leslie."

"Oh, right. As soon as I start talking about how it really is, the conversation's over."

"That will do."

Leslie, defeated, watched her Dad rise. Through her hot tears there seemed to be two of him. He put his coffee mug by the sink and turned to the door. He reached for his Stetson where it perched on the hat rack by the door and, in slow motion, put it on. Two hats, two heads. Slowly, he turned back to Leslie.

"Leslie."

A tear slid down her blotchy, red cheek, unchecked. She slowly shook her head. She'd never agree to this. Never.

He expelled a long, jagged sigh. He turned and stomped down the back porch stairs. Seeing Wade on horseback, he blew a shrill cattleman's whistle and, raising his arm, signaled his son to wait.

## *TWO*

Kip invited Leslie to a school year-end party, chaperoned, she assured her dad. He would be by soon to pick her up. She had just stepped out of the shower and put on her bra and panties. She stood in her bedroom in front of the full-length mirror on her door. Turning from left to right she scrutinized her body.

Shapeless. And skinny. When will I ever get a real figure? Some girls complain that they're too fat, but at least they have something to put in their bras.

She turned to face the mirror again. That stupid Gordon Evans said that if I stuck out my tongue I'd look like a zipper. She stuck out her tongue.

*He's right.*

Leslie rarely wore anything but jeans but this party was a dressy event. Her satin teal dress, accented with a long pearl necklace and drop pearl earrings, and sandals made her feel older, more sophisticated. She looked in the mirror again.

*That's better.*

Leslie heard the doorbell ring, it was Kip arriving a few minutes early. The murmur of his and her dad's voices floated up from the living room. When she made her appearance, her father's eyes shone. Kip stood suddenly, eyes bulging.

Leslie blushed. *I should dress up more often if it causes this much reaction.*

Although the party was a success, at times, sad feelings crept up on Leslie. She would be giving up these friends when she went to Rosemount--kids she had known almost all her life. With this group she felt accepted and popular. Tonight she even felt pretty.

During the evening Kip and Leslie made plans for the summer--swimming at Long Lake, picnics, riding with friends. Kip had a summer job, but they'd still get together.

Leslie and her best friend Janelle had made plans too, mostly long horseback rides, maybe even an overnighter in the hills.

Leslie looked forward to the coming vacation. The most important thing I have to do this summer is to show Dad I'm reliable. I'm going to help around the ranch. I'll help Maureen with the garden. And I'll be cheerful. I want him to know he can trust me. I won't cause him any worry. If I'm good and work extra hard, maybe he won't send me away.

Leslie decided to approach her dad about Rosemount once more. On the last day of school, while her dad relaxed with his newspaper after supper, she sat on his footstool and presented him with her report card.

John's eyes glowed with pride. "Leslie, I'm really proud of you. I know how hard you worked for these grades. I'd like to take you out to dinner, to celebrate."

Leslie took a deep breath. "Dad, you know what I'd really like?"

"What, honey?"

"To stay at Chewack High. Dad, I'll really work hard, I won't get into trouble --"

"Les, I've always thought you worked hard. Sometimes I think you work too hard. Getting into trouble has nothing to do with it. I'm sending you to Rosemount for *your* sake, for *your* good. You'll do so well there with your fine work habits. It'll be wonderful college preparation."

"I have good college preparation where I am. That's why I'm taking honors classes."

"According to the paper," he pointed to a column in the local newspaper, "the number of college bound kids from Chewack is only thirty percent. I don't like the sound of that."

"But I *am* planning to go to college, Dad." Her eyes pleaded with her father. "I don't want to go to Rosemount. Please."

"I've made an appointment for the two of us to visit the school during their open house on Friday, July 25th." He put his hand on her shoulder and looked deep into her eyes. "Let's not talk about it again until we visit the school."

"I don't want to even *see* that school, Dad."

"Les, we're going, Friday, July 25th."

*~*

After breakfast during the first week of summer vacation, Wade approached Leslie. "Sis, now that school's out, I could use your help." Wade had been up since before sunup but had returned to the house for breakfast. Leslie's day had just begun.

"When?"

"Now."

"Why can't one of the hands help you?"

"Because they're busy doing something else."

She'd hoped to go riding with Janelle that afternoon. But, if she was going to prove herself to Dad, she should cooperate. Anything to get him to change his mind about Rosemount.

"For how long?"

"What do you mean, how long? However long it takes."

Her father had already left the table and sat at his desk in the office, off the kitchen, hunched over the accounts. Although he expected Leslie to do her share, he had never insisted she do the hard, rough ranch work. She wondered if her dad and Wade had discussed this.

"Let's *go*," Wade said, taking a final gulp of coffee. "Put on your work clothes, unless you want to get that mucked up," he nodded to her crisp white blouse and light blue jeans. Heading toward the door, he donned his hat.

"I was going to practice the piano right after breakfast."

"Practice tonight. Come *on*."

He stepped to the back porch and whistled for Dutch. The Blue Heeler brushed against Wade's leg. He reached down to scratch the top of her head. "Ready to earn your keep?" Her black and white short fur had a bluish tinge and looked coarse, but was soft to the touch. Now almost four years old, Dutch lived for Wade, always ready to go anywhere with him.

Leslie began to clear the breakfast dishes, but Maureen urged her to go ahead. "Change your clothes and go with your brother, dear, I'll take care of these few dishes."

Leslie changed into work clothes and met Wade at the barn. He had hitched the stock trailer to the dusty Ford pick-up. He had brought both horses from the corral, saddled his mount, Jake, and loaded him into the trailer. Both John and Wade worked fast but never looked hurried. Leslie was amazed that her brother could have done so much in such a short time.

"Shake a leg," he called. "How can changing your clothes take so damn long?"

Leslie quickly curried her mare. She took a second to kiss the long, narrow nose. "I love you, Polly."

The mare's ears followed Leslie as she went about her work. After brushing the coat smooth, Leslie placed the saddle blanket on the mare's back and slid it down to make sure no hair laid the wrong way. After cinching the saddle, she led the horse out of the barn and loaded her into the trailer.

Wade and the dog were already in the truck warming up the engine and listening to country music. As soon as Leslie climbed in they pulled out. Wade grinned at her. "Good girl. I think you set a personal record saddling up."

She sniffed. "I don't know what the hurry is."

"Daylight's burnin'."

Wade drove by the tenant's house where the foreman and his family lived, then passed a double-wide mobile home where another hand lived. Leslie opened a gate and they followed the rough road until it gave out.

They unloaded their horses, mounted and began to climb the rocky slope, up to a summer pasture where they reached a small herd of cow-calf pairs. They began to gather them.

In other situations Wade was the epitome of patience, even when teaching her to drive the car. With horses and stock he was always gentle and kind, though firm, but he had no patience with inattentive help. He yelled now.

"Leslie! Will you watch what you're doing?"

"Les, it may surprise you to know that you're supposed to be smarter than the stock!"

"Damn it! Are you splitting the herd on purpose?" he broke away to gather the strays.

"Stop yelling at me!" She knew she wasn't doing a good job. She just couldn't seem to keep her mind on the work. She'd looked forward to riding with Janelle today but instead she was out here working with a bossy brother.

"Stop screwing around, then. Pay attention."

"I can't even think when you yell at me!" She started to turn her mare. They'd been out for less than an hour but she was ready to call it a day. She'd had it with Wade. "I'm going home."

"You'll stay until the job is done."

"Then stop yelling," she shot back, trying to salvage her dwindling dignity. Wade was her brother, but out here, he was also the boss.

Wade lowered his voice. "Les, don't be so sensitive. I know you'd rather be someplace else, but I need your help. We've got to move this bunch today. Just stay alert and watch what you're doing, okay?"

She sighed. "Okay. Why do they have to be moved?"

"Because the grass is thinning out. I want to save this pasture for late summer."

"Why did you bring them here in the first place? They've only been here about a week."

"Two weeks. These are first-time heifers. We wanted them closer to headquarters to keep an eye on 'em until the calves straightened out after branding."

She rode slowly alongside the herd, keeping her distance. Cattle were touchy about being crowded.

Leslie watched her brother scan the herd; she did likewise, but knew she didn't see nearly as much as he. If you pay attention and used good "cow sense," she had been told often enough, cattle will tell you what's on their mind.

He pointed to a cow standing apart, head hanging. "Look."

"What about her?"

"Look at her udder. She's almost bursting. Where's her calf?"

"I'll go look," she said, swinging behind the herd and up the small hillside where the miserable cow stood.

Leslie kept her distance from the cow, not wanting to spook her.

"Where's your baby?" she asked softly, making a large circle around the cow. Leslie looked down a slope and saw the little carcass, grotesquely bent and partly devoured. Apparently the calf had slipped on shale, falling down the ravine, then couldn't climb back up. It hadn't taken long for a coyote to find it. The cow bawled pitifully.

"Oh, girl, your baby died." Sympathetic tears stung Leslie's eyes. She could never be as tough as Wade or her dad, though she knew it bothered them too when something like this happened. She signaled her brother.

He rode to where Leslie stood and looked down the slope at the little broken body. "Well, that's too bad," he said, resigned. "We'll move her with the others until we reach a place where we can bring the truck and trailer in, then take her home."

"Why?"

"We'll see if she'll take to that orphan calf."

Leslie shook her head. "With over a thousand head, I don't know how you can keep track of every single one."

Wade nodded. "I'm still not as good as Dad. I've seen him scan a herd of a hundred cows, all of the same color, size, and shape, and tell you which cow was missing. Not many can do that. It takes years of experience."

It was mid-June and already hot. Dust swirled around the rough, rutted trail, caking into any crevice it could find. Wade's neck looked as though someone had drawn pencil lines on it. Dark sweat stains blotched the back of his denim shirt. Leslie knew she bore the same trail marks.

She wore sunglasses but her face was slippery with sweat and the glasses slipped down her nose. She tried to concentrate on her job and forget her discomfort.

"That calf is shaking his head," she pointed. "Look there, that other one is, too."

They rode over but the calves split off in different directions. Dutch took off after one, barking and nipping at its heels. Wade dropped a rope over the closest one and, as he slid out of his saddle, his horse kept the rope taut. Wade threw the calf on its side and tied its feet, all in a matter of seconds. The little steer bawled and struggled, then suddenly lay very still and rolled its terrified eyes. Getting closer, they smelled the problem. Maggots. The calf had been dehorned during spring round up, and now a brownish fluid oozed around the horn cavity, hosting the maggots.

"Whew!" Leslie said. "There's a smell to remember. What will you do?"

"Nothing. Maggots eat the dead flesh, then drop off. Maggots are actually used in healing, sometimes even with people. They eat infected skin. We'll try it on you next time you get a cut."

"Oh, nice."

When they crossed a trail that would accommodate the truck and stock trailer, Wade left Les with the herd. "Just keep 'em together--don't let 'em wander off. There's enough grass here to hold them for awhile."

While Wade was gone, Leslie slowly rode Polly around the cattle, gently keeping them grouped together. Time dragged on. She found a shady spot and dismounting, let Polly graze.

A hawk glided against a blank sky, circled, swooped down and plucked up a mouse. Leslie could see the tiny legs and a tail protruding from the hawk's talons.

Mounting again, she slowly made a circle around the cattle, gently prodding them to stay together. Finally, she heard the whine of the truck and the rattle of the trailer climbing the steep hill.

Wade pulled up a short distance from the cattle and unloaded Jake. He rode into the herd to sort out the cow who had lost her calf and dropped a rope around the cow's neck. She instantly pulled against him. It took all of his and Jake's strength and cunning to work her toward the trailer. Once there, Wade threw a rope around the rack and slowly hauled her into the trailer, the cow kicking and snorting every inch of the way. Wade shut the gate between compartments to make room for the horses when they returned from settling in the rest of the herd.

Leslie watched, impressed. "It's easy to see why that trailer gets so beat up."

"Yeah, we could use a new one but it takes so long to customize it, we hate to give this one up." The sixteen-foot stock trailer was indispensable to their operation. Over the years, they had altered it with a welded hitch, racks and special tool compartments. The trailer not only hauled stock, but also served as a portable corral and catch-pen in outlying areas.

By mid-afternoon they arrived at a high summer pasture ringed by tall pine. A spring-fed stream gurgled through the lush green pasture. Later in the summer, when it dried up, the herd would be moved again. There were other summer pastures on Circle C, each could hold perhaps a hundred or more head of cattle.

They headed back toward the truck and stock trailer. Free of herding, Leslie relaxed and enjoyed the ride. She liked these times with her brother, when he was relaxed and didn't have a reason to yell.

Wade sure knew the cattle business; Dad had gradually turned more of the responsibility over to him. When a question came up, the men asked Wade first, unless Dad was right there with them. Wade was a good brother and through the years they had gotten along well. He was dating Teresa Wagner. Leslie liked her.

They were comfortable in their silence, but Leslie wanted to talk.

"Wade, I don't want to go to that boarding school."

"I gathered that."

"It's so stupid! I don't know what's gotten into Dad."

"I guess he feels it will be a better place for you than Chewack." He leaned forward to shoo away flies that buzzed Jake's ears.

"But why?" They had been riding two abreast but the trail narrowed and Leslie dropped back. They zeroed in on her--she fanned her hand in front of her face.

"Why?" she repeated.

Wade turned his head so she could hear. "I guess he's worried about drugs and gangs, stuff like that."

"Don't you think he trusts me?"

"I think he does, Les, but he wants you to be safe."

"What do you think?"

Wade shrugged.

"Wade?"

"Well, I'm sorry you're unhappy about it, but it's Dad's decision."

"That's a chicken answer."

He shrugged again.

"Would you talk to him for me?"

"Les, I tried but I didn't get very far. I don't know what more I can say."

"Tell him you think it's stupid."

"Uh-huh."

"No, really. Tell him you think I'm doing all right here. Tell him how miserable I'd be if I went to Rosemount. Tell him I'll kill myself if --"

"Hey."

"Well, just tell him, politely, what a rotten idea it is."

They rode in silence. Leslie watched Polly's head nod to the rhythm of her feet. The truck and trailer were in sight.

"Wade? Will you talk to him? He'll listen to you."

Wade lifted his hat and ran his sleeve along his brow, then settled his hat back in place. "We'll see. Let's load up now, get this cow home."

## *THREE*

"Dad, are we going to have a Fourth of July party this year? It's almost the last week of June. If we're going to, we'd better plan it now."

Leslie had joined her dad and brother in the ranch office. Two doors led to the office, one from the kitchen and the other from outside, keeping ranch traffic separate from the family.

John and Wade were planning their July work. John sat at his usual place behind the desk. Wade sprawled in one of the chairs opposite it. Leslie sat in the other matching chair.

"Sounds good to me," John winked at his daughter.

"Who should we ask?" Last year she invited Janelle and another girl from school. This year she wanted to invite Janelle and Janelle's boyfriend Wally, and Kip. The Fourth of July was a big day at the ranch, a time when everyone invited friends.

"Wade, are you going to invite Teresa this year? I hope so--I want to get to know her."

"Planned to."

"Who else shall we ask?" Leslie reached for a pad and pencil from the desk.

John began listing the hands --

"Dad, last year Ken's friend was some barmaid from the Roadside Tavern. She squinted all day, it'd been so long since she'd seen daylight."

John stifled a chuckle and shook his head. "Les, who the hands ask is their business."

"Okay, who else? Let's ask Janelle's folks and their kids, and the Jacksons." She added the number of people. "That would make twenty-one people, if everyone can come."

"I would like to invite a friend and her daughter," John said, his voice stiff.

Leslie's amazed eyes settled on her father. "Who?"

"Her name is Lilith, you've probably seen her at the bank. She's a loan officer there. Her daughter's name is Roxanne."

"Oh." Leslie was so shocked she didn't know what to say. She had never thought of her father seeing another woman. Dating! "How old is Roxanne?"

"About thirteen."

"Oh."

"Les, how about you going over the food with Maureen. Let's plan on about twenty-five people. You call Holtons and Jacksons and your friends, we'll take care of the hands and our guests. Wade and I'll take care of beer or whatever, and the fireworks."

"All right. I'll talk to Maureen and make the calls." Leslie left the office, a frown creasing her forehead.

Maureen stood at the sink, her round body in a loose-fitting, faded cotton dress. She wore sturdy shoes to support her considerable weight.

"Maureen," Leslie stood close, dropped her head down. She spoke softly so she wouldn't be heard in the other room, "did you know that Dad is *seeing* someone?"

Maureen nodded. "I suspected so."

"Well, why didn't I know?" Leslie demanded, still whispering.

"I guess you've been involved in your own things."

"When has he seen her?"

"I suppose when he goes into town."

"He always seems to be home in the evenings. Except Saturdays, when he plays cards." Oh, he doesn't always play cards. *Why does it seem like he was sneaking around?* "Why didn't he say something?"

"He probably wasn't ready. Does it bother you?"

"No!" Leslie snapped, too quickly.

"He's been alone a long time, honey."

"Well, we're here. That's not exactly being alone."

"You know what I mean."

Leslie sighed and nodded. "I know. Have you met her?"

"I've seen her at the bank. You probably have, too. What did I hear about a party?"

"Oh! The party!" They forgot everything else and started their planning.

## *FOUR*

The Fourth of July morning sparkled clear and sweet. Ranch work was minimal on the holiday, allowing everyone time to prepare for the party. This would be a day of good food and fun.

Leslie wandered over to watch her father maneuver long-handled tongs to arrange charcoal in the brick barbecue pit. He'd built the fireplace himself years before.

"Can I do anything for you, Dad?"

"No, honey, I'm almost through here."

"When will you start the meat?" She loved watching her father work. He tackled every job with enthusiasm and energy. All her life she had heard of others' respect for her father and she had always been proud of him.

"Maureen said two o'clock, give the people time to enjoy the snacks. Some spread, huh?"

She noticed for the first time that he wore a new western-cut shirt, white, with shiny trim. Even at fifty-six he was still lean, a bit thicker around the waist than Wade, but still strong and tough. Out of habit, he wore a Stetson, his good one today, which covered his dark, short hair. Gray streaked his temples and, except for a little receding, he had nearly a full head of hair. His tan twill pants showed an oval, silver belt buckle with a large turquoise stone in the center.

"I've never seen that belt buckle before."

"It was a gift, from Lilith."

"Oh." Then, trying to recover from the fear of learning more about her father's relationship with this woman, "When are they coming?"

He glanced up. "Here they come now."

A new silver Honda made its way down the dusty driveway, going too fast, making the dust swirl.

Her father hung the tongs on the rack and carefully wiped his hands on a towel. He glanced at Leslie, who stood watching the newcomers.

"Come on, I want you to meet them."

A woman, Leslie's height, about five eight, climbed out of the car. Trim and fit, she wore creased jeans with a subtle plaid blouse and sparkling white tennis shoes. Gray streaked her short, curly hair. On her it looked good. Her face was open and friendly. She smiled as Leslie and her father approached. Her daughter remained in the car.

"Hi," the woman said to John, extending a manicured hand. John took her hand, held it, and turned to Leslie.

"Lilith, this is my daughter, Leslie. Leslie, this is Lilith MacIntyre."

"Hello," Leslie said, trying to keep her smile bright and her eyes off their clasped hands.

"Hello, Leslie. I'm glad to meet you." She leaned toward the car window. "Roxanne, come on."

"I'm staying here."

"Come on," Lilith said through gritted teeth.

Roxanne flounced out of the car and walked around to where her mother stood.

"Hi, Roxanne," John said. He introduced the girls. John and Lilith dropped their hands.

"Hi," Leslie said. *Oh no. I've heard about this girl.* She had to concentrate to keep from staring at Roxanne's crimson, spiky hair. The spikes on top were about two inches long, the sides of her head shaved.

"Hi," Roxanne answered, her voice distant. Her eyes roved toward the food table.

Roxanne didn't enjoy many of her mother's good qualities. They both had the same pretty gray eyes with enviably long eyelashes, but Roxanne was shorter than her mother, and plump. Stretched across her stomach and over her ample bottom, her tee-shirt read "Let's Get It Going." Her jeans looked uncomfortably tight. Her head and the rest of her body looked as though they belonged to two different people. Leslie disliked her immediately.

Janelle and her boyfriend arrived. "Excuse me," Leslie politely said, "more friends are arriving." She hurried away.

Janelle and Wally climbed out of Wally's truck, greeting people and waving. As usual, Wally headed to where the men gathered.

"Sometimes Wally seems like an old man, doesn't he?" Janelle observed as the two girls turned toward the house.

"Maybe he just feels more comfortable around men than with mixed company," Leslie suggested.

"That's what I mean!" Janelle laughed. She was a pretty girl with golden hair, worn straight and short.

"Les, we have to leave early today. Wally promised his brother he would help with their fireworks."

"Okay, but I wish you'd be here for ours."

"Me, too. Where's Kip?"

"He had to go to Oregon for a family reunion. He said he'd rather come to our party but he couldn't talk his folks out of it."

"Oh, that's too bad."

They automatically went up to Leslie's room. She loved her room, her sanctuary.

Leslie's bedroom showed her budding taste in decor. Just this past year she selected matching soft-color floral bedspread and curtains, transforming the bedroom from a little girl's to a young woman's room. An area rug, a gift from Maureen, which bore the same muted colors, lay at the foot of the bed. Near her bed stood a large oak dresser, at the side of the bed a night stand. Her desk was at the other end of the room next to an overloaded bookcase.

The girls stood at the window. They looked down at the guests, observing and commenting on each in turn.

"Who's that talking to your Dad? She looks familiar."

"It's that woman I told you about, the one he's *going* with."

"Do you think it's anything serious? Do you like her?"

"I don't know. I do know I don't like her kid, that fat girl with the weird hairdo hovering over the food."

They watched as Roxanne positioned herself by the corn chips, scooping one after the other into the bacon dip.

"Calorically challenged, Leslie," Janelle said in mock reprimand. "Her hair *is* weird. Her mother's pretty though."

"Hmmmm."

They stood by the window several minutes longer, chatting while watching the growing crowd. Wade had gone into town to pick up Teresa and they were just arriving. Right behind Wade, Janelle's parents and little brothers drove in.

Leslie saw her dad glance up at her bedroom window.

"I'd better see if I can help. Come with me," she urged.

The two traipsed back and forth from the kitchen to the burdened tables, carrying dishes, silverware and food. Maureen gave them the job of shucking corn. They settled happily under the dense shade of a magnolia in the side yard.

John made his way to them, stopping to greet guests and give pats on backs as he strode their way. "Leslie, I think it would be nice if you asked Roxanne to join you."

Leslie looked up at her father. "We're just shucking corn, Dad."

"I know, and I'd like you to ask her to join you. She doesn't know anyone here, Les."

Leslie rose stiffly. She walked over to where Roxanne stood, still by the table.

"Roxanne," she said, forcing herself to be civil, "would you like to help Janelle and me shuck corn?"

"Who's Janelle?"

"My friend."

"Where?"

"By that tree," Leslie said, pointing.

John stood by for a moment, then, apparently satisfied, returned to his barbecuing.

"Would you like to?" Leslie repeated to Roxanne. *Say no, say no.*

"Okay."

*Rats.* Leslie led the way to the old magnolia, introduced Roxanne to Janelle, and resumed shucking.

"So, what do you do?" Roxanne asked, picking up an ear.

"Shuck 'em," Leslie answered. *What a dumb girl.*

"I've never done this before."

Janelle looked up, dumbfounded. "You haven't?"

"No, we buy the frozen kind, in a box."

Leslie's mouth dropped open. "You've never eaten corn on the cob?"

"No, my mom says it sticks in her teeth."

Janelle suppressed a giggle. Leslie concentrated on her ear of corn, not daring to look at her friend. She placed the clean ear of corn in a large dish pan and reached for another. She noticed the one Roxanne placed in the pan.

"Roxanne, you have to take off this stuff, the silk."

"Why?"

"Because it isn't good to eat."

"You could use it as floss," Janelle said under her breath.

Leslie laughed. "Janelle!"

"Sorry," Janelle attempted to straighten her mouth.

Roxanne stared at them. "What?"

"Nothing," Leslie said. "Here, I'll show you."

"Never mind. Do your own stupid corn." Roxanne dropped the unfinished ear on the grass and stomped off. She glanced around for her mother. Finding her, she stood next to her, pouting. Lilith turned to her daughter but Leslie couldn't tell what they said.

"Oh Leslie, I'm sorry. I didn't mean to make her mad. I hope it won't get you in trouble."

"Don't worry about it. She's strange."

Leslie's eyes dropped when she saw her dad look at her, a steady questioning gaze. She looked up again. He still looked at her, the brush he used to apply Maureen's spicy barbecue sauce with hung suspended in his hand. She shook her head and shrugged her shoulders as if to say 'I couldn't help it.' He turned his attention back to the barbecue, apparently convinced.

Leslie made sure that when they ate she sat next to Janelle and Wally, at the end of the table where there was no more room, hoping to avoid any suggestions about inviting Roxanne to join them.

After dinner John again approached Leslie with Roxanne in tow. "Leslie, I'll bet Roxanne would like to see that new foal."

"Oh, sure!" Leslie answered brightly. "Roxanne, one of our brood mares just had a foal. Come on, I'll show you." Leslie smiled, making a genuine effort to be friendly. Roxanne shrugged and followed Leslie.

As they made their way to the corral, the shiny black mare whinnied and dropped her head to her offspring. The little foal leapt around on stilt legs, keeping huge, curious eyes on the girls.

Leslie stepped on the lowest rail of the fence, signaling Roxanne to do likewise. The girls leaned on the wooden fence, their arms resting on top as they watched the horses.

"Is that the pony?" Roxanne asked.

"That's the foal, the mare is its mother."

"Isn't a baby horse a pony?"

"No, a pony is a small horse."

"Well, that horse looks small to me."

"But a pony is a breed of horse; when it grows up it is still small. Ponies never stand more than fourteen and a half hands."

"Hands?"

"A hand is four inches. This horse will grow up to be large, like its mother," Leslie explained, wondering why she bothered.

The foal nudged his mother, found her udder, and began noisily sucking. Roxanne giggled. "Is it a boy or girl?"

"It's a male. When he's weaned, at about six months, he'll be called a colt. If it were a girl, she'd be a filly. Then, when he's four years old, he'll be called a stallion; fillies are called mares. But he'll probably be castrated. Then he'll be a gelding."

At first Roxanne seemed to follow the conversation but then gave up, puzzled. Evidently, it was all new to her. She assumed an air of boredom.

"How long have you lived in Chewack?" Leslie asked.

"About a year. Before that we lived in Seattle. My dad still lives there. Isn't it boring living way out here?" Roxanne looked around derisively. "You're so far from everything."

"No, I don't think it's boring. I love living on the ranch."

"Humph," Roxanne snorted. "I'd rather live in the city. You're close to stores, to restaurants and school."

Leslie, taken aback, said nothing. She couldn't understand this girl.

"Well," Leslie said, "would you like to see anything else?"

"Like what?"

"Let's walk through the barn. It's a real old barn," Leslie explained, swinging open the door, "but my dad thinks it's important to keep it preserved. Old barns are disappearing."

"Why?" Their voices echoed in the vast emptiness.

"Because people don't need them like they used to. We keep most of our hay in a large shed close to the winter pastures. The only hay kept in this barn is for the horses. Most people don't have milk cows anymore, unless they run a dairy operation, and--"

"Why keep an old building like this if you don't need it?" Roxanne interrupted, glancing about with distaste at the rough, heavy timbers. There were several stalls, a tack room, and another equipment room where tools used for the horses were stored. A supply of hay filled the hayloft. Leslie found the smell of fresh hay, horses and leather delightful, apparently it didn't have the same effect on Roxanne.

Roxanne dug into the front pocket of her jeans and produced a wrinkled pack of cigarettes. Glancing around, she pulled a cigarette out of the pack, straightened it, then lit it with a pink plastic lighter. She threw back her head and made a show of blowing out the smoke.

Leslie gaped. "You can't smoke in here!"

"Why not?"

"Because this is a *barn*. You can't smoke in a barn, it might catch fire."

Roxanne stared at Leslie through narrowed eyes. She jerked one shoulder.

"Put it out, Roxanne. And make sure it's all the way out."

Roxanne turned her back to Leslie and dropped the cigarette, grinding it out with her shoe. "Bitch!" she hissed.

They returned to the party, Leslie walking ahead. She rolled her eyes at Janelle who stood chatting with Wally and her parents. As soon as they reached the group, Roxanne joined her mother.

Wally broke away, mumbling about wanting to see someone. Janelle fell in step with Leslie. "How did it go?"

Leslie shrugged. "She doesn't really know anything about ranching. I don't think she likes it here. Oh, well, breaks my heart."

Janelle nodded. "A city girl."

"Let's go back to the barn," Leslie suggested. "Roxanne can't even understand why we would keep 'that old building.' Not only that, she tried to *smoke* in the barn. I told her to put it out and she called me a bitch."

"You're kidding!"

"Nope." Leslie shook her head in disgust.

They stepped into the cool of the barn and climbed to the hayloft, one of their favorite haunts. They fell into easy conversation as they always did. They had known one another since kindergarten and had been best friends since then.

Janelle rolled over on her stomach. "My mom and I talked to Lilith. She seems nice. How could she have such a weird daughter, I wonder?"

"I guess I should talk to Lilith too. I can't seem to get up my nerve. I'm afraid my dad's going to be disappointed in me. I guess I haven't been a great hostess today. I wish Kip could have come."

"Yeah, but it might have been even harder with Roxanne."

Leslie nodded. "Janelle, do you think of you and Wally as --"

"Having a long term relationship?" Janelle laughed. "I don't know. He isn't as much fun as he used to be. Why?"

"Oh, I don't know. I was just wondering."

"How do you think of you and Kip?"

"I'm getting sort of tired of him. He always has to have his own way. You know who I'd like to go out with? Jordan Adkins."

"He's cute. I saw him watching you at the class picnic."

"You did? He seems older, more mature than some of the boys. I was hoping he'd ask me out, but it didn't happen."

Janelle flipped over on her back. "I doubt if he will as long as you're going with Kip."

Leslie sat up and crossed her legs, tucking them in front of her. "Well, it's too late now, anyway. It doesn't look like I'll even be going to Chewack. Jan, I can't talk my dad out of Rosemount. I don't know what to do."

"I can't even stand to think about it, Leslie. What will *I* do if you're not here?"

The barn door creaked open, letting in shafts of light. Dust motes danced in the light beams. Leslie squeezed Janelle's arm. She put her finger up to her mouth, motioning Janelle to be quiet. "Shhh." Janelle's eyes questioned Leslie.

"Les?"

Wade. The girls continued to be silent.

"Leslie!" he called sharply. The door creaked closed.

"Why didn't you answer?" Janelle whispered.

"I think I may be in trouble. How long have we been here?"

"Too long, probably."

"Maybe we'd better go back."

They climbed down from the loft. Leslie swung the heavy barn door open. Wade stood there, giving her his 'what's going on?' look, head slightly thrown back, right eyebrow raised.

Leslie shrugged and started to walk past him. He reached out and caught her arm. "Did you hear me call you?"

She tried to jerk away but his grip tightened. "Yes."

His blue eyes flashed. "Dad wants you."

"Do you know why?"

He nodded his head in a way that told Leslie that he knew but didn't care to say. "I wouldn't dally," he said, "he's acting like a Pit Bull with a toothache."

"Uh oh."

The girls walked back to the yard, Janelle apologetic and Leslie scared. She knew she hadn't done her part at this party. But then, Roxanne isn't *my* guest anyway!

People were in little groups, laughing and talking. A metallic clink and a roar of approval drifted from a horseshoe game. Little kids screeched, apparently in the middle of some wild game.

Wally made a point of looking at his watch, a signal to Janelle. "Les, I think Wally and I have to leave. I'll say good-bye to your dad and my folks and take off. Call me tomorrow."

"Okay. I wish I could go with you," she said, under her breath. Her dad had spotted her and walked toward her, taking long steps, his face dark with anger. He stopped briefly when Janelle bid him good-bye, smiled stiffly, then quickly closed the distance between them.

"Leslie, where have you been?"

"In the barn."

"Why?"

"I don't know. Just to talk."

"Is this your idea of giving a party? Taking off and leaving your guests by themselves?"

"No, but Janelle is my guest too."

"Can you tell me why every time I look around you're not here and Roxanne is alone?"

"Dad, I've tried, but she --" She shrugged.

He stood very close and spoke quietly, his voice like steel. "You listen to me, young lady. Unless you want to spend the rest of this party in your room, you will show Roxanne some attention. For you to go off with a friend and ignore Roxanne is unconscionable. We are giving a party here and have an obligation to our guests. Do you understand me?"

Leslie swallowed. "Dad, I've tried."

"Try harder. Do you understand?"

"Yes."

## *FIVE*

Leslie, red faced and fighting tears, ran into the house and straight to the bathroom. She held a cold washcloth to her face. Would this Fourth of July party never end? When she returned to the kitchen, she found Maureen standing at the sink rinsing out a pitcher.

Maureen glanced up at her. "What's wrong, dear?"

"Oh, Maureen! Dad's mad at me for ignoring Roxanne. I've tried to do things with her, but she's, she's... I can't stand her!"

"Why don't you ask her if she wants to play croquet? Maybe your dad and Lilith would like to play, too."

"Oh, goody."

Maureen turned from the sink to look squarely at her. "We do have responsibilities to our guests, Leslie."

"*I* didn't invite her."

"She's still our guest." Maureen filled the pitcher with a fruit punch, dropping in slices of oranges and lemons. Leslie followed her outside.

She looked around for Roxanne and found her standing near the serving table. Dinner left-overs had been arranged on the table where people were to help themselves. Roxanne didn't need to be asked a second time.

With dread Leslie approached her. "Hi."

Roxanne didn't bother to look up. "Hi." She scooped up a deviled egg and popped it into her mouth.

"Want to do something?" Leslie asked.

"Like what?"

"Maybe play croquet?"

"I've never played it."

"I could show you how."

"What is it, some country-bumpkin game?" Roxanne shrugged and reached for a handful of potato chips.

Leslie turned abruptly. I'd *rather* be in my room. She stormed back to the house and straight to her room.

She threw herself across her bed and pounded her fist against her pillow. Last year they'd had a wonderful time at their Fourth of July party. Why did it have to be ruined this year by those two? Why couldn't we just invite people we all know?

She heard an explosion of laughter but refused to leave her bed to look out the window to see the reason.

After a while, restless, she picked up a book and tried to concentrate. During the school year she seldom had time for pleasure reading and had looked forward to summer and time to read books of her choice. But now she couldn't even enjoy a good book!

An hour dragged by.

She heard footsteps climbing the stairs. Was it her dad? No, there were two sets of footsteps, and women's voices. She heard Wade's door open. "This must be Wade's room."

"Must be," Lilith agreed. "I guess there are two bedrooms and a bathroom upstairs."

Roxanne and Lilith! What are they doing?

"Boy, I'd love to have one of these huge rooms," Roxanne said. They closed Wade's bedroom door.

Her bedroom door opened.

Lilith and Roxanne stared at her.

Leslie snapped her book closed. "Yes?"

"I'm...I'm sorry," Lilith said, embarrassed. "We didn't know anyone was up here. Your dad invited us to look through the house. I've...we've never been in a ranch house." Lilith, obviously uncomfortable, tried to extricate herself and Roxanne from the awkward scene.

"What are you doing here?" Roxanne demanded.

"I'm reading."

"Why?"

"Roxanne," her mother said, "it's none of your business. Come on, let's join the others."

Time again dragged by. Dusk fell, a tomato-red sun slipped out of sight. The rolling violet hills surrounding the house would soon turn dark purple.

Mosquitoes began their nightly attack, whining in high pitch as they buzzed ears, then settled on exposed flesh. The guests, swatting and ducking, searched for long-sleeved shirts. Mothers put long pants on shorts-clad children. Beyond the yard and the murmur and occasional laughter of guests, Leslie heard night noises, a hawk's screech, croaking frogs, the pulsing symphony of crickets. Soon her father and brother would start the fireworks.

She again heard footsteps and knew it was her father. He knocked at her door.

"Come in."

He opened the door, stepped in and quietly closed it behind him. He looked down at her. She had been reading on her bed, sitting with her legs crossed. Her pillow rested on her lap propping up the book. She silently returned her father's gaze, the rims of her troubled eyes red, her face flushed.

Her father didn't look mad. His face was lined with sadness. "We're going to have dessert now and then set off fireworks. Why don't you come out and join us?"

"No, thanks, I'll just stay here. Dad," she looked down and expelled a jagged sigh, then again met his eyes, "I'm sorry. I just can't seem to connect with Roxanne."

He nodded, sadly. "You might be interested to know that Lilith assumed I'd sent you to your room. She was upset with me and said she thought you had tried with Roxanne. She says Roxanne doesn't have any friends and it's no wonder. She isn't a very likeable kid, even according to her mother."

"Lilith said that?"

John sat down on the chair next to the bed. He leaned forward, his elbows on his knees, hands folded loosely. "I guess Roxanne has had a hard time adjusting to her folks' divorce."

"Thirteen's pretty rough, too," Leslie said magnanimously, relieved her father wasn't mad at her.

"Come on down, honey, I want you to be with us now."

Leslie put aside her book and joined her dad. He put his arm across her shoulders as they joined the crowd in the yard. Together they stepped to the dessert table and heaped cake and ice cream on their plates. They sat on the lawn with Wade and Teresa to enjoy their dessert.

Wade and John excused themselves to begin the fireworks. With a whistling shriek, color burst through the air, spraying sparks of red, white and blue. Rockets zoomed skyward, wailing as they arched over the crowd, finally exploding into glorious multi-color splendor. The crowd ahhhed with each colorful burst.

It was late, almost midnight, before the party ended. Leslie made a point of joining her father as Lilith and Roxanne departed.

"It was nice meeting you," Leslie said to both of them in as genuine a voice as she could muster.

"Yes," Lilith said, "I hope to see you again soon. I'd love to have you to our place. It's really small though, nothing like this," she said, indicating the spread of the ranch.

"Well, goodnight," Leslie said.

After helping clean up the party mess, she returned to her room. Although he hadn't seemed angry that she spent so long in her room that afternoon, she knew her dad was disappointed. It probably meant a lot to him to have Lilith and her daughter meet everyone. Then to have things turn out like they did....

Just as she drifted into a restless sleep, it suddenly occurred to her: Her father was really serious about Lilith. He was going to marry her. Lilith and Roxanne would be living here! She sat bolt upright, fully awake. The idea was so revolting her stomach churned. That's why they were inspecting the house! That's why Roxanne said she would like to have one of these bedrooms!

If that happened, which room would be Roxanne's? It would have to be here, in my room, with me. The house only had four bedrooms, she and Roxanne would have to share a room.

The puzzle fell into place. Her stomach knotted into a cold, hard lump. I won't be here. That's why he wants me to go away to school. He knew I wouldn't get along with that creep Roxanne, so he's getting rid of me.

She climbed out of bed and stood at the window, wide-eyed and bitter, betrayed.

## *SIX*

Summer activities kept Leslie busy over the next several days.

At times Leslie felt she had been mistaken about her father's plans to marry Lilith. Once, she was aware that he had met Lilith for dinner on a Saturday night. But their relationship didn't seem to take much of his time.

Is this how someone would act if he were planning to marry? I would think he would see more of her. He doesn't seem to be gone from home that much, though he could be gone from the ranch and I wouldn't necessarily know it.

On the other hand, his getting married and bringing them here is a logical reason to send me away. When Lilith and Roxanne were going through the house it certainly sounded as though Roxanne had her eyes on my room. Dad knows Roxanne and I could never share a room. He's right about that, at least.

One day, soon after their noon meal, John talked on the telephone in the office while Leslie and Maureen cleared away the dishes. Maureen loaded the dishwasher, Leslie wiped the table and counters. The office door stood ajar and Leslie heard her father, apparently talking to Lilith. "Friday? Tomorrow night? That sounds good. I'll ask her. What time would you want us?"

They were invited to Lilith's and Roxanne's for dinner! Panic seized her. I don't want to go! Be stuck all evening with Roxanne, cramped in their tiny place? Trying to play family with *them*?

She glanced at Maureen but doubted the housekeeper heard the conversation above the clatter of dishes.

"Maureen, I'm going to Janelle's. Will you tell Dad when he's off the phone? I'll be back by four."

"Yes, dear," Maureen murmured absently.

Leslie ran to the corral, bribed Polly to come to her with a handful of oats, and quickly bridled her. Jumping on bareback, she hurried out of the yard, breaking into a full gallop as soon as she was out of sight.

Janelle's was about a half hour ride. She slowed as she neared, allowing Polly to cool down. She turned the mare into Holton's small corral and walked the well-worn path to the old style, two-story farmhouse with a wrap-around porch.

Leslie found Janelle hanging laundry on the clothesline in the side yard.

"Hey!" Janelle beamed at her, "I didn't know you were coming over." In the summer, washing clothes was one of Janelle's regular chores. Being the oldest of four children, much more housework was expected of her than was of Leslie. Leslie reached into the laundry basket, shook out a blouse and handed it to Janelle.

Janelle expertly hung it on the line. "This is my favorite job."

"I know," Leslie handed her a tee-shirt, a little one, belonging to the youngest boy. "You've always been a little peculiar."

Janelle laughed. "I'll be free as soon as I finish this. Want to do something?"

"I can only stay a couple of hours, then I have to practice. I have a favor to ask."

"Ask."

"I heard my dad on the phone accepting an invitation for us to go to Lilith's Friday night. Anyway, I think he was talking to Lilith, he always sounds different when he talks to her."

"Different?"

"Just different, his voice is smoother or something."

"So what's the favor?" Janelle shook out the last towel and hung it up. The full lines sagged under their load of wet laundry.

"Well...I don't want to go." How awkward.

"Oh! I get it!" Janelle ran into the house. Leslie heard her call, "Mom!" In only a couple of minutes she returned, grinning.

"Leslie!" she said with obvious theatrics, "would you come for dinner Friday night? My mother says we're having pork roast and we'd love to have you join us."

"Did you tell her why?"

"Of course not. It's not like you never have dinner with us, Les. Why don't you spend the night? Bring Polly--we'll get up early and go riding."

Leslie laughed. "What a nice invitation! Thank you!"

That evening at dinner, Leslie, striving for calmness, said, "Mrs. Holton invited me for dinner tomorrow night, Friday. Janelle wants me to spend the night so we can go riding Saturday morning."

Her father looked up sharply. "Friday night? Lilith invited you and me over for dinner on Friday."

"Oh, I'm sorry Dad. But I already accepted Holton's invitation." This deception didn't sit easily with Leslie. She glanced nervously at her father.

He gazed steadily at her, as though he knew. But he said nothing.

*~*

The next day Leslie rode with Wade to move cattle from one pasture to another. The blue heeler trotted beside them.

"Wade, have you talked to Dad about me going to Rosemount Academy?"

He nodded. "Yes, I did."

"You did? What did he say? What did *you* say?"

"Well, pretty much what I'd said before, something like you really hated the idea of going to a boarding school. I told him I thought you were doing pretty well right here and you were a decent kid." He glanced sidelong at her. "I was stretching it a bit, but I wanted to get my point across."

"Oh, Wade." She made a face and shook her head. "What did he say?"

Wade squinted his eyes and pursed his mouth. "The first thing he said was, 'Don't you get started on me.' But then he said Rosemount was a fine school and he thought it was where you should go. He's worried that the local school is going to hell. He also said that a lot of kids from here weren't going on to college. That worries him."

Leslie slumped in her saddle. "But I've told him I plan to go to college. Anyway, I don't know why it's such a big deal to him. You didn't go to college."

"But I wasn't the brain you are. Remember, he's a college graduate and it's a big deal to him. Les, he just wants you to have choices in your life. He said you two were going to an open house at Rosemount the end of the month. Why don't you wait until after that before you pass judgement on it?"

She tossed her head impatiently. "I don't have to see it to know I don't want to go there!" She looked around her at her beloved rolling hills. A gentle breeze cooled her upturned face. "I just want to stay here, at home," she added softly.

Wade shifted in his saddle and turned to look at her. "I'm sorry I couldn't help, Sis."

She nodded. "I think I know why he's sending me away."

"Why?"

"Because he's going to marry Lilith and she and that stupid Roxanne will be living here. He thinks --"

"Leslie!" He abruptly reined in his horse. "That's ridiculous! Dad wouldn't do that! How can you say such a thing?"

"What? You don't think he would get married?"

"No, I'm not saying that. I think he might get married some day, but he's sure not going to send you away because of it!"

"Oh, no?" Her eyes sparked with anger. "Then what is this talk about me going away? What do you think that means? He *is* sending me away!" She had stopped too, but now roughly kicked Polly into a gallop. Angry tears threatened. That Wade couldn't see the obvious made her even angrier.

Wade caught up with her. "Hold up, Leslie."

She ignored him, leaning forward, encouraging Polly to go faster. There was no way Polly could outmaneuver Wade's quarter horse. With little effort, Wade cut off Polly, bringing her up short. The mare snorted indignantly. Wade grabbed the Appaloosa's reins.

Frustrated, Leslie kicked Polly who, with the big horse in front of her and no place to go, jumped on stiff legs, her ears flattened against her head.

"You abuse this horse and you'll be on foot," Wade growled, still holding the reins. "Now calm down."

Leslie knew this was no idle threat. She glared at her brother through tear-filled eyes. With supreme effort she took a deep breath and nodded to him. She reached up to pat Polly's neck, apologizing.

"Les," he said gently, "I honestly think he doesn't want to send you to this school, but feels he should, for your own good. I know for a fact how much he'll miss you."

Leslie sniffed. "Miss me! He'll be too busy carrying on with Lilith and with that snotty daughter of hers to even notice I'm gone!"

Wade shook his head. "I think you're wrong about that. And I don't think Lilith and her daughter have anything to do with Dad's decision."

She reached out and absently ran her fingers through Polly's mane. The two horses nickered to one another, patiently waiting. The dog walked a tight circle in the tall grass, finally plunking down with a loud sigh. "I guess I didn't win any points at the Fourth of July party."

"Well, you sure weren't the model hostess. I could have smacked you myself. But Les, Dad understood about that. Anyway, that business at the party happened after he'd already told you about going to Rosemount."

She nodded, thinking about what her brother said. She wanted to believe him. "I wish things could just stay like they were."

Wade dropped Polly's reins, backed his big mount and turned. They began riding again, making their way up to the high summer pastures to check on the herd.

"Life doesn't stand still for any of us, Les. Give it a chance. Stop resisting and see what happens."

Wade straightened in his saddle, all business now. "Okay, look alive. Some of the herd are up ahead in that draw."

Dutch ran ahead, found a calf who had strayed a distance from his mother, and nipped his heels. The calf bawled and ran to his mother's side. Satisfied, the dog ran to another small group, working them in the general direction of the larger herd. "Good girl," Wade called.

Although Leslie would have liked to continue the discussion, Wade was apparently through talking. At least he had tried talking with Dad about Rosemount. It hasn't done any good though.

## *SEVEN*

Summer sped by. The days progressed pleasantly enough, but rarely did a day pass without the dread of Rosemount crossing Leslie's mind. She tried not to think or talk about it, but it crept into her thoughts and into her conversation. Even into her sleep.

"Maureen, what do you think about my going to Rosemount?" Leslie sat at the kitchen table drinking a glass of lemonade. The housekeeper didn't miss a stroke in rolling out pie dough. The circle of dough grew with each pass of the rolling pin.

"I hate to think about it."

"But what do you *think*?"

"I think I'm going to miss you terribly."

Leslie ran from the kitchen, up the stairs to her room, slamming the door behind her.

The day of their appointment at Rosemount, July 25th, approached.

"Leslie," her father asked, "did you fill out those forms from Rosemount I gave you?"

"No."

"Well, let's get that done. They need them at the open house. You and I have an appointment with a counselor, and she'll want to go over the forms with you."

Leslie didn't answer. She stared at her lap.

"Les?"

"Dad, it makes me sick to even think about going to that school."

"Now look. We have an appointment Friday that we're going to keep. You'll have a chance to look around the school and see all it can offer you. You're going into this with a bad attitude. Give it a chance. Give *yourself* a chance. Now, fill out those forms and bring them down to me."

In her room, she reluctantly drew out the envelope. She had stashed it far back in a desk drawer. It was crumpled now. She glanced through the many pages then froze when she read, "Rosemount Academy has an existing agreement with The Uniform Store in Spokane. Please make arrangements to purchase the required items before the school term begins."

She scanned the page frantically. School uniform! I'm going to have to wear a uniform! No! No way.

She ran into the office where her father sat at his desk staring at his computer screen .

"Dad! This says I have to wear a uniform!"

He glanced up. "I know. A lot of schools think it's a good idea so kids feel they fit in. You'll get used to it, Les."

She stared at her father. Anger rushed from the depth of her stomach, flushing her face. Her throat felt raw; she could feel her forehead pounding. "Don't you even care what I want?"

"Yes, I do care. But you don't know anything about Rosemount yet. You insist on looking at everything from a negative point of view."

"It won't matter what I think. I'll still have to go."

John said nothing, but looked steadily at her.

She turned and slowly climbed the stairs to her room. At Chewack all the girls wore jeans and a blouse or sweater to school, except for special occasions. She was used to wearing whatever she wanted, whatever suited her that day.

Under special interests she listed "horseback riding, horse training, working with stock, hiking, camping." Nothing that could be done at Rosemount. She didn't mention her music.

The announcement that school started the last week of August jolted her further. Her heart sank. Rosemount started a whole week earlier than Chewack. The first week of school consisted of special orientation, getting acquainted, and activities aimed at making the student feel at home. At home! That's a laugh. *Never.*

She made a momentous decision on Wednesday, the day of her piano lesson.

At the end of the lesson, with great consternation, she said, "Mr. Baxter, this will be my last lesson. I want to thank you for everything."

He had been putting away the sheets of music they had used. His hands stopped in mid-air. "Last lesson? Why?"

"Because I'm going away to school." She blinked quickly to stave off tears.

She had mentioned to him earlier in the summer about going to Rosemount. He had been very positive about the move, saying she would love the school and what a fine music department they had. "Each year several Rosemount graduates are awarded college music scholarships," he'd said. At the time she'd felt as though he were trying to give her a pep talk to cheer her up.

"But that's a whole month away!"

"I know. But since I have to quit, I might as well do it now." She quickly gathered her music books. "Here," she said, handing him one of the books, "this one belongs to you."

"Okay, Leslie. Well, I'm sure you're going to enjoy Rosemount. Mr. Richie is the piano teacher there--you'll learn a lot from him. Leslie, I'll miss you. I've always considered you my finest student. You've..." His voice cracked and he stopped.

Leslie avoided further eye contact. "Good-bye," she whispered and turned to leave.

"Good-bye, Leslie, good luck."

She ran down the steps and climbed into the car. She could feel his eyes on her from where he stood at the window. She swiped the tears from her face. The car jerked as it pulled away from the curb.

That night at dinner Leslie was very quiet. She barely touched her food.

Her father studied her. "How was your lesson today?"

"Fine. It was my last one."

"Your...what? What do you mean?"

She gazed directly at her father, her red-rimmed eyes met his squarely. "This was my last lesson. I've quit."

"Why? Why didn't you talk to me about this?" The meal had stopped. Even Wade's fork was still.

"Dad," her voice was cold, "I'm quitting because I won't be here."

"But that's not for a whole month."

"I don't see what difference a month will make in a lifetime, one way or the other."

"You'd be in better form when school starts."

"It won't matter."

"What do you mean, 'it won't matter'?" He placed both hands on the table and leaned forward, his eyes sparking with anger.

"I mean I won't be taking lessons anyway, so it won't matter."

"You'll be taking lessons at Rosemount. I've already signed you up with Mr... Mr. Richmond."

"Mr. Richie. Dad, my music has always been up to me. I no longer plan to take piano lessons. I've quit." She looked defiantly at her father.

He deliberately speared a piece of roast beef and chewed it, eyeing her but saying nothing.

Wade resumed eating.

Maureen's mouth opened as though she were going to speak, but then snapped shut.

Leslie reached for her milk and took a sip. She could barely swallow.

## *EIGHT*

The three hour ride to Spokane dragged by, long and silent. John, grim, rarely spoke. Leslie only answered when required, otherwise, stared out the window. Occasionally, tears rolled down her cheeks, starting the juices flowing and subsequent sniffles.

"Leslie, will you stop that sniffling," he finally snapped. "I can't believe that the three hundred or so girls enrolled at Rosemount are all crying because they're going to one of the best schools in the country."

"Why is it that when I've said 'all the kids get to do it,' or something like that, you say 'I don't care about the other kids, I care about you.' That's how I feel, Dad. I don't care about the other two-hundred ninety-nine girls. I care about me, how *I* feel. But apparently you don't."

They drove on in painful silence. Rolling hills dotted with sagebrush were broken occasionally by orchards. Crutches propped up branches heavy with ripening apples and peaches.

A mobile home stood alone in the middle of the orchard. Leslie sighed. *That's how I feel, alone.*

Jagged basalt ridges loomed over the desert country. Only where there was irrigation did the landscape change.

They passed a ranch with many horses. The animals stood under the hot sun, no relief in sight. Leslie thought of their own corral and the nice shade of hemlock and pine. A lump caught in her throat when she thought of Polly.

With reluctance in his voice, her father spoke again. "I don't think it said in those forms you read, but your first visit home will be Thanksgiving."

Wide eyed, Leslie turned to look at her father. "Thanksgiving? I won't be able to come home before *Thanksgiving*? Why?"

"Some of the girls live far away. It wouldn't be fair for some to go home for weekend visits and others not. The time will go fast, Les. You'll see."

Silently, she shook her head. *No, I won't see.*

They passed the Double A Cattle Company. Leslie had heard her father talk about this outfit. She thought he had done some business with them but now couldn't get up the energy to ask him about it. What difference did it make anyway?

Almost to Creston now, more cattle country. Ranchers were getting ready for fall round up. Two men hammered on the sides of a ramp, making repairs. I'll miss fall round up.

They stopped for lunch, a strained affair, and Leslie couldn't force herself to eat. Afterward, she couldn't even have described the restaurant.

Nearing Spokane, the road was carved out of hilly terrain. Wave after wave of hills, like a slow roller coaster, shimmered in the heat.

Then, in Spokane, Leslie suddenly became aware of city congestion. Noise, crowded neighborhoods, business districts. Small yards with houses that all seemed to look alike.

I hate Spokane. I hate cities.

They arrived just before the open house began, at one. A gracious ivy-covered brick building facing the curved

51

driveway dominated the campus. Large, rectangular gardens boasted several varieties of velvet roses, pink, radiant yellow and brilliant red.

John parked in the visitors parking lot, and they walked toward the administration building. Many people were arriving as well, some girls with their parents; others alone or walking with other students. Except for Leslie and her father, most people chatted merrily. Girls called out, glad to see one another after the summer break.

"I think only the new girls have their parents with them," John observed.

Leslie didn't answer. She felt nothing but a cold hatred for this place. Her insides felt as though they were shrinking. She had worn a skirt and blouse and now felt awkward and uncomfortable. Some of the girls had worn skirts, others dressy slacks. She would have given anything to be wearing jeans and riding boots.

Entering the administration building, they approached a table where a smiling woman greeted them. John handed her the completed documents. She tore off the first page and handed the rest back to him. "Yes, Mr. Cahill and Leslie. Please go to room 12 down this hall," she said, pointing. "Mrs. Holmes will see you."

Mrs. Holmes, a middle-aged woman smartly dressed in a navy-blue suit with a crisp white blouse, stood at the door to greet the group assigned to her, all new students and their parents. When she had her group together, she smiled warmly. "Please follow me. We're going to take a brief tour of the campus though I know some of you have already visited. Afterwards I'll want to talk to each family individually."

As they made their way through the lush campus, Leslie was surprised with its size. Behind and sprawled on either side of the administration building were a variety of handsome buildings.

"All of you girls will be in McMillian Dorm. I'll just show you a room or two. Later today, you'll be shown your own rooms. As you can see, each room is designed for two students and each room has its own bathroom."

*Big deal.* Others gaily observed the surroundings, nodding and sighing approval.

Occasionally Leslie glanced at her father to get his reaction to what was being said, or what they were shown. He always returned her look and smiled at her, a silent 'See, isn't this nice?' She never returned the smile, and each time it happened her stomach knotted.

After touring the facilities, Mrs. Holmes instructed them to follow her back to the main building to a group of offices. They all took seats, waiting their turn for interviews.

"Mr. Cahill and Leslie? Please come in."

They entered the office where Mrs. Holmes smiled brightly at them as she bade them to sit.

"Well," she said, glancing at Leslie's file, "I see you people are ranchers! There are several girls from ranches here, Leslie, a couple of girls are from Wyoming. The girl I just talked with, Roberta Young, lives close to you, in Omak." She looked up and smiled. Leslie gave a little smile, out of habit, but then dropped her eyes to her clenched hands.

"Have you purchased your school uniform yet?"

Out of the corner of her eye, Leslie glanced at her father.

"We're going to take care of that this afternoon," John said.

"Fine. Here are directions to get to the store from Rosemount. We recommend five blouses, two skirts and one sweater. Any questions?"

John glanced at Leslie. Leslie looked at her father, then at Mrs. Holmes.

"No," she croaked with pounding heart. *I hate it here. I hate it here.*

"We've received your transcript from Chewack High, Leslie. Your records show you are a fine student. We're always glad to have girls with academic interests. But now for the fun stuff. What do you like to do in your spare time?"

Leslie looked up to meet Mrs. Holmes friendly eyes. A lifetime of good manners made it difficult to act in such a distant manner. But she would not, could not, allow herself to be taken in.

"I've listed my interests on the questionnaire."

John scowled at his daughter.

"So you have," Mrs. Holmes chatted on, flipping the pages. "'Horseback riding, horse training, working with stock...' Sometimes a small group of girls, with a supervisor, go to a local riding academy to ride horses."

Leslie eyes widened and rolled off to one side. Forget it.

Mrs. Holmes looked back at the form. "Well. Do you like to swim?"

"Yes, in a lake or river." Not in your dumb pool.

"I see. Do you like to play tennis? We have ongoing tennis and volleyball tournaments. We also have quieter activities, chess, for instance."

Silence hung like fog.

"Leslie," her father said, "you've played tennis, both at school and at the city park."

Leslie merely offered a slight nod.

"Well, I see you have a strong interest in music."

John shifted his position uncomfortably.

"I've quit piano."

"Quit?" Mrs. Holmes rapidly flipped through the file. "We have you signed up for private piano lessons with Mr. Richie. I wish I'd thought to take our tour group to the music department. Some other girls in the group would have been interested, too. You may visit the department after our interview, if you like."

"It doesn't matter. I'm no longer interested in taking piano lessons."

Mrs. Holmes placed the file before her and folded her hands on top of it. "Leslie?" She waited until Leslie met her gaze, then held those hostile eyes with practiced efficiency. "Do you want to attend Rosemount?"

Shock passed over Leslie's face. "No," she answered, barely more than a whisper. She didn't dare look at her father. From the corner of her eye she could see he sat still as a fence post.

"Why not?" Mrs. Holmes asked softly.

"I...I just want to stay at Chewack and live at home. Rosemount seems like a nice school, but I just don't want to come here."

Mrs. Holmes looked from Leslie to her father, then back to Leslie. "Will you excuse us for a few minutes? Please take a seat in the waiting room."

Leslie stiffly rose and left the room. Other people in the waiting room glanced at her curiously, particularly one girl, a small girl with a round face and glasses. Leslie could tell it was all the girl could do not to ask why she'd been sent out of the office. Leslie stared her down.

What were they saying in there? Had she successfully screwed up her chances at Rosemount? I hope so. Oh, I hope so.

In just a few moments Mrs. Holmes opened the door. "Leslie, please come in." Leslie returned to the conference room and took her chair.

"Leslie," Mrs. Holmes began, "you need to understand that many girls are reluctant to come here, at first. But they soon make happy adjustments. Some of our finest students are girls who at first hesitated to attend Rosemount. You are a good student with excellent credentials. Your father and I have decided you would benefit by attending this school and that Rosemount would benefit by having you."

Leslie hung her head. Tears slid down her cheeks.

"Les, I wouldn't have enrolled you if I didn't think it was for the best. I'm sure you're going to like it, honey."

Mrs. Holmes handed her a tissue. Her calm voice was steady, but not without compassion. "I'd like you to go back to McMillian Dorm to see your room. You might meet your room-mate today, too."

The counselor stood. "I'm looking forward to seeing you next month, Leslie. Now I must get on with the next family."

John stood and extended his hand. "Thank you." Mrs. Holmes took his hand and looked at Leslie who had stood but would not look at her.

John gently took Leslie's arm and led her out of the office. She briefly wondered what the others in the room must think. *I know my eyes are red and my face is blotchy. I must look like an idiot.*

"Do you want to see the music department, Les?"

"No, thank you."

"Let's go to the dorm to see your room."

*Let's not*, Leslie thought, but at this point didn't dare say. She knew she was treading on thin ice. Though, on the other hand, what more could he do? Send her away to school?

McMillian dorm, a two-story wooden structure, branched out in two directions. The two wings formed an "L," with the entrance in the crook of the "L". They approached a small nicely furnished sitting room with a desk at one end. Mrs. Dartworth, one of two house parents for this dormitory, sat at the desk. "Your name, please?"

After a stony silence, John finally said, "Leslie Cahill."

Mrs. Dartworth consulted her ledger. "Oh yes, Leslie, here you are, room 213. You'll like that room. Your room-mate is Megan Whitefield, from Goldendale." She handed Leslie the key. "Take your time and have a good look, then please return the key to me. When school starts you'll be issued your own."

They took the stairs to the second floor and found the room. Leslie unlocked the door.

"Boy, Les, this looks pretty nice."

It *was* nice. Although there were no partitions, the room was divided naturally by the arrangement of furniture, single beds, nightstands, four-drawer dressers, and small student desks. The closet was sectioned in two parts with shelves and space for clothes on hangers. The beds had matching floral bedspreads.

A small bathroom had a vanity with four drawers. The shower enclosure had a glass door and one of the doors held a full-length mirror. The room sparkled with cleanliness.

"What do you think?" he asked.

Leslie stiffened. He's trying to be so positive, so encouraging. I know I'm being a real pain, but I just can't help it.

"It's okay."

They returned to Mrs. Dartworth who looked for their reaction. "It's a nice room, isn't it?" she asked hopefully.

"It's okay," Leslie repeated.

Mrs. Dartworth looked from Leslie to John, smiled weakly, and took the key from Leslie.

They stepped out into the mid-afternoon sunshine. "Is there anything else you want to see before we leave?" John asked.

"No."

When they were settled in the car, before he started the engine, John turned to her. "Leslie, I'm disappointed in your behavior today. I wouldn't have recognized you back there. You are deliberately blocking yourself from enjoying this school."

Sad eyes looked at him, then out the window. John started the car and slowly pulled out of the parking lot.

Following the printed directions, they found The Uniform Store. Inside, the store contained racks of uniforms for several local schools. The salesclerk directed them to the uniforms for Rosemount Academy. They found Leslie's size and the clerk directed her to a small dressing room to try on a navy blue pleated skirt with pin-stripes of burgundy and white, a plain white blouse and a navy blue cardigan made of soft wool. Although the woman suggested she show her father how she looked in the uniform, Leslie declined. They purchased the recommended number of items and left the store. No words were spoken between father and daughter.

After many miles Leslie spoke. "Dad, if I promise you I wouldn't date, would never go out, would come straight home from school every day, could I stay at Chewack?"

"Les, don't be silly."

"I'm not being silly, I'm serious."

"Leslie, in the first place, as I've said at least a dozen times before, you seem to think going to Rosemount is the result of something you've done. I'm not sending you to Rosemount as a punishment. You've done nothing wrong. I'm sending you there because you'll get a better education. And so you'll be safe."

"I don't think I'll get a better education. That's why I've been taking honors classes. If I didn't date or go anyplace, I'd be safe."

"Les, you're not thinking clearly. It just isn't a good idea. In the first place, I can't imagine your attitude if you never went anyplace or saw your friends."

"I won't be seeing my friends at Rosemount."

"You'll make new friends, Leslie, and they'll be all around you, all the time. No, I won't consider your idea."

The long drive home dragged on. They stopped for dinner. Hunger finally forced her to eat. They arrived home around nine. Leslie went straight to her room and to bed.

Wade, attempting to be casual, waited for them in the living room. When Leslie didn't even come into the room he knew the answer, but asked their father anyway. "Well, how did it go? Does she like the idea of going to Rosemount any better now?"

John grimly shook his head. "She had her mind made up before she ever saw the place."

"That's too bad. But so did you, Dad."

John looked sharply at his son, then sighed loudly. "My God, this has been a miserable day."

## *NINE*

School would start in less than a month. Her father's mind was made up about Rosemount. It seemed the more she tried to dissuade him, the more he dug in his heels.

And then a tragedy occurred. Traci Murphy, the girl who had been raped on school grounds, had taken her own life.

Janelle called Leslie with the terrible news. "Isn't it awful? Mom and I were in town and heard about it at the shoe store. We didn't even feel like shopping any more. Everybody's talking about it."

"It's so sad," Leslie lamented. "Why would she do that?"

"I guess she left a note to her family. No one knows exactly what it said, but she mentioned taking her own life, that she couldn't live with it any more. I guess she meant the rape."

"How did she do it? What a horrible question, but how did she?"

"An overdose of medication."

"I'm really sorry. I didn't know Traci very well, but I sure feel sorry for her family."

Leslie purposely didn't mention the news to her own family--her father didn't need any more fuel to feed his argument. But Maureen brought it up after dinner the day it appeared in the paper.

"What a shame. I can't imagine the horror her parents are going through. Rape is a terrible thing, but this..." Maureen's round face showed her profound sadness.

Leslie stole a look at her father's grim face. He glanced at her, but said nothing.

*~*

She missed her music lessons terribly. She had quit her lessons to shock her father, knowing how proud he was of her musical ability, to get him to change his mind about Rosemount. But it hadn't worked. She often found herself mentally working out a passage, moving her fingers in concentration.

She would not play the piano within her father's hearing. But often, when she was alone in the house or when only Maureen was home, she sat at the piano and lost herself in music.

Her father never discussed her decision to quit her music lessons. He probably thinks I'll change my mind at Rosemount.

*~*

To Leslie, it seemed John seldom saw Lilith. He usually went out on Saturday evenings, though sometimes she was sure he played poker with friends. Maybe Lilith plays poker, but she doesn't seem the type. Occasionally he had business in town during the day. Maybe he took her out to lunch. It seemed odd that he wasn't seeing more of her. Maybe when people got old they didn't need to see boyfriends or girlfriends--men friends or women friends?--very often. Leslie talked to Kip several times a week plus they dated at least once a week and she was no longer that enthralled with him!

She had overheard a couple of telephone conversations apparently between her dad and Lilith, her father talking in his smooth voice. But the talks didn't seem very romantic to her.

Leslie would have liked to discuss Lilith with her father, but was afraid to mention the subject. For the first time in her life she felt left out, alienated. She felt sure though, that his future plans with Lilith were the reason behind her being sent away to school.

It wouldn't work out between that stupid Roxanne and me, so I'm the loser. I'm the one being sent away, culled out like a dry cow.

*~*

Leslie and Janelle planned to camp out the next Saturday, packing with their horses to the hills on the ranch. They had planned this trip for months. At first, her father had been reluctant about the camping trip, but Leslie knew he hated to deny her this. The situation between them was strained enough. He wouldn't want to make it any worse.

"I'd like to have an idea of where you'll be," he said.

"Okay, we'll decide and I'll let you know. Should I take Dutch?"

"Good idea. Have you mentioned your plans to anyone except Janelle's family and us?"

"No, and we're not going to, not even Kip or Wally."

John nodded enthusiastically. "Especially not Kip or Wally."

But that evening, two days before the planned event, Kip called.

"How about a movie Saturday night?"

"Oh, thanks Kip, but I have plans."

"Plans?"

Kip and Leslie didn't have any real commitment, but they seldom dated others. On the other hand, Leslie felt no obligation to explain her plans to him. As far as she was concerned, he was becoming possessive and she didn't like it.

"Yes, Janelle and I have plans for Saturday night."

"No problem. I'll call Wally, see if he wants to double--"

"Thanks, Kip, but we'll just stick to our original plan."

"Well, what are you doing that's so important?"

"Nothing, really. We're just going to kick back. But we'd planned this time together."

"You'd rather do something with Janelle than with me?"

Irritated, Leslie snapped, "I have plans, Kip. Let's just leave it at that."

"You know, Les, our time together is getting short, now that you're definitely going to *Rosemount*." He emphasized the name with mock importance.

"I know. If you like, we could make it another time."

"I had Saturday in mind."

"Sorry." She offered no further apology.

"Okay. See you around." He hung up.

Her fingers flew over Janelle's familiar telephone number.

Fuming, she related the phone call to Janelle, adding at the end, "I hope that was okay with you, Jan. I would rather stick to our plans than go out with those guys."

"Absolutely. I'm glad you warned me. Kip might still call Wally and suggest it."

After talking with Janelle, Leslie stormed into the living room where her brother and dad watched the news.

"Kip called. He wanted me to go out with him on Saturday, but I told him I have plans with Janelle. He seems to think I should drop everything and do something with him! What is it about boys that makes them think they're so important, anyway!" She directed this last remark to Wade.

"I don't know, Sis, but I think you have the right attitude. I think there're plenty of girls who would do anything for a date, even sacrifice time with a good friend."

"Humph," she snorted.

After she left the room, Wade casually said to his father, "I think she has a good head on her shoulders, Dad. She's not like a lot of boy-crazy girls. I think she's doing fine at Chewack."

Wade and John's glances held for a few seconds. "She's definitely going to Rosemount, Wade. I know she's fighting it, but I'm convinced as soon as she allows herself to, she'll be as enthusiastic about that school as she is about Chewack."

Wade shrugged. "I'm not so sure."

"She'll adjust."

*~*

The camping trip was everything the girls hoped it would be--challenging horseback rides, simple but tasty meals and plenty of time to chat. That night, tucked into their sleeping bags under the stars, they finally murmured their goodnights. But sleep wouldn't come to Leslie. She tossed and turned so much that the dog, who was lying on top of her sleeping bag, crept over to Janelle's quietly sleeping form.

One single thought churned over and over in her mind--Rosemount Academy. What am I going to do? An answer came to her, but she rejected it. There's no way I could pull that off. But one obstacle after another faded as she worked out solutions. Finally, the plan seemed workable. She fell asleep then, comforted that at least she had a plan. She would say nothing of it to anyone. Not even Janelle.

The next afternoon, on the ride home, Leslie glanced over to her friend. "What would you think about driving to Rosemount?"

"To Spokane? Les, that's a long way."

"I know. About three hours each way. We could leave early."

"When?"

"How about tomorrow morning, or Tuesday?"

"I don't think my folks would let me drive the car that far."

"I don't think my Dad normally would either, but since I'm so against going to that school, maybe he would think I just want to show you to make it seem better, or something."

"Why do you want to show me?"

"Don't you want to see it?"

"Sure. But it's not going to make me feel any better."

"But then you could sort of picture where I am."

"Okay. Let's ask."

That evening, after returning from the camping trip, Leslie approached her father.

"Dad, do you think I could use the car so Janelle and I could drive to Spokane? I want to show her Rosemount."

She saw his mind whirling.

"I guess it would be okay. I want you to get an early start though and stop every once in a while to take a break. How about going on Tuesday, to give yourself a day of rest after your camping trip."

"Tuesday's fine. If we leave here at six, we'd be there about nine, snoop around for two or three hours, then leave at twelve or one. We'll be home by supper time. Thanks, Dad."

Leslie smiled at her father. It seemed odd. It had been a long time since she'd smiled at him.

## *TEN*

Leslie couldn't remember just how to get to the school, so her Dad had drawn a little map of Spokane, showing the streets she should take. The school was on the far side of the city, past the downtown area.

Approaching Rosemount, as they turned down the winding driveway, Janelle exclaimed, "Wow! Leslie, you didn't tell me how snazzy the place is."

Leslie was surprised at her friend's reaction. "Oh. I never thought of it that way. Do you think so?"

"Let's put it this way: I wish I could come with you."

"If you could come with me, Janelle, I wouldn't mind leaving Chewack so much."

School wasn't in session, but several cars were parked in the parking lot, probably staff preparing for the school year. The girls parked and began wandering around the campus.

"This building is the gym and there's a swimming pool, too." Leslie tried the door and found it unlocked. They stepped inside.

"My gosh, it's big. I've never seen such a huge pool."

"It's Olympic size."

They went from building to building, sometimes taking quick peeks when they found unlocked doors.

Janelle looked wistful. "It's really a nice place, Les,"

"I'd give anything not to come, Janelle. This place has caused me so much grief so far I hate to even think of the day my dad brings me for good. It makes me sick every time I think about it."

"I dread it, too. We haven't gone into that big building yet. What is it?"

"It's the Administration Building but I don't want to go in there. I'm afraid that lady who interviewed me will be there. I don't want her to see me."

"Why?"

"Because it was such a terrible interview and I could never explain why we're here."

Janelle shrugged. "Oh well, it doesn't matter. It's a neat place, Les, but it depresses me."

"Why should it depress you? I'm the one that has to come here."

"I know. That's why."

When they returned to the car, Leslie said, "Let's drive around a little bit. I want to know where things are."

"Things?"

"Yeah, like Greyhound."

"The bus station? Why?"

"Maybe that's how I'll get home. I don't think my Dad will always be taking me back and forth."

When they stopped to get gas, Leslie looked up the address for Greyhound in the phone book. She asked the cashier for directions. It was only about two miles from the school. Noting the city bus route signs on Newhalem Street, just a couple of blocks from the school, she drove to the

Greyhound terminal and slowed as she passed. "Well, there it is."

Janelle looked at her friend and shook her head. "Les, you're weird."

She pulled into a pick-up zone. "I want to pick up a schedule. I'll be right back."

"Les --" she heard Janelle say. She hurried out of the car and slammed the door.

She ran into the station and picked up a printed schedule.

"Can I help you?" a man from behind the counter asked.

"No, thanks, I just need a schedule."

"Where to?"

"Ah, I'm not sure."

The man gave her a blank stare. "Well --"

"Thank you!" she called merrily, clutching the schedule while hurrying for the door.

Climbing back into the car, Leslie said, "Well, anything more you want to see before we head back?"

"No, not really. Are you sure you don't want to do anything else? Check airports? Car rentals?"

Leslie laughed. "Now there's an idea! Oh, look. There's a pawn shop. Let's go in." She pulled the car off to the side of the street.

"Leslie! Yuck! The place looks creepy. This isn't the greatest part of town, either."

"It's the middle of the day, Janelle. Let's go in."

Janelle shrugged.

They stepped into the dingy shop. A shifty-looking man with a huge belly stood behind a cluttered counter and eyed them as they entered the shop. His once white shirt was stained and tight across his middle. He wore a hand-gun in a holster under his arm.

He showed yellow teeth, imitating a smile. "Well, well. Our clientele has definitely taken a turn for the better. Looking for something special, girls?"

"No, just looking."

"Take your time."

Leslie glanced around the dark shop. Under a glass counter, men's and women's jewelry, mostly wedding rings, shared space with hand guns ranging from tiny to almost foot-long. Rifles hung on the wall behind the counter. The smell of gun oil hung heavily in the air.

Musical instruments, mostly guitars, a few dusty televisions and radios lay scattered about. An assortment of suitcases were piled in a corner. One large suitcase caught Leslie's eye. She looked it over and opened it, turning her head aside when a strong musty smell rolled out. The suitcase was well used, but apparently made of real leather and in fair condition. And it was very large.

"How much is the suitcase?" Leslie asked.

"Les...." Janelle whispered, shocked.

"Ten dollars."

"Okay, I'll take it."

The huge suitcase took almost all the trunk space.

"What do you plan to do with that ugly thing?"

"I'm going to use it for my clothes and stuff."

"You already have that luggage your dad gave you for Christmas."

"But nothing this large. I'll have a lot of stuff to take, you know."

On the way out of town, they stopped along the Spokane River. They climbed out of the car and sat on the bank. Preoccupied, Leslie sat with her legs drawn up, her chin resting on her knees.

"What are you thinking about?" Janelle asked.

"About how much I don't want to go to Rosemount."

"Les, I wish you didn't have to come here, too, but it seems like a nice school."

Who could ask for a better friend than Janelle? "I'm really mad at my Dad for making me."

"I know. I am too. But when I told my mom that she got all over me. She said parents have to do what they feel is best; unless they do, they're not doing their job. She says your dad is doing what he feels is best for you."

"Big deal."

"I know."

They fell silent. Leslie fell into her habit of wondering about Lilith and Roxanne. If it weren't for them, I probably could have talked Dad out of sending me to Rosemount.

Finally, Leslie sighed. "We'd better go."

The drive home was quiet, each wrapped in thought. They stopped for lunch at a cafe in Wilbur. "Well," Janelle remarked dryly as they returned to the car, "that was a forgettable lunch."

"Really," Leslie agreed.

*~*

School would start in two weeks. Leslie waffled between not knowing what to do with herself and being frenzied with activity. At one point she came up from the basement carrying several cardboard boxes.

"Whatever will you do with those?" Maureen asked.

"I'm sorting through my stuff. I need to use your large garbage bags, too. I have a bunch of stuff for Goodwill."

"Honey, why do that now? Just get your school clothes ready."

But Leslie returned to her room and behind the closed door sorted, discarded, and boxed her belongings.

Searching for her brother, she found him hunched over a tractor. "Wade, can I have that backpack of yours? You never use it anymore."

"That old gray one? Why?"

"'When I go back and forth to school, I'll use it. I'd rather use a backpack than a suitcase."

He shrugged. "Okay, if that's what you want. It's pretty grungy though."

Leslie brought it up from the basement, took it outside, and brushed it off. She tried it on, but the straps were adjusted for Wade's height and build. She found her brother again and asked him to help her fit it.

"You can't really fit it until you have it packed, Les, but here, this is what you do." He put it on her. "See this hip-belt? You pull this snug so the weight rides on your hips. Then you tighten the shoulder straps, then ease them off a bit. But I can't imagine you'll be wearing it much, just putting your stuff in it for the ride home." He patted the pack, still on her back. "There you go."

"Thanks, Wade." She returned to her room, adding the pack to her things-to-take pile.

*~*

"Leslie," John announced cheerily on Monday at breakfast, one week before school would begin, "I'd like to give you a farewell party. I thought you could invite some friends and we would have the family, the hands..."

"No, thank you."

"You don't want a party? Honey, it would be nice for people to be able to say good..."

"I don't *want* a party," she snapped, glaring at her father. "Tell you what--after I leave, you guys can have a great party to celebrate. You can invite *your* friends."

The hurt written on her father's face burned a hole in Leslie's heart. Tears filled her eyes, but she continued to glare.

Wade, too, showed shock at her outburst. Maureen fidgeted with the coffee pot.

Without a word, John left the table, strode into his office, and closed the door.

## *ELEVEN*

Leslie now knew her life would soon be changed forever. Really, it already had. With a heavy heart, she measured everything she did in terms of how many more times: how many more times she would be able to ride Polly... she would see Janelle... she would enjoy the privacy of her room?

Her relationship with her father had deteriorated to brief, necessary conversations. Gone were the friendly chats, the bantering they had enjoyed before. Their good-night kisses were merely perfunctory, lacking affection, at least on Leslie's part. She didn't have much contact with Wade anymore. She had been too preoccupied lately to help him. Chores used to be the time when they saw one another and when they'd had the opportunity to really talk. Maureen was always there, of course, and everything seemed the same between them.

She had almost stopped seeing Kip. They had only talked on the phone a time or two since she and Janelle had gone camping, when he had asked her out. *It doesn't matter, soon I won't be seeing him at all.*

Her music, or lack of it, caused her great anguish. She played by the hour when her father was out of the house.

Maureen tried many times to cheer her up. "Leslie, shall we run into town to get you some supplies, maybe a nice leather notebook?"

"No, thanks Maureen. The one I have is fine."

"Well, then, you'll need a dress or two, maybe a skirt and sweater..."

"I've got enough clothes. I don't need anything, Maureen." Except a father who understands how I feel.

Maureen looked up fondly at Leslie. They were folding clothes in the laundry room. Maureen handed Leslie one end of a sheet, then stood back so they could fold it. "Honey, I'm going to miss you so."

"Me, too," Leslie croaked.

"Leslie, I want you to know that I did talk to your father about your going to Rosemount. I asked him to reconsider. I probably shouldn't have, but I did."

"Thanks for trying, anyway. I don't think it matters to him what anyone thinks. Especially me."

"Well, honey, he's doing what he feels is best for you. I'll pray for you, pray that you'll have a quick adjustment and that you'll be happy there." She quickly ducked down to the dryer to pull out more linens.

"Thank you," Leslie said, her voice thick with emotion.

*~*

John sat at his desk, phone receiver in one hand, his other hand ready to dial.

Leslie stuck her head into the office. "Dad, can I use the car to go into town?"

"Sure." He hung up the phone and looked at her hopefully. "Or I could take you in."

75

She'd never thought of the possibility of this offer. Normally, he wouldn't have taken the time. She drew a deep breath. "Thanks, but I'm meeting friends."

On the road, she went over again what she had to do. Her first stop was to Paul Silva's. He was a creep and she couldn't stand him, but he was the only one who had what she needed. He lived with a bunch of guys, and girls too, probably, just past the downtown area in a run-down house. Leslie had known who he was at school but had never talked to him until she'd called him last week to make these arrangements.

As she walked up the cracked sidewalk, she could hear the throbbing beat of hard rock. She rang the doorbell. No response. She knocked on the door, but it didn't make a dent in the noise already pounding the air. She banged on the door. Nothing.

What if he isn't home? What will I do?

She opened the door and yelled. "Paul! Are you here?"

He came from the other room, zipping up his pants. "Yeah?"

"I'm Leslie. I'm... I'm here for the new I.D."

"The what?"

Is this guy brain dead? Uninvited, she entered the house. "Paul, I called you last week about it. I need an I.D. for an eighteen year old."

"Oh. Right. Just a minute." He came back with a shoe box and set it on the cluttered table. The house was as awful on the inside as it looked outside. Dirty and smelly.

"How about this one?"

She'd at least expected him to have selected one for her in advance, to have given it some thought. He'd had a whole week. She looked at the driver's license he held out to her.

"She doesn't even look like me."

He took it back, looked at the card, looked at her, dropped it back into the box, then rummaged around again.

"Where did you get all these?"

"Friends, or I found them...sort of."

Oh, boy. Stolen. She barely knew Paul. He'd dropped out of school last year but was older than most of the kids at the high school. But she knew he dealt in fake I.D.'s, along with other things.

"Here's one. It's a lousy picture--it could be you. It could be me."

She looked at it critically. The picture was poor, fuzzy, somebody with a crooked smile and short hair. The name on it read Linda Carpenter. How odd. Same initials as mine. "Okay. You said twenty dollars." She handed him the money.

"Thirty."

"You said twenty."

He shrugged and took the money.

"And you promised not to tell anyone."

He nodded. Bored. "So who would I tell?"

Next stop, the bank. This might be tricky. She'd signed her dad's name on the withdrawal slip. She hoped Lilith wouldn't be there.

She was, but at her desk on the other side of the bank.

She stepped up to the counter. "I need to close this account. I'm going away to school in Spokane. I'll open an account there."

"All right," the teller said cheerfully. "We'll make a check out to you and to your father."

She hoped the color didn't drain out of her face, as she felt it had. "No, just to me. The account is 'either/or.' He won't be in Spokane with me." Her heart pounded. The lady seemed to be looking into her brain. "But he's signed the withdrawal. It was his idea I do this."

"I wonder if I should call him," the teller thought aloud.

Leslie felt like running, but stood her ground. "I don't think you can reach him right now. He's a rancher. He's up on the summer range someplace and won't be home until late." She sighed. "He's taking me to Spokane early Monday morning."

"Well, I guess it would be okay. Do you know the name of the bank in Spokane? I could make it payable to them."

A scream ricocheted in her head. "No. I'll look for one when I get there. Just make it payable to me." *It is my money, after all. But Dad and I agreed I wouldn't touch the money without our talking about it first. Oh, well. Rules don't seem to apply any more.* Her stomach churned.

After an interminable time the clerk prepared the check. Just as Leslie turned to leave, Lilith looked up and saw her. Leslie gave her as genuine a smile as she could muster and started for the door.

"Leslie!"

*Now what?* She stepped over to Lilith's desk. "Hi."

Lilith put out her hand.

*She wants me to give the check back! But it's so weird-- she's smiling.* It occurred to Leslie then, Lilith wanted to shake hands!

Leslie transferred the check to her other hand and shook the proffered hand.

"Good luck to you at Rosemount. It's a wonderful school. I wish I could send Roxanne."

"Thank you." *I wish you could send her too. Then I wouldn't have to go.*

Leslie glanced at her watch. "Well, I've got some other things to take care of. Good-bye." With great effort she kept herself from running out the door.

Next stop, Goodwill. She pulled out of the car trunk two large plastic bags--old clothes, a few stuffed animals, odd and ends of her past, many items she had cherished. She left the bags on Goodwill's counter, too disheartened to speak with the woman there.

One more place to go. Her appointment was at two...she had almost an hour to kill. At the drug store she whiled away the time looking at magazines. What innocent people. All wrapped up in dress designs, perfume, deodorants. "Make Play with Your Child Meaningful." "What Husbands Expect in Sex." Nothing that would fit her situation. How to handle being exiled from your own home.

When she was sure no one was looking, she pulled out her new identification card. Would it work? The girl in the picture didn't look much like her. Look how short her hair is.

Finally, it was time and she stepped into the beauty salon.

Lori smiled. "Be right with you."

Within a few minutes Lori gestured Leslie to sit in the chair. Wrapping the bib around her, Lori touched Leslie's thick, dark brown hair. She usually wore it in a ponytail, but it was loose today. "So, you said you wanted a trim?"

"No. I want it cut. Very short."

"Your long hair is so beautiful. You sure?"

"Yes."

"*Very* short?"

"Very."

Leslie kept her eyes closed most of the time so Lori wouldn't see the tears.

"Just need a change, huh?"

"Yes." *Please don't talk to me.*

"This will really change your appearance."

"I know." *Shut up. Shut up.*

Long minutes of silence, broken only by the snip of scissors. "Well, what do you think?"

It was short all right. About an inch and a half all over. Leslie stared in the mirror, unable to believe the reflection was her.

"It's fine."

"It makes your long neck look so graceful. I think you've aged five years, Leslie."

Leslie casually looked in the mirror. She turned her head this way and that. "Oh, I don't know. You think so?"

"Definitely."

\*~\*

When she walked into the kitchen, Maureen stopped stirring her applesauce and gaped. "Leslie, what in the world? I can't believe it's you!"

"Do you like it?"

Maureen stammered. "Well...yes but you look so different, so much older! Your eyes look huge. Why did you do it?"

"I just thought it would be easier."

"Does your father know?"

"No. Why should he? It's my hair."

Maureen's mouth formed a straight line as she went back to her stirring.

Wade noticed it next. "Leslie, what the hell --"

"What? Don't you like it?"

"I had to look twice to see if it was you."

Her father came into the kitchen, hearing the commotion. His face darkened. "What have you done?" His harsh voice dumbfounded her. Of all the things to get mad about.

"Dad, I just had my hair cut."

He grabbed her arm. "What are you doing to yourself? Why would you do such a thing?" Anger made his voice raspy.

"I...I just wanted to have my hair cut!" Resentment rushed to the surface. Her day had been full of tension--this was the final straw. "What difference does it make? You won't have to look at it!"

For a brief moment she thought he might strike her. God knows she'd asked for it often enough lately. When she was little he had turned her over his knee and given her an old-fashioned spanking a time or two. Never very hard, but enough to get her attention. But over a haircut? He continued to grip her arm. He stared at her, then blinked. He dropped his hand.

"Dinner's ready," Maureen said.

*~*

Two days, now. What would be the best thing to do with this day? This one precious Saturday...

She rode Polly to Janelle's and they rode for hours. Leslie savored the rolling, golden hills. Standing in her stirrups, her eyes followed the hills as they faded from view, golden to deep purple to fuzzy gray, row after row, endlessly. She lingered at the stand of pines, drawing in their tangy scent. Only one or two puffy clouds hung in the pure, blue sky. The day was hot, but a perfect breeze kept it from being uncomfortable.

Both girls were quiet. Leslie suspected that Janelle wanted to talk, but was reluctant to barge into her friend's thoughts. It was just as well, Leslie was so self-absorbed, she couldn't think of much to say, or how to express what she felt.

She couldn't remember ever keeping a secret, not a real secret anyway, from Janelle. Now schemes and plans crammed her troubled mind, things she couldn't share with her best friend.

Finally, Janelle broke the silence. "I called you yesterday but Maureen said you'd gone into town. Why didn't you call me to go with you?"

"Oh, I didn't think you'd want to." It hurt to lie to Janelle, but she had no choice.

"You didn't even tell me you were going to have your hair cut!"

"It was just a last minute thing." She avoided her friend's hurt look. It's happening already. We're being torn apart. Thanks to Dad. Tears stung her eyes.

Dinner that evening was awkward. Maureen tried to get something going a couple of times: "Well, Leslie had a nice ride with Janelle today."

Her father tried to show enthusiasm. "Good, Les. Where did you go?"

"To the hills. I wanted to see them one last time."

John sighed. "Honey, it isn't for the last time."

"Yes, it is."

Maureen, again. "Leslie, I bought your favorite pork roast for tomorrow night."

Leslie's mind reeled with remarks about the condemned person's last meal, but she said only, "Thanks, Maureen."

She was tired, tired of this. Oddly, she wished it were over, that she was already gone. Her soul hung in shreds. Nothing seemed the same anymore.

Wade tried his hand. "Les, want to ride into town with me after dinner? I'm just going in to buy a radiator hose for my truck, but then we could go wherever you wanted, stop at Dairy Queen, whatever."

"No, thanks, Wade. I have some things to do." She didn't, but her heart was so heavy she couldn't bear expending any more energy trying to be cheerful for Wade. This business was killing her.

\*~\*

Just one more day. A little more than twenty-four hours. She surprised Maureen by accompanying her to church. She enjoyed the hymns but couldn't keep her mind on the sermon. Some of her friends attended this church, but she didn't feel like mingling. Why bother? She would never see these kids again.

After the noon meal she wandered into the corral and spent a long time grooming Polly, all the while murmuring love to her wonderful horse. The horse turned her slender head and whiffled softly in Leslie's ear.

Later, she tried to read but couldn't concentrate. Finally, she helped Maureen make applesauce.

"Leslie, I can manage this. You have better things to do with your time."

"I'll peel, you stir. Your hands have been in the water so long they look like prunes. Maureen, I don't know what else to do with myself."

After dinner Leslie helped Maureen with the dishes, again overriding the housekeeper's objections. "I want to do it, Maureen." One last time.

She sat in the living room with her father for a few minutes watching the news on television. Wouldn't it be wonderful if there were some huge disaster and I wouldn't be able to go. A tornado, an outbreak of some terrible disease-- that we'd all live through, of course. Maybe a plane crash into Rosemount. No such luck. War was happening in other places of the world, buildings were being blown up, some nut opened fire into a shopping mall, but except for one girl's broken heart, nothing much was happening here.

Several times she felt her father's stare. Probably trying to get used to this hair cut. She couldn't get used to it, either. Out of habit, she tried to brush her hair back and came up empty handed.

Leslie stood and turned to leave the room. "I'll finish packing."

"Can I help you do anything?"

Leslie thought her father looked depressed, too. *Good.* "No, thanks."

In her room she packed the final cardboard boxes. She neatly labeled them and stacked them in her closet. She packed the suitcases her father had given her and the large suitcase she had bought. Tomorrow's clothes were folded on a chair.

Everything was ready. She showered, then slipped on an old pair of pajamas, ones she wouldn't be taking. From the large suitcase she took out a tablet and a pen and began writing letters. The first to her father, then to Wade, and finally, to Maureen. It didn't take long. She had given each letter thought and knew exactly what she would say.

Tears streamed down her cheeks, she had to stop several times to dry her eyes. At the end of Maureen's letter a tear dropped on the bottom of the page. She almost started to rewrite the letter, but didn't have the heart to go through it again. Maureen probably wouldn't even notice.

## *TWELVE*

Leslie awakened with a profound sense of dread. How am I going to get through this day? Panic seized her.

Just take it one minute at a time. Make yourself be calm. She swung her legs over the side of the bed and sat there, head hanging, chin touching her chest. Move. Do something.

She forced herself to dress. Moving around felt better. As she descended the stairs she heard Wade's voice.

"Dad, do you think this is the right thing to do?"

Leslie froze.

A loud thunk--probably her dad's coffee mug hitting the table--followed. "I wouldn't be doing it if I didn't think it was the right thing to do. How many times do I have to say this?"

Wade's voice again. "It's not going to be the same around here."

Maureen rushed out of the kitchen. She glanced up the stairs and, seeing Leslie, her hand flew to her mouth. She scurried into her room.

Leslie continued down the stairs and entered the kitchen. Her father had stepped to the stove. He took a plate from the stack and dished up Wade's eggs, then his own. He glanced up, saw Leslie and he dished up hers, too.

"Not so much, Dad. I'm not hungry."

"Eat what you can."

Maureen returned to the kitchen, sized up the situation and without a word dished up her own plate. Leslie noticed her eyes were red-rimmed and her mouth drawn in a straight, severe line.

John looked at Leslie. "Are you all packed? We need to leave by eight."

"I'm ready."

Other than this exchange the meal fell silent. After eating only part of her breakfast, Leslie left the table, returned to her room, and packed her last minute things. She brought all her bags to the upstairs hallway, carefully closed the door to her room, and began carrying her luggage downstairs.

Wade sprang from the table to assist her. "Here, I'll help you with those. Holy cow, Les--you taking all this?"

"It isn't so much."

"Aren't you using that pack?"

"I'm taking it. It's in the large suitcase."

Wade touched the scarred, old suitcase with the toe of his boot. "Where did you get this thing?"

"I bought it."

John joined them in the downstairs hallway. "Why did you do that? I would have gotten you another piece to match this set."

Leslie shrugged. When they stepped out of the cool house, they found the air depressingly heavy. John glanced at the overcast sky. "Could rain today."

Wade nodded. "Might as well, it's so muggy. I'm sweating already."

Leslie seemed oblivious to the small talk as they loaded her bags into the car. She and her father returned to the house and entered the kitchen. Leslie fell into Maureen's waiting arms, resting her head on the soft, warm shoulder. "Oh, Maureen."

Her father left the room.

"There, now, honey. Some day we'll laugh about how sad we all are today, but you'll see. You'll love it there." Leslie silently shook her head, still protected by Maureen's warm embrace and comforting scent.

Leslie pulled away then, looked squarely into Maureen's eyes, drew a long breath. "Good-bye, Maureen. Thank you for everything."

She looked around. "Where's Wade?" She glanced outside. The last she saw him he had been helping put the bags in the car. He must be in the barn. Typical.

She stepped into the quiet semi-darkness of the barn. Wade stood in the doorway of the tack room. He tried to smile, but only managed a crooked attempt. He held out his arms and she folded into them. "Good-bye, Wade."

He awkwardly patted her back. "Good-bye, Les. Give 'em hell." His voice was husky with emotion.

She stiffened and looked up at him. Through tears, her eyes blazed. "I'm not giving them anything."

Startled at her vehemence, Wade blinked. He held her shoulders and looked deep into her eyes. "Les, if you keep this up you'll only hurt yourself. Lighten up. It's okay to give in to it now. You've tried everything and, I want you to know, I've tried too. Now it's time to go along with it."

Her eyes slid off to the side and he gave her a little shake, forcing her to look at him. "If you don't Les, you're the loser."

"I'm the loser, anyway."

Wade stared at her, obviously trying to think of something comforting to say. He dropped his arms. "Well, see you on Thanksgiving."

She shook her head slowly. *You just don't get it, do you?*

Hearing the car engine start, she left the barn. Without looking around, she climbed into the front seat and buckled herself in. It had been her intention to say good-bye to Polly, but she didn't have it in her. She would remember her mare the way she had seen her yesterday, tall, proud and beautiful. Running free, at home.

## *THIRTEEN*

The ride to Spokane seemed longer than ever before. The golden desert country stretched out as far as they could see. Heat waves rippled the highway. Cattle bunched in shade, where they could find it.

Uncomfortable silence hung between father and daughter.

Finally, John said, "I'd like you to call home at least once a week."

"Home? I don't have a home anymore."

Her father whirled on her. The car swerved with the sudden movement. "How can you say that! Your home is where it's always been." Momentarily, he had his hands full straightening out the car.

"You've told me 'home is where your hat is.' I've packed my hat."

Miles sped by, excruciating, silent miles.

Stopping at noon at a roadside café, Leslie ate a fraction of her lunch; it was all John could do to finish his.

An hour later, at Rosemount, they wound down the now familiar curved driveway but instead of driving into the visitor's parking lot, they pulled up to the dormitory and unloaded the bags from the trunk.

"I'll get the car out of the way to make room for other people. There's a place to park over there," he gestured to a small parking lot close to the dormitory. "Why don't you go on in and get your key."

Leslie nodded. She signed in and was issued her key to room 213. Her father joined her, and they returned outside to get her bags.

"I'll take the big one, can you handle the other two?"

"Yeah." Leslie picked up the two bags and led the way. There were stairs, but Leslie turned toward the elevator because of the bulky baggage.

"I'll bet after a while you'll prefer the stairs, rather than wait for the elevator," John commented.

Leslie nodded. She could barely swallow; her heart blocked her throat.

John stood aside while she unlocked the door. Her room-mate apparently hadn't come yet. Good.

The sparkling clean room smelled of freshly laundered linens. Leslie mechanically noticed these things but did not embrace them as her own. This was not her room.

"Do you want me to help you unpack? I'm in no hurry, I'd be glad to."

"No, thanks." She stared out the window, unable to look at her father or even around the room.

Her father turned her toward him and gently touched her chin with his finger, lifting her head. Leslie raised her eyes to his, eyes that immediately filled with tears. One huge tear slid down her cheek.

"Leslie. This is not the end of the world. Honey, if you let yourself, I know you'll like it here. I've been meaning to tell you--if you want to take piano lessons here you still can. I wish you would. I asked Mrs. Holmes to save the spot with Mr. Richie."

Leslie remained silent. She'd said it all.

John sighed and clumsily patted her shoulder. "Well, if there's nothing else, I'll take off. Okay?"

Eyes cast down, Leslie nodded.

Her father drew her to him. His voice was a thick whisper. "Les, it'll be all right."

Tears streamed down her face, wetting his shirt. Then, with finality, she pulled away. She glanced up at him but couldn't force herself to meet his gaze. She looked past him, over his shoulder, at the wall.

"Good-bye, honey. Call me tomorrow. Okay?"

She nodded. "Good-bye, Dad," she managed. *I love you.* It wouldn't come out, she couldn't say it out loud. She tried again. *I love you.* Nothing.

After he left she went into the bathroom, sat on the toilet and wept bitter tears.

She glanced at her watch and a shock rushed down her spine. She stood, reached for the sparkling white washcloth and washed her face with cold water.

She heard a commotion at the door. Oh no!

Leslie opened the bathroom door to four smiling faces.

"Why, hello!" the mother said cheerfully. "You must be Leslie. This is your room-mate, Megan, I'm her mother Mrs. Whitefield." She fondly put her hand on her husband's arm. "This is Megan's dad, Mr. Whitefield, and," she patted the younger girl's curly, blond head, "her younger sister, Amanda. Isn't this a wonderful place! Rosemount is my alma mater, too."

The family was all smiles, everyone seemed delighted with life, delighted to be here, delighted to leave their daughter at such a wonderful place. And no one seemed more delighted than Megan.

Leslie recovered from her shock and made an attempt to sound rational. "Hello, I'm Leslie Cahill. Excuse me, I need to run downstairs with this suitcase. My dad brought it up by mistake. I need to catch him before he leaves." She slipped her purse over her shoulder.

Mrs. Whitefield's pretty, happy face looked puzzled. "How could that happen?"

Leslie's mind roiled, her words followed. "Oh, I packed this suitcase with my old clothes for Goodwill. I hadn't even noticed he brought it up. Excuse me, I need to hurry before he leaves."

Mr. Whitefield stepped forward. "Here, I'll take it for you." He seemed nice, happy. The whole family had these perpetually smiling faces, though now the girls had perplexed looks along with their smiles.

"No, it isn't heavy, I'll get it. See you soon."

"Wait," Mrs. Whitefield said, "you've forgotten your key." Leslie had set the room key on one of her smaller suitcases.

"That's okay," Leslie said, working the large suitcase through the door, "you'll be here. I'll be right back."

Her heart pounded. She took the elevator back down. In order to leave she had to go through the same entrance they had entered such a short time ago. There probably was another door, but she didn't know the building well enough to know where it was, and she didn't have time to look around for it.

"Leslie, what are you doing?" Her heart stopped. Blood rushed to her face. She forced herself to be calm.

"Oh, Mrs. Dartworth. I need to catch my dad real quick. He brought up this suitcase by mistake. It's stuff for the Goodwill." She looked outside, where her dad had parked. His car was gone. "Oh good, there he is."

Mrs. Dartworth attempted to look, but a crowd gathered around her desk, students picking up their keys.

Leslie hurried out. "Dad!" she called. "You need to take this one with you." She felt like an idiot, talking out loud to herself. One woman absently looked around, but by now many people were arriving. No one seemed to notice the circumstances of one particular student.

The two blocks seemed more like two miles. The bulky suitcase banged against her leg as she hurried along. Finally, she stood at the bus stop on Newhalem. She put the suitcase alongside the bus shelter where it was less conspicuous. She had no idea what the fare would be; she had several coins ready.

The bus rocked toward her and slowed down with the sound of rushing air. The door slid open.

"You bringing that big thing in here?" the driver called out.

"Yes, I can sit in one of these seats," she said, indicating a side-facing seat. She struggled up the two steps, lifting the scruffy bag in front of her. "How much is the fare?"

"Seventy-five cents. Where're you going?"

"To the Greyhound Bus station." Careful. Be careful.

"You a Rosemount student?"

Panic. "Yes, but right now I'm meeting my aunt at Greyhound. I have to give her this suitcase." Where did that story come from? It just rolled out.

"Well, keep it out of people's way."

The Greyhound Bus terminal looked smaller this time. She stepped up to the counter.

"I see you're back." It was the man who had talked to her when she picked up the schedule before.

Leslie, startled by the recognition, managed a smile. "Yep. One way to Pendleton, please."

"You just made it. Leaves at one-ten, arrives in Pendleton at seven. That'll be thirty dollars."

Only fifteen minutes to spare. She hadn't thought the timing would be so close. She sat in the waiting room. It seemed like everyone stared at her. You probably look scared. *I am scared.*

She would have to change her plans about this suitcase. That man recognized her and she didn't want to give him more reason to remember.

"Pendleton, all aboard!"

Heart pounding, she handed the heavy suitcase to the driver. He stowed it in the luggage compartment, and she climbed aboard. I feel so unreal, like I'm inside a stranger's skin.

## *FOURTEEN*

Wade returned to the house to find Maureen sitting in the living room, idle. He stared at her a moment. Maureen was never idle. When she did sit she normally read, or mended clothes, or did *something*. She looked up at him and blinked. He sat heavily on the davenport.

He had plenty of work to do--fall round up was just around the corner. He'd mumbled something to the others and returned to the house.

He sighed. "Hell of a deal."

"Yes."

"I wish I felt as sure as Dad that this was the thing to do."

"Me, too."

"I tried two or three times to talk to him, but he was so damned sure."

"I tried once, too."

"How do you think she'll do, Maureen?"

"I honestly don't know. She's one of the brightest girls I've ever known. She's also very sensitive. It's what makes her the way she is, so special."

"She can be tough, though. And stubborn."

"Yes, that too, as she's shown us these past weeks. If she puts her mind to it, she'll make a good adjustment, otherwise...." She shook her head.

Wade sat forward with his elbows on spread knees, his big hands folded between them. "I should have fought harder, argued with Dad more." He stared at the floor and shook his head. "I let her down."

"I don't think it would have done any good. He's worried about conditions at Chewack; nothing would have changed his mind." She uttered a sad, rueful chuckle. "Where do you think Leslie gets her stubbornness?"

Wade slapped his leg. "Well, I've got work to do. I'll be in the equipment shed." He tromped out.

"I'll be right here."

*~*

Wade heard Maureen's voice on the shop's intercom. "Wade, are you there?"

"Yeah?"

"Come to the house right away."

"Why, what's wrong?"

"Just come."

"On my way." Gravel spun as he turned the pick-up toward the house. His heart thudded in his chest. His body felt prickly. Prepared for bad news--his gut rarely lied--he banged into the kitchen.

"What, Maureen?"

Maureen stood in the middle of the kitchen, her apron twisted between her hands. Tears streamed down her face. "The school called. They think she's gone."

"Gone? Who called? Did Dad and Les get there?"

"Yes. John and Leslie picked up the key to her room, and they carried her bags up. Then John left. The housemother, or somebody, said that Leslie came back down with a big suitcase for her father to take back. But then... then...."

"What?"

"... then no one saw her after that. They became alarmed after she didn't show up for orientation."

"Goddamn it!" He suddenly felt weak. He leaned over the kitchen counter, staring out the window. "She's run away. That's why she acted so weird this morning. She'd planned it all." *Do something. You've got to do something. I have to talk to Dad. No, I don't have time to wait. Think. Damn it. Think! I've got to find her. Where would she have gone?*

Maureen dabbed her eyes with her apron. "Mrs. Holmes, the woman who called, wondered if Leslie could be with her father. Do you think your dad might have changed his mind?"

"No."

"I don't think so, either. I understand her other bags are still in the room. They would have gone back for them. Maybe they're just off together. But that doesn't make sense, either." Maureen, still in the middle of the kitchen, smoothed her apron, then knotted it up again.

"Maureen, I'm going to Spokane, to Rosemount. Then I'm going to look for her."

Maureen looked as though there might be hope, after all. "I'll pack some food for you. Someone has to call the school to let them know what you plan to do."

"Call them. Tell them I'm on my way."

"What about your father? Will you wait for him?"

"There's no time for that. You tell him when he gets back. Tell him I'll call as soon as I talk to...who should I see?"

"Mrs. Holmes. Here, I'll write her name and number for you." She darted about the kitchen, grabbing food from the refrigerator, something to make sandwiches with.

"What's the address of the school? I don't even know where it is."

Maureen rushed into John's office. "I think I can find it here in his files."

Wade ran up to his room and returned to the kitchen, still stuffing clothes into a duffel bag.

"Do you have money?" she asked.

"Not much, do you?"

"Here, take this." She handed him sixty dollars of her household money.

"I'll use the credit card for gas."

"Fine. Let me get you the phone card, so you don't have to keep coming up with quarters to call us."

He headed for the basement stairs. "I'll get my sleeping bag." He returned, shaking his head. "Her sleeping bag's gone. Damn that kid."

"Do you have any idea of where she would go?" Maureen packed several sandwiches, some fruit and cookies into a small cooler. She poured coffee in a thermos, sloshing it over the opening in her haste. "Lord knows what I've packed-- at least you won't starve."

"It's fine, thanks. No, I don't know where she would go. Did she ask you anything, maybe about a certain place, anything like that?"

Maureen stared into the distance, thinking. "No."

"Get me one of her pictures." His mind was kicking into gear now, he could think more clearly.

He heard a garbled scream from upstairs. He took the stairs two at a time and bumped into Maureen in Leslie's room. The housekeeper's hand covered her mouth.

"What? What is it?"

"Look around. Everything is packed up. Her shelves are all bare, her dressers are empty."

"Why would she do that?"

"I don't know." Maureen looked around the room in disbelief.

Wade's eyes fell to his sister's bed. There, neatly placed were three envelopes, letters for all of them.

Gingerly, he picked up the envelopes. He handed Maureen's to her and opened the one addressed to him.

Dear Wade,

Thank you for being such a great brother. Sometimes I thought you were sort of mean but you were always there for me. Have a good life. With Teresa? Hope so.

Would you see that Polly is taken care of? Thanks.

I love you.
Leslie

He handed his letter to Maureen and took hers from her shaking hand.

Dear Maureen,

Thank you, Maureen, for all you've done for me. I've thought of you as a mother and I love you very much.

I would like you to have the vase on the window sill. When I was little I gave it to my mom for Mother's Day. After she died, I kept it in my room. I'd like you to have it now.

In the closet are boxes of clothes and
things that I've marked "church." I thought your
church might use them for their rummage sale.
                    Love,
                              Leslie

He hated to do it, but he ripped open his father's letter.
If there was any clue, he had to know.


Dear Dad,
        I'm sorry I've been such a pain lately. It's
just that I don't want to leave you and my home.
I know you think it's the best thing for me, but I
don't agree.
        You've given me a wonderful life--I've
loved my home, and I love you. Thank you for
everything.
                    Your loving daughter,
                              Leslie
"Oh shit." He wiped his eyes and handed the letter to
Maureen. "Give this to Dad when he gets home. Did you find a
picture?"
        "No, she's packed away everything. The pictures are
probably buried in those boxes."
        "Get that one in the office--her school picture." Wade
opened Leslie's clothes hamper. He gingerly picked up the light
cotton pajamas she'd worn that last night. He took a ragged
breath and left her room.
        They met in the kitchen. He placed the pajamas in a
clean plastic bag. "I'm taking Dutch. I'll get a bag of her food."
        "Here's the picture."
        They both stared at it.

"Damn. With her new haircut she doesn't look like this anymore." Wade shook his head. "She thought of everything."

Wade slung the duffel bag over his shoulder and grabbed the sleeping bag. He ran out the back door, tossed them into the back of the pick-up, and returned for the cooler and the dog's food.

"How long will you be gone?" Maureen trailed after him to the truck, carrying the picture and the plastic bag with Leslie's pajamas.

He jammed the cooler and dog food in the built-in tool box in the bed of the truck. "Until I find her. She's got such a head start, it might take awhile, two or three days. I'll call from Spokane. Dad should stay here, Maureen. Don't let him go. She might call and he should be here to handle it from this end."

"I'll try. Take care, Wade." She wiped her eyes. Usually briskly efficient, she looked wilted, drawn.

"You, too. I'll find her, Maureen." Wade whistled for Dutch, opened the driver's door and watched as she scampered in. He turned to Maureen and enveloped her in a long, solid hug. Maureen, whose head didn't reach his shoulder, seemed surprised, but comforted.

Her voice, against his chest, came out muffled. "Wade, now you be careful. I know how you feel, but it won't help if you're in an accident. You drive carefully. Try to calm yourself once you get on the road."

"Yes, ma'am."

By the time he actually left, scarcely half an hour had passed since Maureen had first called him. His mind sorted through the different possibilities. *Would she head for a big city, or some small place? She's probably ditched that old suitcase and is using my backpack now. God, I hope she's not planning to hitch a ride.*

*What is she thinking? What will she do?*

## *FIFTEEN*

The bus rambled on interminably. When the bus stopped at Cheney, Leslie fully expected to see her father's angry face. She envisioned him climbing onto the bus and looming over her. She squirmed in her seat. But, after picking up three passengers, the bus continued on.

Leslie's mind tumbled from ecstatic to frantic. On one hand, she was elated. *I did it! My timing was perfect. I can't believe it went so well!*

On the other hand, guilt consumed her. Never had she disobeyed in such a serious way. Disobeying hardly described what she had done. But she'd been forced to. It was her dad's idea, sending her away. She could be home right now, doing all the familiar things she'd always done and loved.

Did Dad know yet? Was he worried?

She rubbed her sweaty hands on her jeans, then clenched them tightly together. She could feel the blood throbbing in her temples. Her eyes darted to see if her purse was still there by her feet. She picked it up and clutched it to her. She was wracked with anxiety.

Have they seen my room yet? What did they think about all my clothes and things being packed away? At least that snotty Roxanne won't be pawing through my stuff. When that dip-head moves into my room, she won't have the satisfaction of moving my things out.

My chest hurts. I have to stop thinking about home, or I'll never make it. Am I too young to have a heart attack?

Okay, now what? I'll be in Pendleton around seven. What will I do then?

*Don't forget. Your name is Linda Carpenter. Linda Carpenter.*

The bus stopped again in Ritzville where the passengers disembarked for twenty minutes.

I could just get off here, ask the driver for my suitcase. But then what? Call Dad and say I'm sorry? Boy, sorry wouldn't describe what I'd be after he got through with me. What would he do? Probably take me right back to school. They'd probably put me on restriction for the next two years. All I'd ever see would be the inside of a classroom and the rest of the time they'd lock me in my room with that room-mate they saddled me with, what's her name, Megan. Megan and her grinning family. Geez, they were sickening with their love for that school. What's wrong with those people, anyway?

*I have to keep going, that's all there is to it. There's no turning back now.*

A bank near the bus depot reminded her that she needed to cash her check. Never before had she handled that much money. She put the envelope of cash into her purse and hugged the purse close to her body.

She bought a Coke and tried to calm herself. It was so hot! Her skin felt sticky with sweat, mostly from nerves too probably, but the weather didn't help.

All aboard again. She took her seat and tried to plan. Until now, all her energy and planning had gone toward the getaway. Now her future loomed, anxiety seized her. Her heart pounded. She turned her head and stared out the window, fearing the other passengers could read her thoughts.

When the bus door swooshed open in Connell, a blast of heat rushed in. Good thing the bus had air-conditioning. *I can't stay on this bus forever. What will I do in this heat with no house to go to? How will I even take a shower? What have I done!*

In Pasco they were given a twenty-five minute dinner break. The very thought of eating made her sick, but she knew she must eat something. Several passengers headed toward a small restaurant next door. She fell in line behind them. She couldn't remember ever feeling so hot. She could feel the heat of the sidewalk through her tennis shoes.

A group of men, probably transients, mingled outside a mission across the street. Two or three of them noticed her and it looked like they were talking about her. One of the men staggered toward her, his arms extended, shouting something in Spanish. She hurried to catch up with the others as she continued to watch him over her shoulder. The man stood in the middle of the street, swaying back and forth, leering at her. A car came up behind him and honked. Diverted, he waved his arms at the car and lurched toward the mission. Leslie shuddered.

Inside the café, the noisy air-conditioning didn't make a dent in the heat. She ordered a BLT and a glass of milk and hurried through her dinner.

Safely back on the bus again she thought of Wade. How had he reacted? With anger probably, like her father. What about Maureen? She wouldn't be mad, she would understand. Well, maybe she'd be a little upset. Oh, Maureen, I wish we could talk. I could phone home. *No, I can't.* What are they all doing? Do they even know I'm gone yet?

If only the Whitefields hadn't come just then. I wonder if they suspected anything. Would they have told anyone? Maybe they caught on right away and reported me!

The stop in Walla Walla took a few minutes. Several more people got off, two climbed on. Where was everyone going? Leslie quickly scanned the passengers and the people around the terminal for a familiar face. So far, so good.

Pendleton! Leslie had been here once with her family for the Pendleton Round up. After the rodeo they had stayed in a nice motel with a swimming pool. Her dad could hardly get her out of the pool to go to dinner. She'd give anything to dive into a pool right now.

The bus slowed, lurched, and the door whooshed open. *Well, here goes.* On legs that felt like rubber, she stepped off the bus and waited with the others for her suitcase.

\*~\*

Wade's mind raced. Dutch sat beside him in the front seat and watched the countryside fly by. The dog had traveled as far as Chewack but otherwise had rarely been off the ranch.

*What should I do first? It'll be after eight before I get to Spokane. I need to check in at Rosemount, see what I can piece together. Just take it one step at a time. Don't get ahead of yourself.*

Just outside Electric City he stopped to let the dog out. He pushed the seat forward and reached for her water dish and the water jug he kept behind the seat. She quickly lapped the water up, then wandered over to find a suitable place to do her business.

It was hot here, even hotter than at home. And no sign of rain. The back of his shirt was sweat-soaked. Maureen had packed some iced tea in a quart mayonnaise jar. Slices of lemon floated on top. Good old Maureen. He drank right out of the jar.

"Come on, Dutch, let's go." The blue heeler wagged her tail and jumped back into the front seat.

It was eight-twenty by the time he reached Rosemount. Even then he'd broken speed limits all the way. Once he reached Spokane, he lost time wandering around trying to find the school. He parked the dusty pick-up in the visitor's lot and walked to what looked like the main building. Stepping inside, it looked as though the building had been deserted. Well, he couldn't mess around here all night looking for someone. "Hello!" he called sharply.

Mrs. Holmes stepped into the hall. "Mr. Cahill?"

He touched the brim of his wide hat. "Yes, ma'am. I'm Wade Cahill."

"Oh, good. You're here. Your housekeeper called and said you were on your way. Let's go into my office, Mr. Cahill."

Wade took off his hat and brushed it against his knee. "Sorry I'm such a mess. I didn't take time to clean up."

"Yes. I can imagine how upsetting this news was...is. Mr. Cahill, I can't tell you how sorry we are --"

"Look, Mrs. Holmes, I need to keep moving. Just tell me what happened."

Mrs. Holmes outlined the different events that Leslie's room-mate's parents had approached her with, their concern after the orientation, and then her frantic search. She concluded with, "You're probably aware Leslie didn't want to come to Rosemount."

"Yes ma'am, I know."

"Do you suppose she and her father could be somewhere? The dormitory housemother said that she heard her call out to him." She shook her head. "I feel so bad about this. I guess in all the confusion...."

Although angry that such a thing could happen, Wade could understand it. "She was probably counting on confusion. Once you'd called and we looked in her room, it seemed to us that Leslie had planned this."

He stood to leave. "I'd like to take a quick look at her room, just to see if there's any clue. Maureen said Les left some of her bags. I'd like to see those, too."

"You're welcome to see her room, but really, there's nothing there. We've already checked it out. She left two bags and the room key. I brought them down here." She gestured to the two bags in the corner of her office.

"I'll be right back. I have to get my dog."

Mrs. Holmes looked up, surprised. "Dog?"

"I'll be right back."

Wade returned, carrying a plastic bag. Dutch scampered beside him. "Here, Dutch." He opened the plastic bag and let Dutch smell Leslie's pajamas. The dog poked her nose into the bag and made loud snuffling noises. "Where's Leslie?" Wade knelt down and opened the larger of the two suitcases containing blouses, skirts, sweaters, slacks, night clothes, a pair of shoes. Dutch buried her nose in the bag. Her tail wagged furiously.

"Here, Dutch" he said again when he opened the second, smaller suitcase. There, neatly folded with the tags still on them were the school uniform skirt, five blouses, and sweater. Dutch smelled the clothes but not as enthusiastically. She looked up at Wade, her eyes a question.

Wade shook his head and rubbed his eyes. "Well, there's sure no doubt that she planned all this. She had her stuff all sorted--which to take with her, which to leave and even the uniform clothes to return."

"It does look that way, now. What can I do to help, Mr. Cahill?"

"I'd still like to see her room. I need to get the dog used to looking. It'll be good for her to be somewhere we know Les has been." He stood, towering over Mrs. Holmes.

"Of course. It's in McMillian Dorm, just a short walk. I'll come with you so you can go right up without any questions."

"Fine." He glanced at the dog. "Here, girl."

When they rode the elevator at the dormitory, Dutch braced herself as the elevator lifted, her legs splayed for balance. She looked up at Wade in surprise.

At room 213, Mrs. Holmes knocked. Megan opened the door and stared at Mrs. Holmes and the large, dusty man. "Yes?"

"Megan, this is Leslie's brother, Wade Cahill. Please step out for a minute so that he can take a look at the room."

Wade and Dutch brushed past the girl. "Thanks. Dutch, where's Les?" He stood in the middle of the room. He had no feeling for it at all. This definitely wasn't Leslie. Dutch, though, sniffed her way around the room, concentrating on one particular spot. She snuffled into the bathroom and returned to the one area again. Her tail wagged and she sat.

The door had been left open and from the hall Mrs. Holmes and Megan watched with interest. Megan pointed to the dog. "That's where Leslie's bags were, where your dog is sitting."

"It is? Okay, thanks. Come on, Dutch, let's go." Wade and the dog stepped into the hall. "This isn't her usual line of work."

Megan bent over to pet the dog. "The dog works? What do you mean?"

Wade smiled briefly. These were nice people and they were trying to be helpful. "She's a stock dog. Helps gather cattle and keep 'em in line. I'm hoping she'll help me find Leslie."

"Gee, that's neat."

As they returned to the Administration Building, Wade considered the different possibilities. Leslie would have needed a clean getaway. Her main goal would have been to get clear of this school, away from the possibility of being stopped.

"What would be the quickest transportation, the bus?"

Mrs. Holmes carefully considered the question. "Yes, I think so. The airport is quite a distance from here. The train is on the other side of the downtown area. The Greyhound Terminal isn't far from here, just a few miles. I'd be happy to show you where."

"My truck's right here. Would you mind riding in it?"

"No, of course not." Wade held the door open and cringed when this tidy lady climbed into his dirty work truck. He put the dog in the back.

"Sorry about the mess. I didn't have time to do anything with it before I left."

"It's fine. I imagine on a ranch a truck like this gets a lot of hard wear."

"Sure does. Where to?"

She gave him directions and he sped off. There were no parking places nearby so he parked in the loading-only area. He took the framed picture, lifted the dog out of the back and set her on the sidewalk, then stepped into the terminal. Mrs. Holmes' shorter steps could hardly keep up.

Wade strode across the room and showed the picture to a woman behind the counter. "Howdy. Can you tell me if this girl caught a bus here?" Dutch sniffed back and forth between the counter and the door, wagging her tail.

"When?" The young woman had been sorting forms. She seemed annoyed with the question.

Wade looked at Mrs. Holmes, his eyebrows raised.

Mrs. Holmes put her thumbnail to her lip, thinking. "Probably around twelve-thirty or one, maybe later."

The woman at the counter barely looked up. "I wouldn't know. My shift started at six this evening."

"What bus do you have that leaves around one?"

"To where?"

"For God's sake, I don't know. That's why I'm here. What do you have that leaves around one?"

"We have a bus leaving for Pendleton at one-ten and one leaving for Seattle at one-thirty."

"Let me see those passenger lists."

"We don't keep passenger lists."

"Is anyone here now that might have been around at one o'clock or so?"

"No, this is a new shift. Come in tomorrow morning. Talk to Pete. He never forgets a face."

Wade's mind whirled. Tomorrow! "What time?"

"He usually comes in around 7:00."

"Look, is there any way I can talk to him tonight? This is an emergency."

"Just a minute." She left her window and talked to another employee, an older man.

The man approached them, peering curiously through the top of his glasses. "Can I help you?"

"You bet. I need to talk to Pete to see if he recognizes this girl." Wade pointed to the picture. "My sister. I need to know which bus she caught."

"What makes you think she took a bus?"

"My dog knows she was here."

The man leaned over the counter noticing Dutch for the first time. "That dog shouldn't be in here."

Wade put his elbow on the counter and leaned toward the man within inches of his face. "Look. I need to talk to Pete. What's his number? I'll call him at home."

"I can't give you that number. It's against regulations."

"What's Pete's last name?"

"Larson."

"Larson spelled with an 'e' or an 'o'?

"O."

"Fine. Thank you."

Wade strode to the telephone booth and snatched the telephone book hanging by a chain. "It would be Larson. There must be a hundred of them."

Mrs. Holmes caught up with him again and peered over his arm. "There, P.B. Oh dear, there's Peter L. Larson and P. Walter Larson. Do you have some quarters? Here, I do." She quickly reached into her purse and drew out some change.

"Thanks." He'd have to remember to get a bunch of quarters to make local calls.

He dialed the number for P. B. Larson but there was no answer, nor an answering machine. "No answer."

Mrs. Holmes held her finger on the list of Larsons. "Here's the next number."

"Is Pete there? Ah, excuse me, but do you work at Greyhound? I'm not sure I have the right party. No? Okay, thank you."

He dialed the next number. His heart pounded when a woman answered. "May I speak to Pete?"

"No Pete? Sorry. Thanks."

Wade hung up and looked down at his dirt-caked boots, and sighed. What now?

"Here," Mrs. Holmes offered. "Let me write that first number down. We can try again in a little while."

Wade looked at this kind lady. "I appreciate your help, ma'am. I'm sure you have a family waiting for you."

"No, I called them and said I'd be late. Mr. Cahill, may I make a suggestion?"

"I wish you'd call me Wade. Every time you say Mr. Cahill I look around for my dad."

She laughed. "Okay. Wade. Why don't we go next door and have a cup of coffee, take a minute to think."

Wade stopped at the truck and put Dutch in the front seat.

They sat in an old-fashioned cafe where no two tables were alike. A waitress poured coffee into mismatched mugs.

Wade took off his hat and placed it on an empty chair beside him. He ran his fingers through his hair. "I should be on the road right now. She's already had a six or seven hour head start. But there's no sense going the wrong direction." He shook his head. "Which was it--Seattle or Pendleton?"

"Which direction do you think she'd go? Does she know anyone in either place?"

"No, I don't think so. My gut feeling is Pendleton. But if she really doesn't want to be found, maybe Seattle..." He shook his head again. "I can't believe this."

"Has she ever run away before?"

Wade was shocked. "No, of course not. Leslie's a really good kid. She wouldn't have done it now except for having to go to that damned school." He realized what he'd said and dropped his head. "Sorry. It's just that she didn't want to come here, she liked her old school, at home." He rubbed his eyes.

"I know. That was clear when I met Leslie."

"Excuse me, I'll try that number again."

For over an hour they drank coffee, with Wade trying the number again every fifteen minutes or so without success.

"Well, it's almost ten, Mrs. Holmes. You should get on home. I'll take you back to the school."

They left the terminal and climbed back into the truck with Dutch between them. The dog gave Mrs. Holmes a quick sniff and then stared out the window, apparently fascinated with Spokane's night lights.

At Rosemount, as they pulled into the winding driveway, Mrs. Holmes pointed to the now almost empty faculty parking lot. "There's my car, the little blue one."

"Thanks, ma'am, for all your help. I really appreciate it."

"What will you do now?"

"I'd lose time if I drove to either Seattle or Pendleton without knowing. I guess I'll have to take my chances and keep trying old Pete until I get an answer. Maybe I can meet him someplace and show him the picture. Otherwise, I'll see him at seven in the morning."

As Mrs. Holmes started to climb out of the truck, her high heel wedged in a link of chain lying on the floor. "Oops."

"Oh, geez, sorry. Did it mess up your shoe?"

"No, not at all." She calmly disengaged her shoe and climbed out of the truck. She turned back to him. "Wait just a minute, will you?" She stepped to her car and reached in for a yellow tablet from the front seat. A pen was attached to the first few pages. She tore off the top page and handed the tablet and pen to him.

"Here. You can keep track of things better with this. Wade, you'll find her. Good luck to you. I'll be in touch with your father." She extended her hand.

Wade took her small trim hand in his. "Thanks, ma'am. Thanks for everything."

Wade slowly pulled out of Rosemount. Nice lady. Les would have liked her.

Now what? It's so late now I'll just check into a motel, that one by Greyhound.

He checked in, and noticing the telephone on the night stand, remembered to call his father.

"Cahill." John always answered the phone this way. His voice was strained now; Wade could feel his father's tension.

"Dad, Wade."

"My God, Wade, why did you wait so long to call? Where are you? What have you found out?"

Wade briefed his father on the action he'd taken so far. "It's so late now--I'll try once more to call this guy. Otherwise, I'll be at Greyhound at seven tomorrow morning."

"Okay. Call here to let us know which direction you're heading. My hunch is Pendleton, too. And Wade, take care of yourself--you sound beat."

"Will do. Don't worry, Dad, I'll find her."

"Okay, son, keep in touch. I'm going crazy here. How could she have done this? God, I can't believe this is happening."

"Hey Dad, what do you make of her packing all her stuff away?"

"I can't figure it out."

"Me neither." It was too tender a topic to pursue. "Okay, I'll call you after I talk to this Greyhound guy."

Wade tried Pete's number once more with no success. He fed the dog, took a shower, and fell into bed.

## *SIXTEEN*

Leslie sat in the small terminal for awhile to get her bearings. Her fellow passengers all seemed to know where they were going and within minutes the small depot emptied.

I wish I knew where to go. I need to keep moving, to get out of this terminal. But where?

*First, get rid of this awful suitcase.* She found the ladies' restroom, opened the large suitcase and lifted out the gray backpack, her sleeping bag and foam pad. She tied her sleeping bag and pad to the top of the pack and kicked the old suitcase back against the wall. Hoisting the pack on her back, she was appalled as its weight. It hadn't seemed this heavy at home.

Returning to the waiting room she struggled out of the backpack and again sat on a chair. She drew her map of Oregon out of the pack's top pocket. Now where?

It's seven-thirty already. Too late to really go anywhere. I'll find a place to stay tonight and get an early start tomorrow.

She stepped up to the counter. "Excuse me. Can you tell me where the nearest motel is?"

"We've got a couple, not far away. The closest is the Longhorn, just around the corner. Another one, May-Del, is about three blocks south."

Leslie pointed in what she hoped was a southerly direction. "Down that way? Okay, thanks."

"This is a tough neighborhood, honey. Don't dally."

"I won't. Thank you."

She could feel the woman's eyes on her back. She struggled into her pack and left the terminal.

I'm only walking three blocks. How will I manage miles with this heavy pack?

Approaching the May-Del, she belatedly wondered, "How do you check into a motel?" No one was at the counter when she entered the office, but a woman came through the doorway from what appeared to be living quarters. Leslie had obviously interrupted her dinner.

"Yes?" the woman said around a mouthful of food.

"Hi. I'd like a room for the night."

"Just you?"

"Yes. I'm meeting my aunt in the morning. She told me to stay here."

The woman stared at her for a minute, then shoved a registration form to her. "Fill this out. Pay now. Check out at twelve."

Leslie completed the registration form. Name, Linda Carpenter. She used the address she had memorized on her fake identification card. She paid from the cash she kept in her small purse.

Once in her room she collapsed on the bed. It smelled of stale cigarettes. The air conditioning cranked loudly, constantly dripping water into a pan on the floor. She swallowed hard. Finally, she was unable to hold tears back any longer. What am I going to do? How will I get around? I can't keep taking busses and staying in motels for the rest of my life.

It's so weird. I've always loved school and here I am, running away. If Dad hadn't made me leave, I would be getting ready right now for my next year at Chewack.

She punched the pillow. *He made me do this.*

I wish I could talk to Janelle. She sat up, reaching for the telephone on the night stand, then jerked her hand away. I can't, I think telephone companies can trace calls.

She pressed her arms against her stomach.

I feel so bad about not telling Janelle. I know I could have trusted her; she would never have told on purpose, but she would have been upset. She and her mom are so close, her mom would have known something was wrong and could have gotten it out of her. Is she mad at me? Does she even know yet? Jan would never have done something like this. But then, she didn't have to. Nobody was forcing *her* to go to Rosemount.

Harsh sobs racked her body. She tried to be quiet so no one would hear. Finally, cried out and numb, she crawled into bed. Exhausted, she fell asleep.

In the middle of the night loud voices awakened her, motel guests returning, apparently after a night at the tavern. Drunk and swearing, they banged around trying to get into their rooms. Leslie crept out of bed, cautiously lifting one slat of the blind. She double-checked the lock on her door and slipped back into bed. This time she couldn't get back to sleep as quickly as before and her worries returned. What should she do next?

She had quite a bit of money, but it wouldn't last forever. She'd already spent close to a hundred dollars. She should decide where she wanted to live, then get an apartment. How do you get an apartment? She'd heard friends talking once. You need the first month's rent and a damage deposit. How much would that be? I have to find a job. Doing what?

She woke in the morning almost sick to her stomach. I've got to settle down, force myself to be calm. She took a deep breath. Okay. First, I need to rearrange my pack. I should put my money in different places. She took out her money, put a few bills in her wallet, other bills in various places in the gray backpack.

Then she worked with the pack, adjusting it so that it fit better. The adjustments helped, but it still hung heavily.

I can't afford to stay in motels. I'll have to start doing what I'd planned--camp out. But where?

Knowing it would be awhile before she would have another opportunity, she took a shower, washed her hair, and dressed in clean clothes. What should I do with these dirty clothes? There's so much more to this than I'd thought. How do you check out of a motel?

As she walked past the motel office, she saw the woman inside. Leslie stepped into the office, placing the room key on the counter. "Good morning. I'm leaving now. Oh, can you tell me where the closest grocery store is?"

"One block over. Where's your aunt?"

Leslie could feel her face redden. "I'm meeting her at ten this morning. Thanks." She quickly closed the door behind her.

I'm going to have to try to anticipate everything I say and do. That woman knew something was fishy. Okay. Go to the grocery. Get something to eat for breakfast and lunch. And dinner. How will I carry all that stuff?

*~*

Wade was on the road early in the morning. I'll eat at that greasy spoon where we had coffee. It's close and I can keep an eye on the bus depot.

He stepped inside the bus terminal. One man stood behind the counter. "Is Pete in yet?"

"Nope. Comes in around seven."

"Okay. Thanks."

After a hearty breakfast--eggs, hash, ham, coffee--he asked the waitress to fill his thermos. At his truck, he set out the dog's food and water, and sat behind the wheel, all the time keeping an eye on the terminal. Finally, just before seven, he climbed out of his truck, taking Leslie's picture with him.

Wade stepped up to the counter. "Pete?"

"What can I do for you?"

Wade introduced himself and stated his mission, showing the man Leslie's picture. "Do you remember seeing this girl yesterday? She might have caught a bus and --"

"I've seen that girl. A couple of times."

"Oh?"

"Yeah, the first time a while back, about a month ago, when she came in for a schedule. Then yesterday. Had her hair cut in the meantime. She took the one-ten to Pendleton."

"Pendleton. Okay. I tried to call you last night but I couldn't reach you."

"No, my wife and I stayed at her mother's last night. She a runaway, your sister?"

Wade hadn't had the heart to put that tag on Leslie, but it fit. He nodded. "I guess so."

"Well, good luck to you."

"Thanks, Pete, and thanks for the information. You've got a sharp eye."

"I never forget a face."

Wade stopped at the phone booth just inside the terminal.

"Cahill."

"Dad, Wade. The man at Greyhound recognized her. She took the one-ten yesterday for Pendleton. I'm on my way."

"Oh, thank God you found him. He's sure, huh?"

"No doubt about it. Dad, have you called the police?"

"Not yet. I've thought about it. What do you think?"

"I don't know. I hate to get the law in on this. I'm afraid of what it will do to Les. Another thing, if she suspects someone is after her, she'll be even harder to find. She might head for Seattle and really get swallowed up."

"I'll hold off, then. We'll play it by ear. I hope I'm not making a mistake. Today I'm going over to Janelle's, see what she knows about this. Can you think of anyone else? Maybe Kip?"

"I doubt if she told Kip anything, but Janelle is a good idea. If she told anyone, it would be her. Well, I better get moving."

"Okay, Wade. Let's set up some kind of schedule. Try to call at six every night, let me know how you're doing."

"Right. Six. I've got to go, Dad. Look at the time I've already lost. I'll talk to you later."

*~*

Leslie trudged along the highway. Her heavy pack pulled at her shoulders, but at least she'd had breakfast and bought extra food. She'd gone up and down the aisles looking for light-weight food, finally settling on dried apricots, cold cereal, a package of sweet rolls and three oranges. She only had a plastic bowl and no way to cook, anyway. She'd have to remember to fill her water bottle every chance she got.

Not much traffic on this road. Good. One car passed and honked. It probably looked strange, a girl walking along the highway with a pack on her back. As soon as she could, she should get off this highway. She didn't want to look suspicious.

It was hot, even this early in the morning. Her back--her clean blouse--was already drenched with sweat. A hot wind began to blow, stirring up sand and road debris. She reached around to one of the side patch pockets for her sunglasses. They should help keep junk out of her eyes, at least.

An old blue pick-up stopped. The driver, a man, leaned toward the passenger window. "I'm going as far as La Grande. Want a ride?"

Her father had warned her repeatedly about hitchhiking. His voice echoed in her mind. "Les, there's never a time when you can't call home for a ride. Anytime. Day or night. Just don't take a ride from a stranger."

Those old rules didn't apply any more. "Okay, thanks." Why not take a ride? She put her pack in the back and climbed into the cab.

"Where you heading?" The man, older than her father, seemed to size her up as his cold gray eyes narrowed. His mouth smiled but his eyes remained unchanged. She hadn't remembered to be prepared with a story.

"To La Grande. I'm meeting my aunt there."

"What's her name? It's a small place, I probably know her."

"Ah... Alice Young. But she's just visiting a friend. I don't know her friend's name." Her mind reeled.

The man cut over to I-84 and began the long uphill climb to La Grande. The old pick-up whined as they climbed the steep grade. It was a good thing she had a ride. It would have been tough walking this long, steep hill. In clear places, out of the shelter of hills, wind slammed against the truck. The man gripped the wheel to steady it.

After they'd driven about a half hour, the land leveled out onto flat, barren countryside. They were almost in town when the man said, "Looks like a duster brewing. Good thing you'll be off the road."

"Duster? You think so?" Stupid question. The wind had picked up and all there seemed to be was sand.

"Yep. This time of year, we get 'em all the time." He turned to her, then looked back to the road. He reached across the seat and slid his hand onto her thigh.

Leslie jumped at the touch. She looked down in horror at the gnarly, hairy hand. She could feel the heat of it through her jeans. In panic, she glanced out the window and saw they were at the edge of town. "This is fine. Let me out here."

"No, I'll take you to where your aunt is staying." He turned off the highway onto a road leading to the residential district. He stopped at a stop sign. Leslie seized the opportunity to jump out of the truck, leaving the door open. She quickly reached in back for her pack. A few other cars were around and a woman began to walk across the intersection.

"Thanks a lot." She slammed the door and waved as though nothing had happened.

He drove off without looking at her.

Leslie stood at the intersection looking after him. Dirty old man. She shuddered. *Creep.*

She waited until the truck was out of sight then looked around the small town. A little city park looked like a good place to stop and consult her map. If she could just think clearly she could decide what to do next.

How about staying in La Grande? Maybe I can find work here.

She visited the park's restroom. With a jolt she looked at her own reflection in the mirror. She barely recognized the haunted girl staring back.

I don't even look like myself. My eyes are weird. People know. They know about me. That man knew I'm in trouble--that's why he dared to touch me like that.

Her eyes filled. She couldn't bear to watch herself. She stepped into a bathroom stall and wept. Finally, she gathered herself together, washed her hands and face and combed her hair.

At the first place she came to, a small café, she left her pack just inside the door. She stepped up to the counter. "Hello, I'm looking for work."

"What kind of work?"

"Well, as a waitress, or --"

"We don't need a waitress."

The next place was a real estate office. Leslie thought ahead this time to be prepared. She took her purse out of the top pocket and left the pack outside. "Hello, I would like to apply for a job. I can use a computer and do filing."

"Sorry, this is a small office and I do all the work myself."

The next, a hardware. "You from out of town? No, we just hire local kids."

At the Dairy Queen. "Sorry, no openings. You could complete an application but you have to have a local address." Store after store, they all seemed to know she was a stranger.

At the grocery store the clerk looked at her suspiciously and shook his head. "Nope."

Leslie felt like running out of town. She felt desolate, alone. Panic crowded her throat. She passed a telephone booth and yearned to give herself up but managed to keep walking. I'll find something. Not in this town, but I'll find something.

The wind's intensity steadily increased. By the time she found the road leading south out of town, her billed cap had blown off twice. She'd had to turn it backwards to keep it on.

Tumbleweeds and road debris stuck, suspended, against barbed-wire fences. Small rocks rolled down the black-top.

This is stupid, trying to get any place in this wind. But what else can I do? Where can I go? I have to keep moving.

In less than half a mile the wind made it impossible to walk in a straight line. Leslie leaned into the wind, concentrating on keeping upright, her balance off-kilter because of the heavy pack. A tumbleweed skidded in front of her, swirled, then tangled in her legs. She shook it off and kicked it aside.

Suddenly, a gust of wind slammed against her, sending her sprawling on her back. Her sunglasses flew off. She kicked like a turtle, trying to right herself. Struggling, she managed to work herself into a sitting position. Frightened, she crawled to her glasses and put them in her shirt pocket.

She picked herself up. The wind caught at her again, tearing at her clothes and sandblasting her skin. Gritty sand worked its way into her squinting eyes.

She could just make out a bridge, part of the road that crossed over a large gully.

I could climb under that until this wind stops.

She stumbled and lurched her way toward the bridge, then climbed down a bank toward the abutment. Wind howled and pulled at her as she awkwardly slid on the gravel beneath the bridge. Once down, she looked up at a landing. The gap between where she stood and the platform came to her shoulder.

How am I going to climb up there?

A hand reached down. "Here." It was a black hand with a creased, light palm.

She froze. With huge eyes she looked up. A black man knelt on the platform, his hand extended. "Hand me your pack," he yelled above the wind. She hesitated. The hand gestured impatiently.

In a daze, she took off the heavy pack and lifted it up to him. He took it, set it aside and held his hand out to her again. He leaned over so she could hear him shout. "Put your foot on that brace, there." He grasped her forearm and she locked onto his arm. He gave a heave and she was on the platform with him.

He moved toward the center where there was more protection from the wind and squatted down, leaning against the cement wall. He calmly watched her. She moved toward him and followed his example, shoving her pack between them.

There was no sense talking, or shouting, in this raging wind. They sat in silence.

Finally, the wind quieted. There were occasional gusts but the worst was over.

He glanced over to her. "Going camping?"

She sighed. "Sort of."

He looked at her carefully, his dark eyes penetrating. "Running away?"

"What makes you think that? What are you doing here?" That's right, bounce questions back. And get out of here as soon as you can.

"I'm on a trip, camping out. But I'm not sixteen."

"I'm not sixteen, I'm eighteen."

"Right."

"No, I am." She made a move to take out her fake identification, then stopped herself. She didn't have to prove anything to this man.

"You're going about it all wrong."

"Why, what do you mean?"

"I mean an innocent like you won't last another two days."

She glared at him. He wasn't a large man, about her size. His stubble of a beard was sprinkled with gray. He'd taken off his knit hat to shake out the sand, showing kinky hair receding about half way back. Leslie found she wasn't afraid of him but was unnerved by his attitude. He seemed to know too much, like he could read her thoughts.

She looked out from their perch. The windstorm had definitely eased. She reached for her pack.

"So now what? More walking? To where?"

"Thanks for your help. Bye now."

He reached out and held a strap of her pack. "Hold on. Think for a minute."

"Think about what? I've got to go."

"Listen, I mean it. You'll never make it."

Leslie sat back. A strange sense of trust came over her, but could she trust that feeling? "Okay, what should I do?"

"Go home."

"I can't."

"Oh, come on. I can't believe it's that bad."

"I can't."

"You can't go on like this, either. How long have you been running?"

"A couple of days."

"From where?"

She shrugged.

"What's your name?"

"Linda. What's yours?"

He sat forward earnestly. "Cyrus. Linda, I'm surprised you've lasted this long. You stick out like a sore thumb."

"What can I do about that?"

"You have to have some sort of plan. Have a purpose, or at least look like you do."

"I do. I'm looking for a job. I tried in La Grande but..."

"It's hard for a stranger to find work, especially in a small town. You say you're from Oregon?"

"Washington." Oh darn, I shouldn't have told him that.

"Why didn't you head for Seattle?"

"Because I've heard about big cities like Seattle and the street kids. I don't want... to do that. I want to get a regular job."

"Doing what? Have you even graduated from high school?"

With determination, she looked straight at him. "No, but I will. I can use a computer, do office work. I've done that at home. I tried to get a job as a waitress--I could do that." She bit her lip. "How do people get jobs?"

"They answer ads or see a help wanted sign in a window. Sometimes through friends. But you usually have to live someplace, have a permanent address in order to find work. Not many people hire strangers."

Leslie fell silent. It all seemed so complicated and hopeless.

"Linda, go home."

Leslie shrugged and shook her head. "Do you work?"

He nodded slowly. "I'm a teacher."

She looked up sharply but tried to keep a look of incredulity from showing.

"I get cleaned up a bit."

"Where do you teach?"

"Tacoma. I'm just poking around here for the summer."

"What do you teach?"

"Math."

"This is your vacation? It doesn't seem like much fun to me."

The man laughed, his white teeth stood out against his dark face. "I like the solitude, the freedom from schedules."

"Don't you have a car?" She couldn't grasp the idea of just wandering around out here without a car or at least a horse.

"Yep. I left it at my brother's in Portland. I like to travel unencumbered. So, where to next?"

Her voice was barely audible. "I don't know."

"Is your home life so bad that you can't live there?"

"No. My home life was good. I didn't run away from home. I would *never* have run away from home." Her voice broke, and she swallowed hard. She avoided his eyes.

"What *are* you running away from?" He studied her then, astounded, "School? You're running away from school? Which school?"

She looked at him defiantly. He got information out of her so easily. "Just some stupid school." She stood up, suddenly in a hurry to leave. She'd already told him too much.

He looked up at her, a smirk on his face. "So, you plan to spend the next few years running? Cold weather's just around the corner. Then what?"

"No, I'm not going to keep running. I'm going to get a job and then go back to school. I already told you that."

"Look, Linda--by the way, the name doesn't fit you-- think what your folks must be going through."

"I wouldn't be home now, anyway."

"Oh. A boarding school. What? Catholic? Too strict for you?"

"No, not Catholic." Geez. She had to get out of here before he found out her real name and address.

"Are you camping out?"

She hesitated. "I will, but last night I stayed in a motel."

He threw back his head and laughed.

She straightened her back indignantly. "What? What's so funny?"

"Poor little rich girl. Running away, staying in motels." He laughed again.

"I'm not rich. And it was late, I didn't know where to go. I can camp out, I've done it before."

"Where?"

Oh no. She shrugged.

He laughed again. "Do you have food, water?"

"Some."

"Sit down. You need to think this through. I can't believe you didn't think of these things before you started this high adventure. What kind of work do you think you can do way out here? Gather tumbleweed? Most people find jobs in cities."

"I spent all my time planning on how to get away from the school. I just thought I would go some place and find a job. I have an Oregon map. The towns are all so far apart, though. I guess I started out in the wrong direction."

"Let's see your map."

She drew the map from her pack and scooted over to where he sat.

"Linda, I'm serious. You are the original babe in the woods. You won't survive this. A city girl like you, you don't know what you're doing out here."

"I'm not a city girl," she snapped. Uh oh, he did it again.

"Your family ranchers, farmers?"

She shrugged. "Could I travel with you, just for awhile? I mean, you know the area so well."

His dark eyes widened with disbelief. "Listen to yourself. No, no you can't come with me. In the first place, this is red-neck country. The first cop that saw me traveling with a sixteen year old, a *white* sixteen year old --"

"I'm not sixteen, I'm --"

"-- would throw me in the can with a list of grievances a mile long. Besides, I'm not going where you need to go, where the jobs are."

"Well, then if I can't go with you, can you tell me what to do?"

"Where do you want to go?"

She shrugged. She hadn't the vaguest notion. He looked as though another lecture was on its way. She glanced at the map. "Baker City."

"Why Baker City? You ever been there?"

She shrugged.

"How do you plan to get there?"

"Hike. Hitch a ride. Take a bus. I don't know. How would you?"

"All of the above, probably. But hitching is pretty risky, especially for a girl."

"Maybe I should buy a car."

He groaned and rocked back and forth holding his head. "Girl, girl. You just can't go around saying things like that."

"Like what?"

"Like saying you have enough money to buy a car. You won't, you keep talking like this."

"Well, I don't have much, but maybe a junker..."

"You just don't get it, do you? You tell some people on the road that you have five dollars, they'll relieve you of it without blinking an eye." He winced. "Come on, let's get off of this cement. My skinny butt can't take much more of this."

He climbed down. "Hand me my pack."

She lifted his pack. "My gosh, it's heavy. I thought mine weighed a ton but yours...." With considerable effort, she passed down his pack.

"Okay. Hand me yours." She did, then scrambled off the platform.

They hoisted their packs and headed down a small dirt road, away from the highway.

## *SEVENTEEN*

Leslie's shoulders burned where the pack straps chafed. Her parched throat ached. Her water bottle was almost empty and she'd resolved not to drink any more until the next water source.

They stopped for lunch and while Cyrus ate jerky and an apple, Leslie ate a sweet roll and an orange. She gave in and drank all but the last swallow from her water bottle. She felt him watching her, his dark eyes missed nothing. They had walked in a southerly direction, on a rough, rutty side road bearing tire tracks and cattle droppings. After the brief lunch-break they resumed their steady pace. Walking. Walking. Step after step. He led, she followed. They climbed a steep grade. To where? Where would all this end? At least he was letting her go with him. Had he changed his mind?

Leslie could hardly keep up with him. Her legs were so tired she occasionally staggered. Her ragged breathing made her throat raw. "Where are we, anyway?" she panted.

"Wallowa Whitman National Forest. This is a forest service road, not used much except by forest rangers and a rancher or two." He wasn't even breathing hard.

He stopped, finally. For three hours, since lunch, they'd been steadily walking. "There's a stream on the other side of this big outcropping. Need a drink?"

Leslie nodded. Her legs shook from fatigue.

I need a new body. A new life. Everything seems so unreal. Is this really happening?

Briars snagged her pant legs as she followed him around the huge rock where a small stream gurgled. Sun reflected off the ripples, creating sparkling jewels. She was giddy with relief and gratefully shrugged out of her pack.

"I don't know how safe the water is, but I've drank it before and I'm still kicking." He dropped his pack and knelt down to the cool, clear stream. He dipped his canteen into the stream, then splashed water over his face and neck, then unbuttoned his shirt and slipped it off and more thoroughly doused himself.

Leslie watched for a moment. Muscles bunched in his smooth brown back and arms. He didn't even flinch when streams of cold water ran down his back.

Leslie stepped upstream onto a flat rock and gulped the cool water from her cupped hands, then filled her water bottle. She scooped water into her hands and lowered her face into its soothing coolness. She stepped off the rock onto the pebbly stream bed and wearily sat down. Her shoulders burned cruelly; they felt raw. She wanted to look at them but felt uncomfortable doing so in front of this man.

"My pack feels like it's unbalanced."

He moved closer to her and sat on another rock. "Take your stuff out and we'll repack it. Haven't you ever backpacked before? This pack isn't new."

She was thankful he was willing to help. "It was my brother's. I've never really hiked before, not with a pack, anyway. But I've packed in with horses and mules."

"With who?"

"Usually with my dad or brother. But this summer I went with my girlfriend, for one night." The lump in her throat strained her voice.

She struggled to her rubbery knees and propped her pack up. Self-consciously she began unpacking it, placing the different articles in piles.

"Well, it looks like you've brought sensible clothes, anyway, though hiking boots would have been better than tennis shoes. Riding boots? In case a horse comes along?"

Leslie glanced at him. His eyes were full of humor. She shrugged.

"Try rolling your clothes." He reached for a pair of her jeans and tightly rolled them. "They'll pack better and you can pull stuff out of your bag easier."

"Great idea." She immediately began rolling her clothes.

He shook his head in dismay. "That's your food? That's what you plan to survive on? Apricots, sugar cereal and dessert?" His eyes burned into hers. "No wonder you're so pooped. Food is fuel, kid. You'll never survive on this crap."

"I guess I need a pan or something to cook with."

He nodded and drew from his pack a little cooking kit. Reaching back into his pack he brought out a plastic bag containing several envelopes of packaged meals. "These are called MRE's--Meals Ready to Eat. Open the packages and you have yourself a meal. They use them in the military."

"Were you in the military?"

"Army. We used to gripe about MRE's, say things like 'If the enemy don't get you the MRE's will,' but I really don't mind them."

"Can you buy them at a grocery store?"

"No, I buy them at an Army surplus store before I leave. I pack about a ten day supply in boxes and my sister mails them to me, a box at a time."

"Mail?" She looked around at the surrounding scrub and scraggly pine trees. "How do you get mail?"

"When I know what town I'll be near, I call her and she sends a package, in care of general delivery."

"Oh. Good idea." She sighed. "I can't do it that way, though. I could get dehydrated soups, or those noodle dinners, that kind of stuff."

He nodded. "That would be better than this junk. Whatever you buy, make it real food."

"But it has to be light enough to carry, too."

"That's right. While you're in a town, stop and pick up some milk and apples, stuff like that, and eat them right away."

She nodded. "Okay." Her eyes studied his. "The pack straps hurt my shoulders. They feel raw."

"Let's see."

She sat still for a moment, then slowly pulled her tee-shirt down from the neck to her shoulder revealing a raw welt where the pack strap had rubbed. The other shoulder was as bad, in fact, blood had oozed from one of the welts.

Cyrus grimaced. He reached into his pack and brought out a little cloth bag, producing a tube of antibacterial cream. "Here, rub some of this on. You could cut some strips from your foam pad for cushioning. Do you have a knife?"

"Yes, I do. How much should I cut off?."

"Just a few inches. Make them about three inches across and five inches long."

Leslie followed his instructions. "Now what?"

"Cut a couple of slots near the ends and we'll slip them over the straps."

She handed him the small cushions and he slid them onto the shoulder straps. Leslie hefted her pack on to try them out.

"This will be a lot better. Thanks."

"When you pack your bag, put the heavy stuff on the bottom so your hips take the load."

She repacked. "It's sure harder carrying the load yourself rather than having a horse haul it for you."

They sat in silence. She sat on the ground, her long legs drawn close to her body with her chin on her knees. Exhaustion made her quiet, broody.

Cyrus broke the silence. "Let's break for the day. You need to give your shoulders a rest. This doesn't make a bad camp, right here. Can you build a fire?"

"Of course."

"Okay, let's see you do it."

She glared at him. Did he think she was a complete idiot? She began to gather leaves and twigs, then small branches, finally heavier branches. She reached into a side pocket of her pack and pulled out a book of matches. Leaning over the pile of leaves and twigs, she carefully lit a match, cupping it in her hand, and held it under a leaf. A feeble flame caught and she cupped it until another leaf made the flame grow stronger.

She carefully added a few twigs, then the smaller branches. She hovered over the fire to protect it from the slight breeze.

"I'm impressed." He'd sat watching her, legs sprawled in front of him with his back against a scabby tree. His jeans were dirty at the knees. Dark blotches of sweat and grime covered his shirt.

She looked at him triumphantly, grateful she'd been able to start the fire. It wasn't always this easy.

"But you should get some wooden matches and put them in something that won't get wet."

She nodded. "I'd better make a list." She took out pad and pen from her pack and jotted down the items they'd discussed: pan, dehydrated soups, wooden matches, antibacterial cream. She added toilet paper, having realized earlier that important item was missing.

"Here, you can use this for your matches." He handed her a plastic container, something medicine had apparently been dispensed in. "While you're at the store, get a few plastic bags from the produce department. They're handy. When you come across some paper, tear it up and keep it in a plastic bag. Just a small supply. That way, if it rains and you can't find dry leaves you'll have a better chance of building a fire."

What a wealth of information this guy is. She watched as he poured water from his canteen into his sauce pan. He placed three flat rocks around her fire and placed the pan on them, just like she had done when she camped with Janelle. It felt good to see something familiar, something she knew how to do.

They sat silently until the water heated and then he took out a selection of MRE's, all identical with heavy, brown plastic bags. Only stenciled print on the package identified their contents.

He gestured to the pile of packages. "Here, pick one."

"No, thanks. I'll use my own food."

"I have extra. Take one."

She looked at the selection he offered: Chicken and Rice, Red Beans and Rice, Omelet with Ham, Meatballs, Beef and Rice. It seemed so long ago since she'd eaten a regular meal. She argued with herself about whether or not she should take one. She chose the Meatballs.

She hefted the package. "This stuff is heavy. How can you carry it all?"

"Better than starving. There's lighter stuff on the market, hikers food, but there's not as much to it, and it's a lot more expensive. He cut the top off his main package, removed the inner plastic-packaged Red Beans and Rice, and placed it in the hot water.

Leslie reached in her pack for her knife and did the same, imitating him, placing the package containing meatballs into the pan with his.

"Is this how you did it in the Army, make an open fire to heat them?"

"No, not usually. We'd either eat them cold or heat them up on a truck or tank radiator. An open fire would have been a luxury."

Fascinated, Leslie sorted through the rest of her packet. The meatball item was only the entree; there was much more inside. "Just like Christmas."

A package of powdered drink mix made her realize she didn't have a cup. She jotted it on her list and put the beverage package aside.

He gingerly picked the packages out of the boiling water. "These are probably hot enough. You can eat them right out of the package, but I'd rather eat from a bowl."

Again, she imitated him and cut off the top of the heated package and poured the contents into her bowl. "Ummm. Not bad. It's good, actually."

"I get tired of them sometimes, but they're easy to fix and filling. When I get too sick of them I'll go into town and eat a real meal in a restaurant and get some fresh stuff from a store. Then I'm set for a while longer."

"Look, I even got some freeze-dried peaches. Did you?"

"No, I got applesauce this time. What's your desert?"

"Desert? Oh, wow. I got a brownie. What's this stuff?" Leslie poured assorted small items from a five-inch square package: book matches, salt, instant coffee, a little package of sugar, a moist towelette, and a small package, only a few squares, of toilet paper. "This is so cool. I wish I'd known about these."

"It's called being prepared."

"Well, I had a lot on my mind. Getting away wasn't easy."

He nodded. "I can imagine. Don't you think they're worried?"

Leslie glanced up sharply, then deliberately began cleaning up the dinner mess. She carefully put the unused items in a pack pocket.

He tried again. "Don't you think your family's looking for you? They must be frantic."

"I doubt if they even know, or care." Her voice cracked. *I've been replaced, culled out.* She kept her head down, intent on her clean-up chores though now they were swimming through tears.

"I don't believe that. How about calling home?"

She shook her head. "I can't," she whispered.

"Of course you can. I'll go with you, if it would help. Hell, I'd wait with you until someone comes for you."

"No, I can't. Please, I can't talk about it. Do you have a family?"

"I'm not married, if that's what you mean. I have a big family though. I'm uncle to more kids than I can count and my folks are still living. I'm the oldest of thirteen kids."

Her head jerked up. "Thirteen!"

"How many in your family?"

"Just two kids. I have a brother, but he's eleven years older than me. It's just my dad, brother, and me. My mom died when I was six, in a car accident. But we have a housekeeper. She's just like family."

"What do you think they're doing now? Don't you think they're worried sick?"

She shrugged. "Like I said, I wouldn't be home now, anyway."

He looked across at her, his somber dark eyes questioning.

She turned away, making a big production of rinsing her eating utensils and placing them in her pack.

*~*

Wade was relieved Leslie had gone all the way to Pendleton. He'd worried that she might get off the bus early, to throw them off. In Pendleton, he checked the two closest motels and sure enough, she had stayed at one of them, checked out at eight just this morning.

This morning! If I'd only come to Pendleton right away instead of waiting to talk to that Pete guy at the terminal, I would have found her, right at the motel. I should've gone with my gut feelings.

His mind reeled with the feeling of failure.

He spent precious time in Pendleton, beating the sidewalks, checking out stores, anywhere where she might have been. Some store owners started to raise objections with the dog, but a look or word from Wade seemed to change their minds. Leslie had picked up groceries at one store, the store manager recognized her picture, but then Wade ran out of leads.

So far, she seemed to be heading in a southerly direction. He followed suit and drove to Pilot Rock and then further south to Ukiah. No clues. He asked around both towns, showing Leslie's picture and getting nothing but strange looks in return. They stopped several times, but while the dog absently peed and sniffed around, she never showed any signs of recognition.

At one point, he came close to despair. After he'd asked around in Ukiah and came up with nothing but blanks, he'd pulled up at a small combination gas station and store on his way out of town. As usual, it irritated him to wait for an attendant to pump gas. In Washington people pumped their own damn gas. He went into the store, picked up a six-pack of beer and showed the woman behind the counter Leslie's picture.

"Ma'am, have you seen this girl?"

She glanced at the picture. "No." Then she gave him a long, hard look. It made him feel guilty, like he'd done something wrong.

He paid for the gas and beer, and left the store.

A short distance away he stopped the truck at a wide place in the road and cracked open a beer. He ran the cold bottle along his neck. I'm losing her. Her trail's getting cold. What if I can't find her? His eyes stung. What is she doing now? Oh God, keep her safe. He glanced at his watch and took a long swallow. Five o'clock.

I'm not so sure anymore, sure that I can find her. He felt his blood rush and his stomach take a dive. What will I tell Dad? I have to call him in an hour. He got out of the truck and walked around it, checking the tires for want of anything more useful to do.

Steady, now. Get a hold of yourself. You've barely started. She must not have come this direction, that's all. This is such big country, but nothing's clicked since Pendleton. He reached in the front seat for the Oregon map and spread it on the hood.

I'm still convinced she's heading south; otherwise, why Pendleton at all? Why not Portland?

La Grande. She could have taken a bus to La Grande. Or hitched a ride. No, don't hitch a ride, Les.

He called home at six, right on schedule.

"Cahill. Wade?"

"Yeah, Dad. I went to Pendleton, to the bus terminal. I'm so many hours behind her I couldn't get the shift that was on duty when she passed through. But she was there, all right. Spent the night in a motel. She dumped that old suitcase."

John's voice perked up. "Really? Tell me about it."

"I was asking around the depot if anyone had seen her, and I heard Dutch's tail thumping behind the counter. She was giving the suitcase a once over, swinging her tail like crazy. The clerk asked if it was Leslie's. She said someone had left it in the john."

"Why would she leave the suitcase?"

"The pack must have been inside, ready to go."

"Pack?"

"She'd asked me for my old gray pack. Said she needed it to get back and forth to school. You know that picture you had in your office doesn't look that much like her anymore. That haircut...."

"Wade, do you think she cut her hair so --"

"I think so, Dad."

"She must have planned this for some time."

"Did you talk to Janelle? Any clues there?"

"I talked to her. Apparently Les didn't tell her. She seemed genuinely shocked. After we talked awhile though she mentioned going to Spokane with Les. But then she clammed up."

"Yeah? Then what?"

"I guess I came on a little strong. I scared her and she cried. But damn it, Wade, this is no time for loyalty. Her mom told her to tell me anything she could think of. Finally, she said that when they were in Spokane Leslie had driven to the bus depot, then to the city bus stop. She thought it was strange at the time, but Leslie'd said she just wanted to know where things were. They stopped at some pawn shop, and Les bought that old suitcase. Janelle didn't think Leslie would do anything like this. It sounds like she was planning it way back then. My God. I can't believe she was so desperate."

John's voice turned ragged. "I don't think Janelle knew any more, but she promised she would call me if she thinks of anything."

"This must be the first secret between those two."

There was a long period of silence. Then, "What did you do after Pendleton, or are you still there?"

"No, I headed south to some little one-horse towns. This country is so huge, really big ranches, with little towns scattered around. I mostly check stores thinking that she'll need supplies, at least a cold drink. It's hotter than hell here during the day."

"No clues?"

"Not since Pendleton."

"What's next, Wade?"

"I'll just keep looking. I'm heading east now, over toward La Grande. It's a bigger place. I'll spend the night there and check it out tomorrow."

\*~\*

Darkness settled in. At times Leslie felt awkward, yet she felt safe enough with this man. Knowing he was a teacher gave her reassurance. "Is this what you do, then? Just walk around out here?"

He laughed. "Yeah, isn't it great?" He turned serious. "After dealing with kids all year, I need a break. I enjoy it, especially here in eastern Oregon. It's nice having two consecutive thoughts without interruptions."

"Until I came along."

He shrugged. "Oh, well. A little variety doesn't hurt. What do you like to do? I can tell you've spent time outdoors."

She nodded in agreement. "I ride a lot. I have a great horse. Polly. I got her for my twelfth birthday. She's a registered Appaloosa, dark brown with a white and brown patch over her rump that looks just like a blanket. And she's got a freckled nose." Her throat tightened.

"Appaloosa. They're originally from the Palouse country, in eastern Washington, right?"

Leslie swallowed, trying to clear her throat. "That's right. They were originally Indian ponies."

"What else do you like to do?"

"I like music. I play the piano. Anyway, I did."

"You pretty good?"

She shrugged modestly. "I guess. I quit my lessons, though."

"How come?" Cyrus casually stirred the fire and added a stick of wood.

"Because I was leaving to go to that stupid school."

He looked up sharply. "Couldn't you take lessons there?"

She rested her chin on her knees. It hurt to remember all this. She slowly raised her head and nodded. "My dad wanted me to take lessons there, but it wouldn't be the same."

She looked past the flickering flames. She could barely distinguish his dark face. "What do you like to do? Besides wander around."

"During the school year I'm busy with teaching, working the football and basketball games, correcting papers at night. And I get together with my family."

"Do you live with them? Your family?"

"No, I live alone, but close to one of my sisters and two of my brothers and their families. My folks live about five miles from my place."

"That must be fun, having a big family."

He nodded thoughtfully. "It can be. But it's not all fun and games. Are you close to your brother?"

"Pretty much. He's so much older we've never really played together. I always thought it would be fun to have a brother or sister closer to my age. But he takes me places sometimes. I work with him. I did, anyway."

"Work?"

"During the school year I can't--couldn't--do much." She gave up trying to keep her status current. "I'm so busy with school and music. But during the summer, especially this summer, I rode with him. Working cattle."

"You work with your brother more than your dad?"

Should I be telling him all this stuff? Oh, well. What hurt could it do? He doesn't know where I live. Lived.

"I used to ride with my dad a lot, but now Wade--that's my brother--has taken over a lot of the outside work. My dad does more of the paperwork, running the ranch from that end. His knees are beginning to bother him, and he doesn't ride as much as he used to."

She took a long drink from her water bottle. She wished she had some cocoa. That would taste good about now.

She glanced at him. "Sometimes my dad and brother argue about me. My brother thinks I don't do enough around the place. He thinks I'm dodging work when I practice the piano. I usually practice a couple hours a day during the summer, an hour during the school year. To him it's just a hobby."

"Two hours! That's a lot. You must be good. What does your dad say?"

"He says my work is just different and that I'm doing what I should be doing." She looked sadly into the fire. The glow from the fire lighted her face. "My brother thinks I'm spoiled. But I did help him a lot this summer. I kept hoping my dad would notice and change his mind about sending me away when he saw how hard I was trying to--oh, I don't know--fit in."

She stood abruptly. "I'm tired. I think I'll turn in."

"Yeah. It's time to call it a day."

She rolled out her thin foam pad, now a few inches shorter, and her sleeping bag. She took off her shoes and slipped into the bag. She was wide-eyed. This was all so weird.

"Linda, just so you know. Tomorrow morning we go our separate ways."

She felt as though he'd punched her in the stomach. Her mind tumbled. What would she do? How would she know where to go?

"Linda?"

"I know."

She turned her back toward him. Several feet away, he rummaged around, getting his night things ready. He settled in and sighed as he made himself comfortable.

She curled into a tight ball. She was so lonesome and here she was, with Cyrus. What would it be like when she was really all alone? Tears streamed down her face. She tried to silence her sniffles. Finally, she sat up so that she could breathe. If Cyrus noticed, he didn't say anything.

She lay down again and tried to think of something to occupy her mind. She remembered her music. Straining to concentrate, she recalled a piece she had played just before she left, Chopin's Minute Waltz. Her fingers moved with the music as she floated along with it. She drifted into a sound sleep.

## *EIGHTEEN*

Leslie awakened with a sinking heart. She knew Cyrus was serious about their not traveling any farther together.

If only I could talk him into it. What will I do? It's so different out here, everything seems so much bigger and rougher. The ranch seemed big, even rough, when I'd go riding or camping, but then I could always go home. Home.

She tried to ease her stiff, sore back and shoulders. Where the straps had dug in, her shoulders throbbed. She gingerly touched the welts, now crusty where they had oozed.

She could see her breath in the cold morning air. Fog blanketed the nearby hills where tree tops hid in the morning mist. Dew dampened the outside of her sleeping bag. She remembered that fall was just around the corner. Panic rose in her chest.

She glanced over to Cyrus' bag, crumpled on the ground, empty. She slipped out of her bag, put on her shoes and jacket and went in search of a suitable bush. She glanced around, wondering where he was. A clinking toward camp told her that he'd returned, maybe starting a fire. She relieved herself behind a scraggly bush, then slowly walked back.

Cyrus glanced up as she approached. "Good morning."

"Morning."

"I'm going to heat water for tea. Want a cup?"

"No, thank you."

"We'll share a tea bag, okay?"

"Well, okay." She rummaged in her pack and pulled out one of her oranges. "I'll split this with you." She began to roll up her sleeping bag.

"Why don't you let the dew evaporate before you roll it up?" He glanced up at her. "What are your plans, Linda?"

"Like I said. Find a job. When I get settled, I'll go back to school." Not knowing what to do with herself, she sat on the ground near the fire.

"But right now, today. What will you do?"

She watched the fire, could feel its feeble warmth against her face. She scooted closer, knees drawn up to her chin.

"Go to the nearest town and get some supplies."

"Why don't you get to a phone booth and call home? Whatever the problem is, I'm sure you've made your point."

She didn't answer and kept her eyes downcast, afraid he could see her hopelessness.

Hunkered down by the fire, he drew out his little pan from his pack and poured water into it. He'd apparently refilled his canteen from the stream; she'd need to do the same.

He studied her for a moment. "Huh? How about it? How about giving the folks a call?"

"Nothing's changed. We'd just go through it all again."

"Go through what?"

Tears suddenly streamed down her face. She tried to keep up with the deluge with the backs of her hands, but there seemed no end to them. She felt defenseless, alone, and in the middle of nowhere.

He moved closer to her. "Linda. This probably looks hopeless to you, but these things can be worked out."

"You don't know that."

"I'd be willing to bet."

She gathered herself, sat up tall, her legs crossed in front of her, eyes blazing through tears. "My dad sent me away to school because he plans to get married and the woman has a daughter, younger than me, and we don't get along. Well, it isn't that we don't get along, I just can't stand the snotty bitch, and my dad knows it wouldn't work out 'cause we could never share a room. It was just easier to send *me* away. He doesn't say that's the reason, of course, but I know it is. My brother doesn't agree with me, but he doesn't really know. Maureen says Dad's lonely after all these years since my mother died."

Cyrus, startled with the outburst, tried to take it all in. He leaned forward in concentration. "I find that hard to believe."

"So did I at first, but there was no changing his mind. I tried all summer."

"I don't mean that. I mean, I can't imagine he would send you away because he's getting married. People combine families all the time. My family's such a mishmash of everybody's kids I can't keep them straight."

She shrugged.

"Did you tell him this--what you've told me? What you thought his reason was?"

"No. But I begged him not to send me away, and he wouldn't listen."

"What did he say? What did he give as a reason?"

"Oh, some phony baloney thing about I'll be safer, and I'll get a better education. It's so stupid. I'm a good student and I get good grades. And just because Traci got raped doesn't mean I will."

Cyrus cocked his head and wrinkled his brow.

She heatedly continued. "What could he say? She's in and I'm out."

"Traci?"

"No, Traci's the girl that got raped. Then she killed herself. It doesn't really have anything to do with anything, but it was just one more argument my Dad used as an excuse to send me away."

"Well," he said, but with less conviction now, "I'm sure all this could be worked out. From what you've told me, your dad sounds like a reasonable man. What you're doing--running away--isn't helping anything."

"At least I'm not at that stupid girls' school."

"That's right. And where are you? Sitting on the hard, cold ground waiting for a measly cup of tea."

"Well, so are you."

"But I'm not on the run. I've got a job, a home, a place to go when I'm through. What have you got?"

"I'll get a job, a place to stay. I won't go back. I've made up my mind."

"Why not call home and talk to him? What hurt would that do?"

The image of her father's determined face flashed through her mind. "If you knew my Dad, you'd know why. I can't, that's all." She stood. "Well, thanks for everything."

"Hold on. Aren't you going to have your tea?"

"No. I'll just take off now." She turned and began rolling her bag.

"Sit down, Linda." It was a teacher's voice, leaving no room for argument. She returned to the fire and sat down.

"What do you plan to do--fly out over these hills in all directions like a balloon losing air? Do you even have the faintest idea which direction to go?"

"I'll manage."

"Right. Drink your tea." He'd poured her tea in what must have been a spare tin cup. "Here, get out your map. You want to go to Baker City?"

She hesitated, then nodded.

He went over the map with her, tracing the way with his long black finger. Dirt caked under his pale fingernail. She glanced at her own nails; they were dirty, too. Mr. Baxter would give her a bad time if he saw her hands. "Hands are a pianist's life," he'd say. She swallowed hard and fought to keep the tears back.

"Are you listening to me?"

She nodded, unable to speak.

"Stay on this road--see, it's that broken line there--until it comes out to the paved road. Go east--that's left--and you'll come to Crazy Horse. It's only a small combination store and gas station. You could get some supplies there, but Baker City is a bigger place. At Crazy Horse you'll see a junction and a sign pointing to Baker City."

"How far is Crazy Horse from here?"

"About twenty miles."

Twenty miles. Oh, God. "Then how far from there to Baker City?"

"Another forty or so. Linda, this is crazy."

She shrugged. She'd manage, somehow. "Do you think I could get a job in Baker City?"

"I've no idea."

He tore off a piece of jerky and gnawed on it while she ate one of her sweet rolls. She carefully peeled the orange, handed Cyrus half and slowly ate her half, section by section. The tea tasted good and soothed her stomach. She'd have to remember tea, add it to her list.

*~*

Wade awakened before first light. Mist veiled a moon peeking through the high pine treetops. He'd slept on the pick-up bed, figuring it would be more comfortable than the rocky ground. Plywood covered the ridges in the truck bed offering some comfort. The dog slept with him--he'd left the tailgate down so she could get in and out during the night. He stiffly climbed out of the truck. He was camped just outside La Grande.

A bird shrieked, either at him or at another bird. Maybe at the dog. Now it was two birds screeching. What a racket. The large, fluffy camp robbers flew between trees, wings flapping against branches as they darted back and forth, watching him. Probably waiting for handouts.

He'd had dinner in La Grande and checked some stores for traces of Leslie. By the time he'd got there though, most of the stores were closed. This morning he'd check them out thoroughly.

Dutch was having the time of her life. She wagged her tail when Wade poured dry dog food into her dish and filled her water bowl from the jug.

He splashed cold water on his face and ran a comb through his hair.

Somewhere along the way I'm going to have to take a shower. I'm getting pretty ripe.

He rolled up his sleeping bag and tossed it in a corner of the truck bed.

It's time I get some supplies. And cash. I wish this knot in my stomach would let up. I guess that won't happen until I find Les.

What is she doing this morning? Is she scared? Does she think of us, of home? Never in a million years would I have thought she'd do this.

*~*

Leslie tried to bluff her way through the ordeal of saying good-bye to Cyrus. "Good-bye, and thanks for everything."

They solemnly shook hands. She could see hesitation in his dark eyes, but then he said firmly, "Okay, Linda, take care of yourself."

She couldn't stop her chin from quivering, so she turned quickly away and put on her pack.

With a heavy heart and feet of lead, she trudged down the rutted road. She felt his eyes on her. She wanted to turn around to look at him one last time, but didn't dare.

She watched her footing, not wanting to fall with her heavy pack. Step after step, she marched on. A quarter of a mile. A half mile.

She glanced at her watch. I've probably walked a mile. Nineteen to go. Oh God. Try to keep your mind on where you're going. Don't look back.

She trudged on. With the cold nights, the cottonwoods had begun losing their leaves and they fluttered around her feet. A slight breeze made the dry leaves spin miniature cartwheels along the road.

The fog had burned off and now the day was clear. Mid-morning heat closed in. She stopped to take off her jacket and stuff it into her pack. A deer fly darted around her face, attracted by sweat. She fanned it away impatiently.

What am I doing? Why am I doing this? It's because of you, Dad. It's your fault. If you hadn't made me go to that dumb school, I would be home now, with you. I hope you *are* worried.

Unchecked tears streamed down her cheeks.

I wonder which is worse--this or Rosemount. At Rosemount, I would be mad, anyway. And lonely and sad. I'm lonely and sad, but at least I got my way about something--I'm not at that stupid school!

She pounded on, her dismal thoughts drumming with the pace of her feet.

And I don't have to listen to how simply wonderful Rosemount is from the grinning Whitefields. I wonder if Megan and I would have become friends?

Her pace became irregular. At times she found herself standing still, staring at the road, deep in thought. Finally, she could walk no farther. Cyrus had told her the stream where they camped last night flowed close to this road. She left the road and followed the rushing sound.

The stream had grown into a boisterous little river. Approaching, she remembered how it would be with Polly. She would dismount and lead her mare to the stream and let her drink. Leslie loved to watch Polly slurp water. Her arms ached with the need to stretch them around the mare's strong neck. She craved the wonderful horsy smell.

I wouldn't have had Polly at Rosemount, either.

She felt drained of all energy, all hope. She slipped out of her pack and propped it up against a tree. She sat down and leaned against it, bringing her legs close to her chest. She lowered her face on her knees and wept.

Her anguished sobs ricocheted off the pines. She couldn't bear to hear herself, the awful, lonely sobs, made even worse by the echoes. She continued to cry, but silently. Her tears wet the knees of her jeans.

Her heart felt hollow, somehow emptied out. I've made such a mess of things. How can I go on? Even if I wanted to call home, how could I now, way out here? Anyway, I'm not sure Dad could ever forgive me.

She tried to bring the image of her father's face into focus again, but all she could manage was a dark, angry look. Nothing pleasant came to mind. She tried to find Wade's face. She remembered his puzzled look in the barn. Maureen's face was easy; as usual she looked comforting. But remembering Maureen's comfort brought on fresh tears.

What were they doing now? They'd been getting ready for fall round up. I suppose once they got rid of me they could get to work. Were Lilith and Roxanne living there already? At least Roxanne won't be rummaging through my stuff. By now Maureen would have sorted through the boxes and given a lot of it to her church.

Her stomach boiled and churned. Her breaths came in hiccups, like a baby who's cried for a long time.

Her food was running low. Cyrus had tried to give her another MRE, but she'd refused, saying that she would stop at that little store at Crazy Horse for a few supplies. How far had she walked today? Probably only five miles or so--fifteen to go. She would never make it today; she couldn't go on.

The sun came out from behind the trees and warmed a cleared area. She nestled down, pushed aside the larger rocks to make room to stretch out. With the sun on her face and a cooling mist from the rushing water, she escaped into an exhausted sleep.

She awoke shivering. The sun had passed over and was now reaching the tips of the trees across the river, casting shadows. Thoughts flooded her mind, dark ugly thoughts.

This is all Dad's fault. And Wade didn't help--he would never cross Dad. Well, I did.

She tried to get up, but fell back, exhausted.

I haven't taken a bath in two days. Do I have the energy to do that? Maybe it would perk me up.

Self-consciously looking around, she slowly took off her clothes. Slipping off her panties last, she hurried into the icy, cold stream. Gasping, she forced herself to sit down. Her skin shrank from the cold. The nipples on her small breasts grew hard and wrinkled.

Teeth chattering, she bathed herself and washed her hair. She'd forgotten her shampoo, but lathered the soap in her hands and used that to wash her hair. I'm glad I cut my hair-- long hair would be a pain, now. She stopped lathering. I goofed. I should have waited and cut my hair after I left so they wouldn't know I look different. But then she remembered the satisfaction she'd felt when her father was upset with her new look.

She didn't linger long in the frigid water. Standing by her pack, drying herself with her towel, she felt refreshed. I'll wear a clean shirt and panties and wash the dirty ones. Hopefully they'll dry before morning.

Doing something helped, it helped purge the poison she felt building up. She didn't have the heart to go on today but vowed she would get an early start in the morning.

As the late afternoon slowly turned to evening, she ate from her meager food supply. Her spirits plunged again. She would be all alone tonight. All alone forever. An empty, lonely future yawned before her.

She sat up with a little fire as long as she could. Her laundry of shirt and panties hung on sticks near the flames. She didn't want to go to bed too early, afraid she would wake in the middle of the night. Night noises surrounded her, clicking and chattering sounds. She heard a coyote yelp in the distance, then an answering howl. But she didn't fear the dark; she feared her thoughts.

She couldn't concentrate so tried recalling pleasant events from her childhood. There had been plenty of wonderful incidents, she knew, but her mind was such a tangled jungle she couldn't recall even one with clarity.

Finally, climbing into her sleeping bag, loneliness overwhelmed her. Oh God, I'm sorry. Please just let me die tonight. I've messed up so bad, there's no way anything can be right again. I could never go home and face Dad. Anyway, home won't be the same with *them* there. Please, please just let me die tonight.

Sleep wouldn't come. She groaned with the realization that this was only the third day of her escape. I can't go on, I can't. Please, God, let me die.

She again tried to recall happy times, but her torment crowded into every thought. Music. I'll do that again. She picked one of her most difficult pieces and concentrated. When misery tried to intrude, she hummed the tune out loud to block it out. Finally, she fell asleep.

She awoke sometime during the night. What? What was that? She propped herself up to listen. Ribbons of moonlight streaked across the river, lighting up the night. What had she heard above the rushing of the stream? Something crackled. The cold air finally forced her to snuggle down into her sleeping bag to get warm. It's nothing, she finally convinced herself. Just a deer or a raccoon.

She started on her piano piece again. She could hear Mr. Baxter's voice. "Think the notes, Leslie. They won't be true until you think them, feel them..." She drifted off again.

*~*

Wade found encouragement in La Grande. She'd been there, all right. He'd taken her picture into a grocery store and asked several clerks if they had seen Leslie. One of them, an assistant manager, said yes, she'd been in--what was it, one or two days ago? She'd asked for work.

The man held the picture at a distance. "This photograph must be old. She looks two, three years older than the girl in this picture."

"She had her hair cut short. Could that be the difference?"

"Yeah, that's it."

"Did she seem all right?"

"Looked all right to me, a little nervous maybe. We couldn't give her a job, we only hire local kids as baggers."

"Can you remember which day she was in?"

"Well, let's see." He hung his head, thinking. "This is Wednesday. I'm pretty sure it was yesterday, Tuesday, sometime around noon."

"Do you have any idea where she went after she left here? Did you see her again?"

The clerk shook his head. "Nope."

"Okay, thanks a lot."

He stopped at the truck and reached for the bag with Leslie's pajamas. "Dutch, where's Les? Come on, let's find Les." The dog bounded out of the car and sniffed around, finally leading him to a small cafe.

He opened the door, stepping aside to let the dog in. Dutch hurried in, nose to the floor.

"Hey, get that dog out of here!" an indignant waitress yelled. Customers peered over their breakfasts and newspapers, looking curiously at the dog, then at Wade.

"Hold on. I'll just be a minute." He watched as Dutch vigorously sniffed a spot by the door. Her tail thumped on the door jam. She circled the room and made loud snuffling noises by the counter. Then she returned to the spot near the door.

"Okay, girl, come on." He opened the restaurant door and stepped to his truck, parked on the street, and let the dog in the front seat. He returned to the cafe.

He held the picture out so that the waitress could see it. "Have you seen this girl? She looks a little different now with shorter hair."

The waitress looked at the picture. "No, who is she?"

"My sister. I need to find her. My dog picked up her scent in here."

He glanced around the restaurant making eye contact with all those watching and held up the picture for them to see. "Anyone else here that might have seen her, probably yesterday, maybe around noon?"

The waitress shouted into the kitchen. "Stella!"

Another waitress appeared at the window opening between the dining area and the kitchen. She wiped her hands on her apron. "Yeah?"

"Com'ere. This man wants to know if you seen his sister."

Wade held up the picture so she could see it.

"I seen her in here yesterday, looking for work. She had a big gray pack with her. She set it there, by the door."

One man left his seat and took a closer look at the picture. "I saw a girl yesterday walking down the street wearing a pack. I think that was her."

"Oh? Which way was she walking?"

"Going south on Center Street."

"Okay. Thanks a lot. Anybody else see her?"

A woman at a booth called out, "Let me see the picture." She handed a half piece of toast to a small child in a highchair.

Wade walked over to her booth and handed her the picture. The woman nodded. "I saw this girl at Bob's yesterday, around noon."

"Bob's?"

"The grocery store. Bob's."

"Oh. Right." He tipped his hat. "Thanks, I appreciate it."

Wade checked more places and learned she'd looked for work at a dusty little hardware. At the hardware Wade watched as Dutch circled the store and returned again to the counter by the cash register. The dog didn't have much reaction, no joyous recognition, but some definite interest.

Dairy Queen said she'd been there but hadn't filled out an application. He checked at a few other, unlikely places too, but apparently he'd found the ones where she'd tried to find work.

While checking, he was all business, not allowing himself to get emotional. But when he'd exhausted all the possibilities in La Grande and climbed back into his truck, he smacked the dashboard with his open hand. The dog jumped. He reassured her with a pat.

Oh God. She was here. Just yesterday. She's looking for work. What is she thinking about? How will she live? Please, watch over her.

Okay, get your butt in gear and start looking. From La Grande he scoured the nearby towns: Island City, Alecil, Imbler, then way up to Elgin. This was big country. More wide open space, more sage, than Washington. He felt her trail getting cold, so he circled back south, stopping in Summerville and Hilgard. His spirits, so high after learning she had been in La Grande, plummeted. No trace. Where could she have gone?

He called his father at six. "Dad, she's been in La Grande, tried to find work there."

"Wait, let me find it on the map. Okay, here it is. You sure?"

"Yeah, but she didn't have any luck and apparently didn't stick around."

"Wade, what the hell is she doing? Why is she looking for work?"

"Well, I guess she looks at this as permanent, Dad. At least she's smart enough to know in order to survive she'll have to work."

"Lilith told me Leslie was in the bank a day or so before we left for Spokane. She withdrew all her savings, a little more than two thousand dollars. That should do her for awhile--she shouldn't be looking for work this soon."

Wade rubbed his eyes. He was beat. "I don't know, Dad, maybe she just figured she needed to settle somewhere. Maybe the money's for an apartment. I don't know."

John sighed. "I drove her to this, Wade."

"You did what you thought was best."

"I was apparently the only one who thought that."

A long silence followed. "Well, it was your decision. All we can do now is take it from here. Try not to blame yourself, Dad."

"There's no one else to blame."

Silence hung in the long distance between them.

John's voice was thick. "So what happened after La Grande?"

"Nothing. I checked a lot of small towns. I'm going to keep circling around, try to pick up her trail again. I have a few hours before dark."

"Could she have taken a bus?"

"No busses stop at these dinky places."

"Maybe she got a ride."

"I'm hoping like hell she didn't."

"Okay, son. Take care of yourself. She'll probably stop at night, you do the same. Where are you staying tonight?"

"I'll go over to a state park, take a shower and crash. I need to find an ATM for cash, I didn't bring much with me."

"Sure. Why not stay at a motel?"

"If you saw the local's idea of a motel, you'd know why. The only one I've seen looks like a pay-by-the-hour place."

John snorted. "Okay, let's keep this schedule, but call any time. I'm sticking close to home. Maureen can always reach me."

"Right. Have you started round up?"

"Yeah. They're up to their asses. I'm pretty useless, but I butt in once in awhile. We called around and found some extra help."

"Okay. Good. Goodnight. And Dad, don't worry, I'll find her."

## NINETEEN

Propped up on one elbow, Leslie looked at the world through morbid eyes. "Shit."

This is so stupid. Cyrus was right--it's crazy to be way out here. How can I find work if I'm wandering around this dumb wilderness?

She lay back, miserable.

I could stay right here until I die. The way I feel it shouldn't take long. She pulled her arm out of the warm sleeping bag to peek at her watch. Five-thirty.

She had to go to the bathroom. By the time she struggled out of her sleeping bag and found a bush, she no longer felt like crawling back into bed. It felt good to stretch her stiff, sore back. The morning air was chilly; she slipped into her jacket.

She sat on a large, flat rock and watched the river rush by. Birds played vocal ping-pong.

I need to get food, but Crazy Horse is probably another fifteen miles or more. How am I going to get the energy to walk that far?

Stop whining and get moving. Wade's image flashed through her mind.

Jerking her head around, she expected to see her brother standing there.

He said that to her, just this summer. He'd wanted her to help him move some cattle, but she balked and later, on the trail, had complained she was hot and tired. He'd nudged her horse and said that then: "Les, I need your help. Stop whining and get moving."

That day she hadn't much choice, not with him looming over her. Actually, today she didn't either. She did have to get moving and keep moving if she was going to get supplies. Death by starvation wasn't that appealing.

She rolled up her sleeping bag and pad and tied them to her pack. Breakfast consisted of the remaining sweet roll, now in crumbs, and a few dried apricots washed down with water. Finding the road again, she began the long walk to Crazy Horse.

She walked steadily on the rutted road within hearing of the river's rush. The walking wasn't too difficult; the road made a slow descent.

She forced herself to keep walking for two hours. Occasionally, to ease her shoulders, she clasped her hands behind her back and lifted the pack. She snacked on a few apricots and a handful of cereal. She had to wash the cereal down with water.

I'll never eat Fruit Loops again.

The heat forced her to stop and change into shorts. There, that's better. More meat for mosquitoes though.

In places the small road, tinder dry, was like powder, and where she stepped, clouds of red dust drifted across her bare legs.

She tried not to think about home but instead, attempted to concentrate on what she had to do next. Meeting Cyrus had been so helpful. She wished she could have stayed with him.

But, as he said, what good would that do? They had two different goals. He called this fun! After his vacation, he would return to a home and his job. What would she do? Never mind. Just think about now.

She marched on, determined not to stop for another two hours, or at Crazy Horse, whichever came first.

Two hours later, she stopped again for a brief rest and a snack. She left the road to top off her water bottle at the river, then returned to her forced march, as she began to think of it, hoping with each turn to come to the paved road.

Finally, in the early afternoon the forest service road met the paved road. She turned left and could see in the distance Crazy Horse and the small store with gas pumps in the front. She was so relieved she hardly noticed the weight of her pack.

With triumph she stepped into the store.

It wasn't much of a store, as Cyrus had said. But she bought a quart of milk, four local apples, a box of hard tack, and a small package of processed cheese. She stepped outside to eat. Her hands shook from fatigue but also from excitement in finding the store.

A car pulled in for gas. The driver, a young woman, waited for the store clerk to pump the gas for her. They seemed to know one another. Their voices were so low Leslie couldn't hear them, but at one point they both glanced her way, and she knew they were talking about her. Oh oh. Better line up a story.

The attendant returned to the store, and the young woman came to where Leslie still sat, resting her back against the shaded storefront, finishing up her lunch. "You need a ride? I'm going to Baker City."

Leslie looked up at the woman, astonished. "Sure, that'd be great. I'm supposed to meet my aunt there."

"Okay, I'll just get a few things from the store, and I need to make a phone call. Then we'll be on our way." She disappeared into the store.

A phone call. I could call home. Quick, while she's in the store. No, I can't. I could call Janelle. But she would be full of questions. She might even be mad at me. Anyway, I still think the telephone company can trace calls.

The woman came out of the store with a large Coke. "Okay, a quick phone call and we'll be on our way."

Leslie stood by her pack, waiting, listening. Could she trust this woman? Could she be calling someone, like a sheriff? Don't be silly. How would they know anything? Her chest felt so tight she could hardly breathe.

"Chuck? I'm on my way. I should be there in an hour or so. Okay, bye." The woman turned to Leslie and smiled. "Okay, let's go. We'll put your pack in the back seat. I'm Charlene Webster."

"I'm Linda Carpenter."

"You've been camping, Linda?"

Leslie nodded. "I've been camping with friends. They just dropped me off."

"Dropped you off?"

"Yeah, I decided to go into Baker City to see my aunt. She's been sick."

"How were you going to get there?"

"I was hoping for a ride. Thanks a lot for offering me the lift. Do you live in Baker City?"

"No, I live out here in the boondocks, but my boyfriend lives there." Charlene opened a fresh pack of cigarettes and pried one out, then extended the pack to Leslie.

"No, thanks." But she appreciated being thought old enough to smoke.

The woman lit her cigarette and took a long drink from her Coke. "Where do you live?"

"Oh, I'm sort of between places, now. This is pretty country. Are you a rancher?" I'm getting pretty good at this.

Small talk filled the hour it took to arrive in Baker City. Leslie pointed to a telephone booth in the center of town. "I'll call my aunt from here. My uncle will come and get me. Thanks for the ride!"

Charlene Webster pulled over to the telephone booth, and Leslie hopped out of the car and reached in the back for her pack.

As soon as the car was out of sight, Leslie stopped to look around and get her bearings. I need a car. Riding with that woman, I realized what I'm doing isn't working. I'll never be able to get around enough to find a job.

She stepped into a small dress shop. The woman raised her eyebrows. "Yes?"

"Can you tell me where I can buy a car? A used car?"

"Terry's Car Corner is a couple of blocks down the street." She motioned vaguely. "Oh, and the other way, about two or three blocks down, is a vacant lot where people park cars and trucks for sale. My son bought his truck there."

Leslie had never bought a car, but it seemed safer to buy from a person than from a company. For one thing, wouldn't a company person ask a lot of questions? And wouldn't there be forms or something to fill out? But would it be safer to buy from a company? I don't know anything about cars. What if it's a lemon?

Her feet answered some of her questions as they led her to the vacant lot where eight or so parked cars and trucks faced the street. Telephone numbers were written on "For Sale" signs, and in some cases prices were listed, too.

There's a clunker station wagon. Yuck. She looked further. This car is nice. Which means it will cost too much for me. She read the sign. Four thousand dollars! Yep. Too much for me. I can't spend more than eight hundred, nine hundred dollars at the most. I still have to buy supplies.

She considered the possibility of a pick-up. But if they've used them as hard as Dad and Wade do, the trucks will be beaters.

Another car, a brown compact two-door, might be a possibility. No price listed. She jotted down the telephone number.

She wandered over to the car she first rejected, the old Chevrolet station wagon. The faded finish made it look as though it couldn't decide which color it was... somewhere between a blue and a green. The doors were locked but Leslie pressed her forehead against a side window and looked at the seats. They sagged, but not too bad. No price listed.

She walked across the street to a telephone booth in front of a gas station. She dialed the listed number for the brown compact. How do you buy a car?

"Hello. Do you have a car for sale? ...Um...how much is it? ...Three thousand dollars! Thank you." She hung up.

The clunker station wagon, then. "Hello. Do you have a station wagon for sale?"

"Yes, we do." It sounded like an older woman. Good.

"How much is it?"

"We're asking sixteen hundred."

How do I do this? "I see. That's more than I can pay."

A muffled conversation and then the phone was taken by someone else. A man's gruff voice asked, "How much did you have in mind?"

Leslie swallowed. "One thousand dollars."

"Now, I'm not going to give my car away for one thousand dollars. How do you know how much its worth unless you've driven it?"

"Oh. Can I do that?"

"I'll be there in about ten minutes."

I should clean up. That woman at the shop gave me strange looks. I'm a mess.

She stepped into the gas station restroom and washed as best she could with paper towels and watery, pink soap. She changed into jeans and a clean shirt, the one she'd washed the night before.

Her mind whirled. If I pay even one thousand dollars, I wouldn't have enough money to get an apartment. But if I had that car I could live in it until I found a job. She could feel herself sinking deeper and deeper into a hole.

But I can't go on like this, just wandering around. If I bought a car, I could get around faster and find work. She wrapped her arms around her middle, wishing her stomach would stop aching.

She reached into the various places in her pack, gathering her money. She counted out fourteen hundred dollars, hoping she could talk him into no more than a thousand dollars, twelve hundred tops.

She returned to the lot just as his car pulled in. The man, as gruff looking as he talked, wore baggy slacks with suspenders and a white shirt with the sleeves rolled up. White hair crowded out of the front of his shirt and sprouted from his nostrils.

He eyed her suspiciously. "How old are you? It's against the law to sell a car to anyone under eighteen."

"I'm eighteen."

"Do you have a license?"

"Yes." Leslie had anticipated this and had her fake identification ready. She held it out for the man to see. He merely glanced at it and signaled her to get behind the driver's wheel. He climbed in the passenger side.

It was an automatic, which was a relief though she could handle a stick shift. Leslie had driven so few cars she was afraid she couldn't make a good judgement of this one.

I should probably try more than one. I wish I could ask Wade. If Wade were here, I wouldn't be buying a car.

She drove the car around the block, trying to get the feel of it, testing the brakes and steering around imaginary obstacles. She listened for...what?

They returned to the lot.

"I could pay twelve hundred."

"Fourteen. No less."

Fourteen hundred dollars! That would take almost all of her money! She quickly calculated. She would only have about four hundred dollars left. Well she'd just have to get a job right away, then.

"Do you have cash? I won't accept a check."

"Yes, I have cash." With a sick feeling she handed him the money. They sat in the front seat while he counted it then stuffed it into his pants pocket. He signed the title.

He handed her the document. "You have something like two weeks to get this into the licensing department. Instructions are on the back."

"Okay." How will I do that? Will it cost more money? I'll worry about it later.

He gave her two sets of keys and showed her how to lower the back seat, in case she ever wanted to. He even took the time to show her where the windshield wiper controls were--she would never have thought to ask--and how to turn on the heater.

"Oh good, air conditioning."

"It doesn't work."

Oh well. Anyway, I have a car. The sense of freedom! It's so big. With the back seat down I can stretch out to sleep. I can get around. Now I can get a job! I'll have to get a job. In the meantime, this car is my home.

Relieved that she didn't have to lug her heavy pack, she cruised down the streets of Baker City looking for likely places to apply for work.

There isn't much time left today, only a couple of hours, but I should try to look for work, anyway.

After stopping at three or four shops, it occurred to her that here, too, people were not eager to hire strangers.

She drove to a residential neighborhood and wrote down a house address and street name. Then, when they asked where she lived she could give an address. Let's just hope they don't know the neighborhood.

For the rest of the afternoon she canvassed the downtown area looking for work. Later, tired and discouraged, she climbed into her car, jobless.

*~*

As far as Wade was concerned, the day--Thursday, already!--had been a bust. He'd spent the whole day crisscrossing Highway 84. He'd tried to be systematic about it, but damn, those dinky towns were far apart. He'd pull into town, check out every store, though in most of these burgs there were only two or three stores, at best. He could usually tell when he pulled into town that Leslie wouldn't be there, but he couldn't afford not to check it out.

At each town he jotted the name of the town and his findings on the yellow tablet Mrs. Holmes had given him. Most of the towns had a simple "No" after them. Of the towns where he'd found traces he made brief notes of that, too. He'd started dating his entries. It was getting hard to keep track of time, the days blurred together.

No sign of Leslie. Hadn't been since La Grande. It was as though she'd become air-borne.

He was spinning his wheels, messing around like this. But what else could he do? He snorted in bitterness when he recalled his earlier confidence. Now look. It was already Thursday. She left on Monday, around noon. Where the hell could she have gone?

When I get my hands on that kid, I'm gonna wring her neck.

What was she thinking, trying to find work in such small places? On the other hand, he'd just as soon have her settle in some small place, rather than Portland or Seattle. His stomach tightened, knowing the dangers she would face in a big city. Stick to the small towns, Les.

It had been so long since they'd found a trace, he was afraid the dog would lose interest. Or, if a long time elapsed, the scent would get cold. At the different stops, he frequently let Dutch smell Leslie's pajamas to freshen the dog's memory.

That night he slept out under the stars. He'd had dinner, of sorts, at some greasy hamburger joint, but he could feel his strength slipping. I've got to eat better, but it's hard, being on the go like this.

*~*

Though Leslie's spirits were dampened some from not finding work, she was still elated with her car. She stopped at Safeway and bought a few groceries and supplies, taking pride in loading them into the back of the station wagon. Now she was more conscious than ever about her diminishing money. Still, now that she had wheels, she wouldn't have to lug everything around. What a treat!

At the grocery store she inquired about a park, a place to camp. Now she headed for the county park, eager to be away from strange stares and the awkwardness of asking for work.

At the scruffy park, about five miles from Baker City, the camp sites had very little grass; mostly dirt mixed with ash. The few trees were small and scrubby. A family occupied the best site by the river.

She longed for a shower, but the only bathroom was a smelly pit toilet. Empty cans and bottles had been dumped in many of the fire pits. Smells drifted over from a nearby overflowing garbage can.

Finding a reasonably clean site, she self-registered, following the instructions posted on a bulletin board. She slipped ten dollars into an envelope and filled in her fake name and address.

This camp isn't worth ten dollars. But to just pull off the road and sleep, especially so close to town, wouldn't work. If the police or sheriff saw me, there would be questions.

She dumped crumbs, leaves and ants from an empty box she found by the garbage can and began placing her groceries in it. She'd bought a plastic bottle of juice. As soon as it was empty, she'd fill it with water, to have an extra supply. She placed all her cooking supplies in the grocery box, her new sauce pan, her bowl and utensils.

She found the little container Cyrus had given her for matches. He had been so nice to her. She held the bottle tightly in her hand and raised it to her cheek.

Sighing, she split her supply of wooden matches, filling the little bottle as he'd suggested. She returned it to her pack.

She placed the rest of the matches in her food box, together with some scraps of paper she had begun to accumulate.

Leslie glanced around to make sure no one was watching and then split up her money. She placed two hundred dollars under the front seat, beneath a crumbly rubber mat. Fifty dollars went into the bottom of her pack. She tucked the remaining cash in her purse.

A stub of a whisk broom had been left in the car, and she swept her home. There. Now it feels like mine. She lowered the back seat, making a long bed, and rolled out her mat and sleeping bag.

She built a fire and when her water boiled, she added the noodles from her boxed dinner, then opened a little package with powdered cheese, dried vegetables and seasonings. Not as complete as an MRE, but not junk, either. She finished her dinner with an apple.

It was still too early to go to bed. She felt tired enough, but was afraid of awakening during the night. She put off going to bed as long as she could.

When it was fully dark, she gratefully escaped to her car. Her car. It had been expensive, but it was worth it. She locked the doors, opened the back side windows a couple of inches, and settled into her sleeping bag.

Strangeness enveloped her.

Will I ever feel comfortable again? I'm a stranger to myself. My chest hurts. Is this what a broken heart feels like? I didn't know it actually hurt.

Once their family car had been a station wagon. She remembered a trip that the four of them had taken, Mom, Dad, Wade and her. She must have been about five. It was Christmas time and they were going to Uncle Jack's, Mom's brother. In the back seat she and Wade fought, each trying to stretch out to sleep. Without a word, her dad had stopped the car, rearranged things to make a place for her to sleep, all the way in the back. Then he'd gently tucked her in.

Her eyes stung.

When she was ten or so, after her mom had died, she and her dad used to go to the movies together. Sometimes Wade joined them, but usually he went off with his friends. They had gone to a lot of shows, just the two of them. There was only one theater in their small town, and they were at the mercy of whatever was playing but it didn't matter, they just wanted to go. Sometimes they ate out, too, usually hamburgers at the Dairy Queen.

Then, when she was in junior high, about the time she turned thirteen, she wanted to spend more time with her friends. Not much was said--she'd just asked permission to go to the movies with friends. Parents took turns car pooling. When it was her turn, her father had taken them, and then returned later to pick them up.

Had that made him feel bad, her preferring going to the show with friends? She had never thought of it before. He'd never said anything, but of course, he wouldn't.

Everyone in the camp had settled in for the night. Leslie sighed. How can I get to sleep?

Remembering previous nights, she again concentrated on a piece of music. She pictured herself walking to her turn-of-the-century Chickering upright. She sat on the leather covered bench. By memory, she played a piece she had played in recital. Her father put down his newspaper and listened to her, his eyes closed.

## *TWENTY*

On Friday, Wade made his way to Baker City. Highway 84 cut a wide swath between hills streaked with alkali. The few trees he saw were juniper.

He slowly cruised down Baker City's main street. Well, this is more like it. A place where she might settle. She must be beat, hauling that pack around. How is she getting around? Hitching? Hiking?

He pulled into a gas station. While the attendant filled the tank--it still irritated him that he couldn't fill his own damn tank--he let the dog out and walked around to the restroom.

Dutch snuffed under the door of the women's restroom. Hope sprang as Wade stood, transfixed, by the door. Dutch's tail wagged frantically as she looked up at Wade expectantly.

After a moment or two of waiting and listening, it occurred to him that no one was in the bathroom. He knocked on the door. No answer. With some hesitation he slowly opened it. The room was empty. The dog rushed in.

The dog walked in a tight circle around the small, dingy bathroom. She snuffled loudly at the front of the toilet then spun around at the sink.

Wade ran to the attendant. "Did you see a girl here in the last couple of days? I think she used your bathroom. My dog picked up the scent."

"Yeah, a girl was here yesterday. I doubt if the room's been used since then."

"Can you tell me what she looked like? What did she have with her? Was she alone?"

The attendant shrugged. He was about Wade's age, but stocky. His creased fingers looked as though the grease and grime would never wash out. "Just a kid, I guess. Sixteen or so. She used the john to clean up and change her clothes."

"Was she alone? Was she carrying a pack?"

"Yeah, she carried a big pack."

Wade reached into the truck and held the picture out to the attendant. "Is this the girl?"

"Look, I didn't make a real study of this kid. I just noticed she came out with different clothes than when she went in." He looked at the picture. "This could be her, yeah."

"Do you have any idea where she went?"

The tank was full and the attendant obviously wanted to finish this transaction. "That'll be twenty-five thirty."

Wade handed him his credit card. "She's my sister. I've gotta find her. Did you notice where she went after here? Did she hitch a ride? Have you seen her around town?"

The man shook his head. "Sorry. No."

He parked the truck at the far end of the service station lot and began to walk, following Dutch, who kept her nose to the ground.

Hours later, he was still searching. They'd found several businesses where she'd been, looking for work. People in the various shops either recognized the picture, or Dutch gave definite signs of his being on track. But, in the end, no Leslie.

Could she still be in town? There were really only four main roads out of town. They had walked them all. No sign of her leaving; no sign of her staying.

Should he hang round, see if she's just resting someplace?

He found two motels and checked them. No luck. She hadn't eaten at a restaurant, though she had applied for work in a couple of them. Where was she eating? Where was she sleeping? Damn!

I still have four hours or so of daylight. Maybe I'm wasting time. She might have gotten a ride out of town. I'd better get going. If I don't get any other strong leads, I'll come back.

He'd only driven five miles out of town when his truck broke down. The motor just died. No sputtering, no warning.

God, what are you doing to me?

He looked under the hood, but he didn't have the tools to do a thorough investigation.

A man in a car pulled up and parked behind him. "Have a problem? Can I call anyone for you?" He held up a cellular phone.

"Yeah, that'd be great. Looks like I need a tow. Know any place I can call in Baker City?"

"No, not really. I'm just passing through."

"Oh, wait. I have a receipt from a service station where I got gas this morning." He dug around in the glove box. "Here. Can you call information and get a phone number for this place, Sam's Automotive?"

The same attendant that Wade had talked with earlier answered the phone. "I'll pick you up with my tow truck. If you want, I can take a look at it, see what we can figure out."

The man with the phone made sure Wade was taken care of, then left. Wade expressed his appreciation, but all the while fought a silent rage. Ups and downs again. Christ!

Once back at the station, the news wasn't good. Sam diagnosed the problem as a broken timing belt. There was no way the truck could be fixed before noon the next day.

"Noon!" Wade's heart pounded. His eyes bulged.

The man raised his hands in a hopeless gesture. "Look, mister, I'm sorry. We don't even have the part in stock. I'll order it in right away from the dealer and see if they'll drive it over from Redmond. After I get it, it'll take me two, three hours to install it."

Wade nodded. He tried to be civil. The man was doing the best he could. "Okay. Fine. Let's just do it quick."

He checked into a nearby motel. After he'd taken a shower, he sat on the bed to call his father.

"Cahill."

"Hi, Dad."

"Wade! Where are you? How's it going?"

"In Baker City. Well, I've got good news and bad news."

A short silence fell between them. When Leslie was involved in a good-news-bad-news situation, she always asked which you wanted to hear first. She loved creating the suspense.

"Go on."

"She's been here, in Baker City. She stopped to use the restroom and change her clothes at a gas station where I stopped. Dutch picked up her scent. I spent the day going to almost every store in town."

"Any more signs of her?"

"Yes, but that's all. Just signs. People recognized her picture, could answer my questions. She's been here all right, looking for work."

"When was she in Baker City?"

"Thursday, yesterday."

"Well, Wade, that's real progress. I think this is encouraging. The bad news is that you can't find her right now?"

"No. The bad news is that my goddam truck broke down."

"Is it serious?"

"Serious enough that I can't stay on her trail while it's still hot," he snapped. He sighed. "It's the timing belt."

"How long will it take to get it fixed?"

"I'm having a garage do it. It should be ready by noon tomorrow."

"Well, then, that's not so bad. Son, just take it easy. This day is almost over. Rest this evening. Sounds like you need it. You can do a little more snooping around tomorrow morning while you're waiting for the truck. Just roll with it, Wade."

Wade could hear the disappointment in his dad's voice. He was as frustrated as Wade, but trying to sound encouraging. Wade squeezed the bridge of his nose with his thumb and forefinger. "Jesus Christ, Dad."

"I know. Just hang in there, son."

"This is a lot tougher than I thought it would be."

"But look at the progress you've made. You've found exactly where she's been. Several times. I think that's remarkable."

"Not as remarkable as having my hands around her scrawny neck."

In spite of himself, John chuckled. "Well, son, I know you're discouraged now but you're making headway. I've been thinking though--do you think it's time to call the sheriff?"

"I've been wondering about that. Let's hold off, see what I come up with tomorrow. How are things going there?"

"Pretty good. Mrs. Holmes from Rosemount called. She thought a lot of you. Said if anyone could find Leslie, you could."

"She's a nice lady. How're you doing on round up?"

"We've about got it wrapped up."

"I'll bet that's a relief."

"Yeah, it's been tough keeping my mind on it."

After Wade hung up, he decided to find a place to eat, then return to his room and rest, maybe watch a little T.V. One of the restaurants he'd checked earlier when looking for Les was pretty close to his motel. As he left, he was surprised to find a restaurant right there, in back of the motel. He'd brought the papers from the truck into his room, and now he returned to the room and picked up Leslie's photo.

At the restaurant a waitress approached him. He asked if she had seen the girl in the photograph. "No, I haven't. One for dinner?"

"Yep. If you don't mind I'll ask around first."

"You go right ahead," she smiled.

No luck. Not a single person--wait staff or cooks--showed any sign of recognition. Leslie probably hadn't seen this place, either. The familiar feeling of despair settled over him. The waitress took his order. "Bring me a beer while I'm waiting."

He sat sprawled at the booth, staring at the frosted glass. My God, what lousy timing. Will she ever stay in one place long enough for me to find her?

"Mister, could I see that picture?"

Startled out of his reverie, Wade glanced up to the face of a black man. The man gave him a reassuring smile. He was a small man with a close-cropped beard peppered with gray.

"Uh, sure." Who is this guy?

The man looked at the picture carefully. "Your sister?"

"That's right."

"Her name Linda?"

"No, Leslie." His hopes plummeted.

The man nodded. "You must be Wade."

Amazed, Wade said, "Have a seat."

The waitress brought him his steak dinner. The black man slid into the seat opposite Wade.

The waitress smiled. "You having something more, Cyrus?"

"Just another cup of coffee, Charlene."

Cyrus leaned on the table, sat back when Charlene brought his coffee, and then leaned forward again.

"I met your sister."

Wade pushed his plate aside. "Tell me about it."

As the story unfolded, Wade's hopes soared and plunged. He listened to it all, mostly in silence. Cyrus told him the story from the beginning, the sandstorm, when he and Linda--Leslie--met. "I knew her name wasn't Linda, it didn't fit." He spoke of the welts on her shoulders from the gray pack, her plans, vague as they were. The tears.

"Right up to the end I tried to talk her into going home, or at least calling."

"What did she say? Why wouldn't she?"

Cyrus studied Wade, apparently trying to decide how to say what was on his mind. "She's really angry, Wade. From what I could gather, she felt her father was sending her away to school because he's seeing another woman, a woman with a daughter. Your sister says she and the woman's daughter wouldn't get along so..." He shrugged.

"That's ridiculous."

Cyrus shook his head. "Hey, man. That's what she thinks, at least it's what she told me."

"Well, it isn't true," though a little nagging memory nibbled in the back of his mind of Leslie and his conversation, when she'd expressed this very thing to him.

"Your sister is one determined kid, I can tell you that. I'm in pretty good shape after a summer of walking. I walked that kid for miles, up and down those foot hills, trying to discourage her. I thought she might see the light and I could talk her into at least calling home. She was exhausted, but would she holler 'uncle'? No way. Not a word of complaint. She's tough, that kid."

"She can be tough. Stubborn, anyway. Then you haven't seen her since she left the next morning, on Wednesday?"

"No. But I couldn't get her off my mind." He fell silent, looking down at his folded hands. He raised his head. His dark eyes looked steadily at Wade. "I followed her. From a distance. She only hiked about five of the twenty miles to Crazy Horse. I guess she was done in. She spent the night alongside a river, then continued on in the morning. I kept my distance. I wanted her to work this out for herself. But by the time I got to Crazy Horse she was gone. The woman that runs the store there said she got a ride to Baker City."

"How far is Baker City from Crazy Horse?"

"Forty miles."

Wade shook his head.

"It took me awhile to get to Baker City. I walked part of the way, got a ride for most of it. But by the time I got here, she was gone, or at least I couldn't find her. I've checked around. I heard she was here yesterday but no one has seen her today."

Wade looked at Cyrus with new appreciation. "It was good of you to try."

"Well, I was hoping I could talk her into at least calling home, especially after she'd been on her own for awhile longer. I'm due to get back home, to my job, but I just couldn't leave before giving it one more try. Must be the teacher in me. It's a curse."

"You teach? Where?"

"Tacoma."

Wade held out his big hand. "I'm indebted to you for telling me all this. And thanks for being her friend, Cyrus." His eyes filled. He was so exhausted he could hardly hold up his head.

Cyrus nodded with understanding. "I knew she was a good kid. Eat your dinner--it's getting cold."

Wade roughly brushed his eyes and pulled his plate toward him. "I can't believe I ran into you. When I'd looked earlier I didn't even see this restaurant."

Cyrus grinned. "I just stepped out of the restroom and Charlene told me you were asking around about a girl, maybe the same one I asked about. I figure I've got a day or so before I have to leave for home. I know this area pretty well--I've tramped around here for years." He laughed. "Your sister couldn't believe I thought this was *fun*. Anyway, if you need the company I could tag along, maybe be some help."

"Man, that'd be great. My truck's broke down but it should be ready by noon tomorrow."

Charlene returned and smiled at Wade. "How about a slice of warm apple pie and a cup of coffee?"

Wade nodded. Relief flooded through him. Someone to share the load somehow made this easier. "Make it two. You'd have a piece of pie, Cyrus?"

Charlene cleared Wade's plate. "You don't have to ask him. Of course he will." She winked at Cyrus.

Cyrus laughed.

They ate their pie and drank more coffee.

Cyrus finally pushed away his coffee cup. "During an entire summer of hiking, I usually spend maybe three nights in a motel and, as it happens, I'm staying in this motel. I'll see you in the morning. I've gotta do my laundry."

Wade returned to his room and called his father back. John answered on the third ring. At the six o'clock calls he usually answered before it finished ringing the first time.

"Cahill."

"Dad, I've got more news. I've just met someone who spent time with Les. His name's Cyrus, and he's going to join me for a couple of days."

Wade held nothing back. His dad deserved to hear the whole story, just as he had.

"That's ridiculous," John sputtered, just as Wade had when told the reason Leslie thought she'd been sent away to school. "I must have explained to her a dozen times why I was sending her to that school: She'd be safer, she'd get a better educa --"

"Dad," Wade interrupted, "you don't have to tell me. But for some reason, this is what she thinks."

"Well, she's wrong." A jagged sigh rasped over the phone, then, "I've come to the realization there was another reason, though."

Anger rose in Wade's chest. "What?" If it's true that Lilith and Roxanne had anything to do with this...

"I was afraid, Wade."

"Well, you've said that all along, that you were afraid for her safety."

"No, more than that. I've been afraid of her growing up, of letting go. I...I guess I didn't feel up to being the father she needed, of being able to handle a teenage girl. I worried about her all the time. It scared me to think of what could happen to her."

"You handled me, a teenage boy." Wade's teen years flashed through his mind. There'd been a few rough spots, but generally they'd gotten along. "We managed all right."

"Yeah, but I understood you. Most of the time, anyway. Besides, you had your mother. And Leslie's so different. If her mother was alive, I wouldn't worry so much, but on my own, I..." He cleared his throat. "At Rosemount she could get what I couldn't give her."

"What she wants is what you *do* have to give her."

At the silence, Wade spoke again. "Dad?"

"Yeah."

"We'll find her. I'll bring her home and you two can sort this out. Okay?"

"Okay, son."

After the call, Wade pulled off his boots, shucked his pants and shirt and fell into bed. Dutch curled up on his jeans where he'd dropped them on the floor. He awakened once during the night, worried briefly about his plans for the next day but remembered that he could discuss them with Cyrus. Good enough. He sank back into a deep sleep.

## TWENTY-ONE

Leslie's first thought Friday morning was to return to Baker City. The town had felt so comfortable, so right.

It's a lot like Chewack. That's why it felt so good, I guess. But I have to keep moving. I can't go back. I have to find a job.

She began to build a fire in the fire pit. It was so automatic by this time she hardly gave it a thought. From a nearby faucet she filled her pan, then her water bottle. She placed her little pan of water on the fire pit grate.

She consulted her map.

I've gone about this all wrong. These little towns aren't going to have work for me. I don't want to go to the really big cities, but maybe some place bigger than where I've been so far.

She'd never noticed it on her own, but Cyrus had shown her how to consult the index to cities and towns.

"See," he'd said, "they tell you what the population is. Baker City has nearly ten thousand people. That might mean you have a chance of getting work there."

Before she got her car, she hadn't much choice but to check for work in every little town she passed through, but now she had more freedom. She was definitely heading in the wrong direction; as she headed south the towns got smaller.

I could go to Idaho. Boise isn't too far from where I am now, and that's a big city. But I have Oregon license plates-- they would stand out in Idaho.

The water boiled and she poured it onto a tea bag in her cup. Carefully, she lowered two eggs into the remaining boiling water. She checked her watch. Three minutes. She studied the map again.

Maybe I should try Bend. It's a long way from here, but the population is almost thirty thousand. There must be jobs in Bend.

With a spoon, she removed one egg from the boiling water. She tapped the side to break the shell and, with the spoon, carefully scooped the soft-boiled egg onto a slice of bread that she'd placed in her bowl. Maureen often fixed soft-boiled eggs for breakfast. Toast would be better than plain bread, but this will be good too.

The remaining egg boiled for ten minutes. She carefully removed it from the pan and balanced it on a rock to cool. After cleaning up her breakfast dishes, she placed the boiled egg in her bowl and stored them away in her grocery box.

She brought the back seat upright. She didn't want the car to look as though she lived in it. Tidying up, she thought of home.

The familiar ache returned. She sat behind the wheel with her eyes closed, trying to clear her mind. Her eyes pricked with tears.

After glancing around her camp, she started the car. The thrill returned. Driving south on Eighty-four, she noticed the fuel indicator read half full.

It was nearly noon when she pulled into a gas station in the small town of Harris. Leslie's head throbbed with panic when it cost almost fifteen dollars to fill the tank.

*My money's going so fast!*

Hunger made her give a little restaurant a second glance. *No, I can make my lunch with the food I have. On the other hand, maybe stopping for a real meal now would be a good idea, then I'll have a lighter dinner tonight when I'm camping.*

She entered the little restaurant. The luscious smells made her mouth water. Automatically, she asked if they had a position open.

"No, but we might in two, three months. One of my girls is pregnant. You gonna eat? Our special today is homemade lamb stew."

Leslie nodded and sat at a table set for two. The waitress brought a steaming plate of stew and set it before her. From her table, Leslie noticed a girl enter and walk to the counter. She bought a pack of gum.

Leslie took a bite of the tasty stew and was startled when she glanced up to find the girl standing at her table.

"Hi! Do you mind if I join you? I hate to eat alone in a restaurant, don't you?" Without waiting for an answer, the girl sat opposite Leslie.

Leslie, shocked with the suddenness of having a table-mate, simply looked at the girl.

"Oh! I'm sorry," the girl said, moving as though to get up, "do you mind?"

Recovered, Leslie answered. "No, no that's fine. You just surprised me."

The girl laughed gaily. She was pretty. She had all the attributes Leslie admired: curly, almost frizzy, blond hair, medium length just reaching her shoulders, dark brown eyes with long, dark eyelashes, a perfect figure with a real bust line, just the right height, about five-four rather than a gangly five-eight. She wore a lot of heavy makeup, though, especially around her eyes. Raccoon eyes, Wade would have called them. Her tee-shirt and jeans were well worn, and sort of dirty. Like mine.

"My name's Tanya. What's yours?"

"Linda."

The waitress came to their table. "You having something?"

Tanya nodded. "Yeah, I'll have what she's having. And a Coke."

Leslie took a sip of her milk. "Do you live here?"

"No, just passing through. Is that your station wagon? That's a sweet car."

"Yes, it's mine. How are you traveling?"

Tanya shrugged. "Any way I can." She leaned forward. "I'm on the go, if you know what I mean. Actually, I'm looking for a ride. Could I hitch with you?"

Leslie hoped her shock didn't show. Her first reaction was: No! But how could she refuse? After all, she'd accepted rides from others. "I don't think it would work out."

Tanya didn't show any signs of disappointment. "Where you going?"

Oh! Darn it! I should have asked her that, then I could have said I wasn't going there! Think! Might as well tell the truth. "Bend."

"Bend? Why there?"

"I'm looking for work."

"Really! So am I. You don't have to go all the way to Bend though. There're lots of jobs between here and there."

Leslie leaned forward eagerly. "Really? Where? Doing what?"

"Oh, different things. Restaurants. Offices. I know one place that's hiring kids for tourist work."

"Where?" Leslie's brow creased. "Tourist work?" This girl must know her way around.

"Sure. Near Burns, there's lots of work. That's where I thought I would go. A friend of my Dad's is hiring. It's a lot closer than Bend."

Tanya leaned forward conspiratorially. "Linda, it's a lot safer for us to look for work together. That way, they won't take advantage of you."

"Well, I..."

Tanya sat back. "This time tomorrow, we could be working."

What a relief that would be! "Where would you live?"

Tanya's head bounced back and forth comically. "Depends. Lots of times they have cabins or rooms for kids. That's another thing. They like it when kids come together because they double you up. Anyway, I'd rather know who I'm rooming with, wouldn't you?"

"I guess so...."

"Well, what do you say? No sense in passing it up, huh?" Tanya had eaten surprisingly fast. She signaled the waitress. "I'd like a piece of apple pie. With strawberry ice cream."

The waitress returned to the table with Tanya's pie and ice cream. "You having dessert?" she asked Leslie.

It sounded wonderful, but Leslie's limited budget wouldn't allow anything so frivolous. Not now. Not before she found work. "No, thanks."

Leslie's mind whirled. I don't know this girl. Something doesn't ring true about her. On the other hand, she seems to know what she's talking about, knows her way around.

Go. Now. Get up, pay for your lunch, and leave. Just say "No, thanks" and leave.

Tanya looked up suddenly. "Last night my Dad told me his friend--Steve Johnson's his name--told him that they needed ten kids right away. Before the weekend."

"Why? To do what?" Weekend! It was already Friday.

Tanya shrugged. "I'm not sure but the pay is pretty good. About seven dollars an hour."

"I don't understand what kids would do."

Impatience showed in Tanya's voice. "Like I said, they work in the *tourism* trade. Where there's tourists, there's work."

"Where would the tourists be going?"

"Lots of places. You know, Frenchglen--lots going on there. Then there are the two big refuges."

"Refuge?"

Tanya looked as though Leslie were born yesterday. "Sure. You know, Malheur and Hart."

This girl knows so much, I'd be a fool to let this opportunity pass. "Well, okay, let's go together."

Tanya flashed her a dazzling smile. "Great."

"I'll use the restroom and then I'm ready to go." Leslie had learned to never pass up a restroom.

"Me, too."

They went into the restroom and when they returned to the dining room, Leslie stepped to the counter to pay her bill.

"Oh, listen," Tanya said, "catch mine too, okay?"

Leslie looked at her wide-eyed. "I'm pretty short of cash, I'd better just get mine."

"Go ahead, get mine too. Then we'll stop at the bank, and I'll cash a check."

Caught in an awkward position, Leslie didn't know what to do. The waitress waited, looking from Leslie to Tanya. Tanya started out the door.

Leslie's face reddened. "Okay, I'll pay for both of them."

Just outside the door, Tanya picked up her pack as Leslie left the restaurant.

"Where's the bank?" Leslie was determined to get this straight right now.

"About two blocks away. Let's get in the car and drive over. I can't pack this heavy thing all that way."

All that way! For Pete's sake! I carried mine for days before I got my car!

Out of nowhere--Leslie didn't see where he came from--a boy materialized. He fell into step beside Tanya. He was carrying a pack too, more of a day pack.

"Oh, hi," Tanya said casually. "Linda, this is my friend, Arnie."

Leslie, caught off guard, looked over and gave him a half-hearted smile. "Hi."

She couldn't stand him from the beginning. He looked like a smartass before he even opened his mouth. He had a strange bouncy gait, rising to the balls of his feet with each step. He was skinny with terrible skin. His straight hair was pulled back into a greasy ponytail that straggled between thin shoulder blades. And he acted as though he belonged with them.

At the car Leslie stopped and looked directly at Tanya. "Well, are you ready to go?"

"Sure. Shall I put my pack in the back?"

Leslie unlocked the tailgate and with a heave Tanya tossed her pack in.

Leslie walked to the driver's side and unlocked the door and sat behind the wheel. She leaned across and unlocked the passenger door. Tanya slid in.

Arnie tapped the back window and pointed to the lock. Tanya reached back and unlocked it for him. He popped into the back seat and slammed the door.

Leslie was dumbfounded.

"All set. Let's go," Tanya announced as though this had been the plan all along.

"Wait a minute. This isn't what we talked about."

"Don't worry about it. It'll be fine. Arnie, to go to Burns, should she get back on Twenty?"

"Look...." Leslie sputtered.

Arnie reached a dirty, skinny arm alongside her head, pointing to the main intersection. "Just take a right there."

"Wait. Tanya, I didn't agree to three of us going. You said it would be just the two of us." This is wrong! I don't want to do this! Get out! Get out of my car!

Tanya seemed shocked at Leslie's attitude. "Linda, what difference does it make? Arnie needs to find work, too. He's my friend. My good friend. And he'll be a help with all the people he knows."

With serious misgivings, Leslie started the car.

"So, just take a right..." he pointed again.

"We were going to the bank." Maybe I can get rid of them at the bank. After she pays me back.

"Oh," Tanya said brightly, "I almost forgot. The bank! At this corner, turn left then it's down a couple of blocks."

Following instructions, Leslie found no bank, only a grange hall and a tire store. "I don't see it."

"Arnie, where is that damn bank?"

"What bank? Why do you need a bank?"

"I need to cash that check."

"Well, cash it in Burns. We should get going, Tanya."

Leslie's skin prickled. "This town must have a bank." She felt her life slipping out of control.

"Right. Let's go over one block. Maybe that's where I saw it."

"Tanya!" Arnie shouted from the back seat. "Are we going to lose out on a job because you can't find a fuckin' bank?"

Tanya smiled apologetically to Leslie. "Linda, why don't we go on now, and we'll look for a bank in Burns. It's a lot bigger place than this. Arnie's right, we need to get going. I'll pay you back as soon as we get to Burns and find a bank."

Leslie didn't like it but, under the circumstances, didn't know what else to do.

They drove in silence at first, then Tanya reached over and turned on the radio, switched the station to hard rock and turned up the volume.

Leslie reached over and turned the volume down. "I can't concentrate when the radio's that loud."

Tanya shrugged.

In the rear view mirror Leslie saw Arnie's smirk. "You have to concentrate to drive?" He bit into an apple. Its crunchiness made a cracking sound.

An apple! Leslie looked behind her. He had helped himself to her food!

Tanya chided him with mocked shock. "Arnie! That's Linda's food."

"Well, you guys had lunch." He rummaged through her grocery box and brought out her boiled egg.

"Hey, that's my stuff," Leslie said.

"Don't worry about it," Arnie answered, peeling the egg and dropping the shell on the floor. "We'll pay you back when Tanya cashes her check."

## TWENTY-TWO

Late Friday afternoon, en route to Burns, the three passed a small combination gas station and store. "Stop right here," Arnie pointed.

Leslie glanced at the fuel gauge. "Why? We don't need gas."

"I need something at the store. Stop!"

Leslie had driven a little past the store, but she drove onto the shoulder and made a U-turn.

"Just park over there," Arnie again pointed, this time to a space away from the gas pumps. He hopped out, leaving the door ajar.

Leslie, determined not to have to pay for anything else for these two, stayed behind the wheel. "I'll wait here," she said to Tanya. "You going in?"

"No."

Too bad. If she could get the two of them in the store together, she'd leave. She mentally rehearsed how she would run back, take Tanya's pack out of the tail-gate, drop Arnie's small pack out the door, and take off.

Tanya was friendly enough, but she detested Arnie. By now he had eaten most of her food--gone were the apples, bread, and cheese. He even finished the bottled juice she so carefully allotted herself. She was being taken advantage of, but what could she do?

Did Tanya really have a check? Will they pay me back? I doubt it.

She thought back to the restaurant and burned with the memory. How could Tanya have had the nerve to order lunch and not have the money to pay for it? She even had dessert when I couldn't afford to. And I ended up paying for that, too!

Suddenly Arnie jumped back into the car. "Go. Go!"

Startled, Leslie turned to look at him.

"Go, stupid. Move!"

Leslie's jaw dropped. "Why? What did you do?"

Arnie face grew red with fury. "Just get the fuck out of here!"

"Why?"

"Hey, if we get caught, you're in this with us. You're driving. Now move!" He punched her shoulder.

Frightened, Leslie pulled out. The car jerked, then lurched forward. Tanya had remained silent but now turned to look at him.

"Oh, for God's sake. That's what you got, cigarettes?"

In the mirror Leslie watched wide eyed as Arnie pulled a carton of cigarettes out from under his shirt.

"And these." He tossed a package of Twinkies into Tanya's lap. "And this." He pulled a quart of beer out of his shirt. "Burr, this bugger's cold."

Tanya rolled her eyes. "Great."

He flicked her on the head. "You don't like it then next time you go in with me."

"Ouch. Stop it, Arnie."

Leslie was terrified. I can't live like this. I'm already in trouble. I can't make it worse by breaking the law. I hate this creep. I hate them both. Somehow I have to get rid of them. I feel dirty, being with them.

Occasionally, Leslie glanced at the countryside, at the alkali streaked hills, the endless miles of sage. Mostly, though, she was consumed with this terrible predicament.

When they reached Burns, Leslie asked between clenched teeth, "How do we get to this place, this friend of your dad's?"

Tanya glanced at her watch. "It's too late to talk to anyone tonight. We'll see them first thing in the morning. Saturday."

"So, now what?"

"Well, I don't know," Tanya said defensively. "What do you normally do?"

"I camp out."

"Camp out?" Both of them stared at her.

"Sure. What do you do?"

"Different things. Stay with friends, relatives, whatever."

Arnie snickered. "Camping. Let's go camping!"

Angered with his tone, Leslie turned to look at him. "Staying in camps costs money. We've used my gas and my car all day. How about you paying the camp fees?"

His eyes slid out the window, a smirk spread on his lips.

Tanya looked from one to the other. "Linda, why can't we just camp in the woods, not go to a regular campground?" She gave them a dazzling smile. "I really think it sounds like fun!"

Leslie knew she would end up paying park fees, anyway. They didn't have any money.

Not only that, Burns looked as hopeless as any of the other small towns where she'd tried to find work. But maybe...maybe Tanya really knew a way to get work. But then what? What about these two? She sure wasn't going to hang out with them.

She continued through the small town and drove west. She took a small forest road that wound up a foothill. In a way, it was harder to find a camp site with a car than when hiking. That's what Cyrus must have meant when he said he liked to travel unencumbered. She thought longingly of Cyrus and how she trusted him.

The car strained with the uphill climb.

"How about right here? What's wrong with this place?" Arnie, took a swig of his beer and belched. He'd had several cigarettes and now the car reeked of smoke.

Leslie parked and they all climbed out. Her skin prickled, the way it did whenever she felt trouble. She was afraid of these two.

"We're camping! We're camping!" Arnie pranced around, mimicking a child.

"Arnie, shut up," Tanya said, though trying to soften her admonition with a tolerant smile.

"So, do you set up a tent?" he asked, looking around the car.

"No, I just sleep out." Well, now that I have the car, I sleep in it, but I won't mention that to him.

She was concerned about the sleeping arrangements. Without asking, she knew they wouldn't care to sleep on the ground while she slept in the car. Yet, even with the seat down, there certainly wasn't room for the three of them to sleep in the back.

"So, are we going to roast marshmallows?"

"Not unless you stole some," Leslie retorted. She reached in the back of the car for her box of food. What was left of it. "I don't have much food left."

Tanya stepped over to the box. "Linda, as soon as the bank opens in the morning, I'll cash my check and pay you back." She picked up the box of noodle dinner. "Let's fix this."

"It's really only enough for one person. I only have one bowl, one fork and spoon. Tanya, this isn't what we'd planned to do."

"Well, we can open the can of chili, too. That should be enough. Arnie can eat out of a can, I'll eat out of the pan."

With a heavy heart, Leslie built a small fire and began heating water. Tanya pitched in and helped get things organized. Arnie wandered around and returned to camp empty handed. He hadn't even gathered firewood.

Leslie was annoyed. "How about gathering some firewood?"

Arnie shrugged. "No thanks." He sat on a log and waited for his dinner. What a useless turd.

It was one of the longest evenings Leslie had ever endured. She had nothing in common with these two. They forced chatter about neutral subjects--their favorite music, which they did not have in common, school--Arnie hadn't gone since ninth grade, Tanya's answer was vague. Of course, Leslie didn't shine in the school department, now, either, but didn't care to share that with them.

Arnie smoked one cigarette after another. He'd long ago finished his quart of beer and tossed the bottle into the brush.

Finally, it grew dark.

"You guys have sleeping bags?" Leslie asked. Come to think of it, she hadn't seen any.

"No." Tanya shrugged.

"How do you sleep? On what?" What is wrong with these people? How do they manage?

"We were planning to sleep where we find work. Linda, we just left home today."

Arnie sprang up. He opened the car and struggled until he'd figured out how to collapse the back seat. "Ah ha! Tanya, we can sleep back here. There's plenty of room."

"That's where I sleep."

Arnie looked as though she had lost her mind. "So? There's two of us and one of you. You can sleep on the front seat."

Leslie fumed, but knew there was so sense arguing. She was afraid to be too difficult, afraid of what they might do, especially Arnie. In the morning she would dump these losers.

The night started off badly and got worse. Arnie brought out a stash of marijuana. He rolled a joint and took a long drag, then passed it to Tanya. After taking a drag, Tanya passed it to Leslie.

"No, thank you," Leslie said coldly. She was sitting in the front seat, leaning against the door. At this elevation the evening was cool but she unrolled the windows in an attempt to get rid of the sickening marijuana smell.

"What do you do for fun?" Arnie's voice was strained, altered by the smoking.

"I don't do drugs, if that's what you mean. I don't think it's fun. I ride horses, go places with friends." She shrugged. Why bother.

She would have preferred to sleep outside, as cold as it was here at night, let them sleep in the car, but she didn't trust them. She kept her car keys in her pocket. Even so, there were ways of starting a car without keys, hot-wiring, they called it. Arnie would know all about that.

Then, much later, after they finally settled down, Leslie heard Tanya's muffled voice. "No, Arnie, not now." Leslie's eyes flew open. She lay on the front seat, her long body cramped into an S.

Tanya giggled. "Shhh. Arnie!"

Soon the car rocked and creaked as Arnie took gulping, noisy breaths.

Leslie felt like screaming Get Out! Tomorrow they were leaving. Absolutely. She would not spend another night with these jerks. She no longer cared about the supposed job opportunity. First thing, she would dump these two.

## *TWENTY-THREE*

Saturday morning Wade took a critical look at himself in the mirror at the Baker City motel and saw one tough customer. He hadn't shaved since leaving home.

I can't do much anyway until the truck is ready. I'd better get some shaving stuff.

He dumped out the clothes from his duffel bag onto the bed and put on his cleanest dirty shirt. Might as well do laundry, too.

In the laundry room, right there at the motel, he dumped everything into one machine and dropped four quarters into the slots together with the contents of a little box of detergent. He thought of Maureen.

Okay. Time for breakfast.

He returned to the motel restaurant. "Sit, Dutch," he commanded the dog just outside the restaurant door. He saw Cyrus sitting at a booth, laughing with a waitress.

"Cyrus, you character," the waitress punched him in the shoulder playfully, "isn't it time you went home?"

"Hey, you're gonna hurt my feelings!" he said, rubbing his shoulder.

Wade walked over to the table. "Mornin'."

"Wade! Sit down. Having breakfast?"

Wade ordered his usual.

Cyrus's eyes widened. "Whew! No wonder you're so big. Your sister needed a little coaching on her eating habits, or at least on the kind of food to buy."

"She never has been much of an eater. If something's bothering her, eating is the first thing to go. Our dad used to get after her all the time. Why? What did you tell her?"

Cyrus shrugged. "Just that she needed to buy real food. All she had with her was sugary cereal, junk like that."

Wade's concerned look made Cyrus add, "But she was going to pick up more supplies here, in Baker City."

"She did, too, at Safeway. I asked the clerk, and she remembered Les had bought groceries and kitchen stuff."

Cyrus straightened. "Kitchen stuff?"

"Yeah. A small pan, can opener, stuff like that."

"Good."

Wade shook his head. "Cyrus, I can't believe she's going through with this. What is she thinking about?"

"I don't think she has a real plan. All her planning went into leaving the school. Now it seems to me she's just trying to survive. She says she'll go back to school after she finds a job and a place to live."

Wade stared at him in disbelief. "She's just a kid. How does she think she's going to do that all by herself?"

"It's been done, but it's risky. I teach inner-city kids, and I know kids who live on their own. But most of those kids have to because they can't live with their families. Most don't have the stamina to see it through, stay in school. They have to quit school and work to survive."

Wade leaned forward, his voice urgent. "I've got to find her, Cyrus. Soon."

"Like I told you last night, I'll be happy to help."

"I'd like that. I need to pick up a few things, and check on my laundry. We have until noon, at least, before my truck's ready."

Cyrus nodded. It looked as though he'd trimmed his wiry beard. "We can poke around, see if we can figure something out. Try to get some direction."

"Sounds good. I'll meet you in front of the motel in an hour."

Cyrus looked at Wade's breakfast remains in disbelief. "I've never seen anyone eat so fast."

Wade returned to the laundry room, Dutch at his heels, threw his clothes into a dryer, pushed in more quarters, and walked down to Safeway. He tossed some jerky, chocolate doughnuts, and potato chips into his grocery cart, along with cold drinks and disposable razors. On his way to the checkstand, he grabbed a bag of ice for the cooler.

At the checkout, the same clerk he'd spoken with yesterday spotted him. "Oh hi! I thought of something after you left. Your sister asked me where the closest park was, a place to camp. I told her the county park, just outside of town. I'm sorry, it just slipped my mind."

He shoved his cart aside and glared at her. "Where is the park?"

"Just west of town, about five miles. Go down Main Street, turn left on Hooten Road and you'll see a sign, 'Hooten County Park,' off to your left. I'm really sorry..." she said to his back as he stormed out the door.

At Sam's Automotive, he found Sam in the office. His breath came in gasps. "Is my truck fixed?"

"No, not yet. I just got the part last night. I'll get on it right away. Like I said, I think I can have it ready by noon."

"I just got a lead on my sister. You have something I can drive, just for a little while?"

Sam pulled keys out of his pocket. "Here, take my truck."

"Okay, thanks a lot. Here, Dutch." The dog had run with him to the station and now Wade waited until she hopped into the truck.

On a chance, he took another minute to drive past the motel. Cyrus was just turning the corner, on his way to his room.

Wade pulled up beside him and honked the horn.

Cyrus glanced at the "Sam's Automotive" on the side and opened the door. "You steal this truck?"

"Get in. I got a lead."

Cyrus started to climb in, then noticed the dog. "He all right with me coming in?"

"She. Sure, come on."

Cyrus looked warily at the dog and climbed in, being careful not to touch her.

Dirt flew as they tore down Hooten. Cyrus bounced while he gripped the dash with one hand and dug between the seats for the seat belt. "Take it easy, Wade."

At least the directions she gave him were correct. He turned into the park. No campers, though there was a smoldering fire.

"It doesn't surprise me that no one's here," Cyrus observed. "There's nothing pretty about this place."

Wade hit the steering wheel with his fist. "Damn that woman! If she'd only told me about it yesterday when I first talked to her...." They slowly circled the dingy campground, then parked the truck.

Dutch pushed her way out of the door as soon as it opened and tore through the camp, nose to the ground. She investigated each campsite, giving it a fast circle. At the fourth campsite, she sniffled, wagged her tail, and barked sharply.

"Well, she was here." Wade forced himself to put aside his crushing disappointment and examine the camp more closely. At least Cyrus had a head on his shoulders. And Dutch. More than he could say for himself. Maybe if he'd asked more questions last night, that lady would have remembered.

A campfire had been recently doused at the site where Dutch concentrated. A few unused branches were neatly piled next to the fire pit. A sack of garbage precariously perched on top of a nearby overflowing garbage can, topped by the lid. Cyrus lifted the lid. Wade joined him at the garbage can.

"Yup." Cyrus picked up the plastic wrap from a can opener and a lid wrapping from a cooking pot. He chuckled and pointed to an empty milk carton. "Your sister's doing what I told her to do. She drank a whole quart of milk. And she fixed herself a good dinner." He turned the box of noodle dinner over to show Wade. "She's doing okay."

Wade turned away.

"I think this is encouraging, Wade. We'll find her."

"I've come so close, but then she just slips through my fingers." He kicked a log. "Son of a bitch! What the hell is she doing? Why doesn't she just *go home*?" His voice dropped. "At least call."

"I guess she feels she can't, that nothing's resolved. Once, the morning she left, she made the comment she'd been replaced."

"It just isn't true. That's stupid."

"Hey, it may sound stupid to you, but I'm telling you how she feels. And as long as she feels that way, nothing much is going to change."

Wade took off his hat and ran his fingers through his hair. "Well, I can't help her 'til I find her."

Cyrus nodded and continued to look around. "I see tire tracks, but that could be from people that used the camp before.

I think she camped here alone. Look, your dog is sitting right where your sister sat by the fire."

Wade walked to the truck. "Come on. I don't think Sam needs his truck right away. She's on foot. How far could she go?"

They drove ten miles either way on Hooten without spotting her. They drove down side roads that led to isolated homes. No Leslie.

Dutch curled up contentedly between them on the front seat. Cyrus hesitated, then reached over to rub her ears. The dog rumbled contentment. "That feel good, girl? Wade, maybe your sister went back to Baker City."

"It's worth a try. We could drive up and down the streets, just in case."

When they left Sam's truck at the garage, Wade was gratified to see his truck torn apart, being repaired. A kid was handling the gas pumps so Sam could work without interruption.

Cyrus had to take two steps for every one of Wade's. "Have you checked out of the motel yet?"

"No. And I left a grocery cart of stuff in Safeway." He lifted his hat and scratched his head. "I guess I need to apologize to that store clerk, too. I was pretty rude when she told me Les had asked about that park. Oh, and my laundry."

"I haven't checked out either."

"After I go to Safeway and pick up my laundry, I'm going to grab a quick shower and shave and get my stuff together. Let's meet at the motel office."

When they met again, Cyrus made a suggestion.

"We have about an hour before your truck will be ready. Let's give your dog her lead, let her take us wherever she wants to go."

"Might as well. We pretty much wore out this side of the street. Let's cross to the other side."

Cyrus nodded. "Not much over there, though. Few shops down the street."

They crossed the street and passed a vacant lot with a few cars and trucks for sale. Dutch sniffed her way into the lot. They stood there, watching, as the dog straddled a scent and worked her way around a large circle.

Cyrus smacked his head with the heal of his palm. "Oh, God. She did it."

"Did what?"

"Look at your dog. Leslie bought a car."

"What are you talking about?"

"A car. Your sister bought a car, right here, from this lot."

"She can't buy a car. She's only sixteen. I think you have to be eighteen to --"

"She's carrying I.D. for an eighteen year old."

Wade stared at him. "You saw it?"

"No. When I challenged her, called her sixteen, she said she was eighteen. She started to show me her I.D. but changed her mind. I'm pretty sure she had one. It probably has the name 'Linda Carpenter' on it. She even said maybe she should buy a car. I gave her a bad time for mentioning that she had that much money."

"She had about two thousand dollars with her when she left."

"Two thousand! Still, that's not going to buy much of a car. She said she could at least buy a junker."

"She must have had a car last night, then, at that camp. No wonder we couldn't find her this morning."

They both stared at the place where a car had been parked. Dutch sat on the ground, twitching nervously, staring at them intently.

They half-ran across the street to Sam's Automotive.

Wade leaned against the fender, next to Sam who was bent over the hood. "Sam, did you notice my sister across the street, where those cars are for sale?"

"Nope. Didn't notice." The mechanic grunted with the effort of his work.

"Do you happen to remember what car was there, between the Ford truck and the Impala?"

Sam pulled himself out from under the hood and looked across the street. "Yeah, Adam Harrison finally sold his old Chevy station wagon."

"You know that car?"

"Yeah, it's been in the shop. I replaced the carburetor, brakes, lots of stuff over the years. The car's seen better days, but it's not too bad. It's a real gas guzzler though. I don't know how much he got for it."

"Do you have any records on it? The license number, anything?"

The mechanic called his attendant over and instructed him to look in their records and give Wade the license number and a description of the car. "The finish is in pretty bad shape, but I'd say it's basically green," he said, again bending over the truck's engine.

Wade went with the attendant and noted the name and telephone number of the previous owner. He called Adam Harrison and verified the man had sold his car to Linda Carpenter.

"How was she? She seem okay?"

"Looked okay to me."

"Do you mind my asking how much did she paid for the car?"

"Fourteen hundred."

Armed with this information, Wade called home.

"Dad, I think it's time we called the sheriff. Les has a car, and it's going to be harder for me to find her."

Dismayed with this latest news, John agreed. "I hate to, but we've got to get this stopped." He made note of the car's description and told Wade he'd handle it from that end. "I don't like the sound of this, Wade."

"Me neither. It's been tough enough when she's been on foot. Having her mobile will be even harder. She's using the name Linda Carpenter, Dad."

John's voice came over the lines thick with emotion. "Where did she get that name, I wonder?"

"It's on her fake I.D., I guess. Cyrus called her Linda at first, had to get used to her real name. I'd better get going. We're pretty much staying on the same course as before, hoping she'll do the same."

"Well, now we'll have the Sheriff's Department looking, too."

By the time the truck was ready, half of Saturday was already spent.

Following Leslie's previous path traveling south, crisscrossing Eighty-four, they followed the Snake River which cut through bare, rolling hills, into Ontario, along the Oregon-Idaho border. Ontario held some promise, it was a good sized town with many stores.

Cyrus studied the map. He'd taken the job of noting on the yellow tablet the places they checked, his neat handwriting contrasted with Wade's scrawled notes.

He folded the map and returned it to the dash. "Let's go as far south as it would be practical for her to go, say down to

Jordan Valley, then head northwest, toward Burns. Boy, this is desolate country." He looked around at the endless sage, rock and sand. "I'll bet it looked just like this a thousand years ago."

Wade nodded grimly. "I wish she didn't have a car. In a way, she's probably safer, not having to hitch rides, but it opens a whole new can of worms. She couldn't have bought much of a car. What if she has a breakdown out here?"

They stopped at six so that Wade could call home. "Cahill."

"Hi, Dad. Well, so far, nothing. She can get around a lot faster now. Did you call the Sheriff's Department?"

"Yeah, I gave them her description, the name she's using and the description of the car. They gave me hell for not calling sooner. I hope we did the right thing, waiting."

"I think we did, Dad. If they find her first, it's going to be a lot tougher on her."

"Here, Maureen wants to talk to you."

"Hello, Wade."

"Hi, Maureen. How's it going?"

"We're fine. Are you taking care of yourself? Are you eating well and getting enough rest?"

Wade shook his head. His voice grew hoarse. "Yeah, Maureen, I'm fine."

"Well, I just wanted you to know that I'm praying for you out there."

"Thanks, Maureen. Pray for Les, too."

"Oh, I am, I am! Good luck, Wade. Here's your father."

Wade could picture his father's extended hand, impatiently waiting for the phone.

"Wade? Where are you? What's next?"

"We're in Nyssa. We'll go down to Jordan Valley, then we'll head northwest, toward Burns."

It was dark by the time they ended that day's search and found a place to camp. Wade took out the few supplies he'd bought. "I was in such a hurry I didn't get much, I guess."

"You're as bad as your sister. Here, I've got some extra MRE's."

While they ate their MRE's, Cyrus told Wade of Leslie's reaction to the instant dinners.

"'Just like Christmas,' she said when she saw the little packet with gum and stuff in it."

Wade snorted his appreciation of the story. "She always did like surprises. Tell you something, she surprised us by doing this."

"I'll bet. How's your dad taking it?"

"Hard. I'm worried about him. I'll bet he's aged ten years. He's blaming himself and that doesn't help."

"Well, it works both ways. She wasn't in the right running away. What school was it? She would never say more than 'just some stupid girls school'."

"Rosemount Academy, in Spokane. I went there, first thing, after she left. It's a nice place. Les just had her mind made up that she didn't want to go there."

"It seems to me that once she got the idea it was because of your dad's friend and her daughter, that became more of an issue."

"But that wasn't true, you know. Dad started talking about Rosemount before Lilith and Roxanne were even in the picture. Well, I guess he knew her, but none of the rest of us had met her. Once Leslie met Lilith and her daughter, she took it that way. I guess she just couldn't buy Dad's reasons."

"You know, most kids complain about home, how unfair life is, stuff like that. But your sister speaks very highly of home."

"Yeah. She's a happy kid, or was. She and my dad were beginning to have a few go-rounds, but nothing serious. Typical teen stuff. He's a soft touch with her."

"More so than with you at that age?"

"Oh hell, yes. He wouldn't take any crap from me. You don't mess around with my dad. I could do a lot of stuff during the school year, play sports--mostly football and basketball-- but he kept a tight rein on me. Come summer, he'd work my butt off. Now I know it was so I wouldn't have time to get into trouble."

"I know what that's like. My dad was a roofer, and every summer that's where you'd find me, on some damn hot roof. I thought he was a mean son of a bitch then, of course, but, like you, now I know it was for my own good. Actually, for the good of the family. I got regular wages, but half my salary went back to the family, most of the rest went toward my college fund. I'm the oldest of thirteen kids."

"Thirteen!"

Cyrus laughed. "You and your sister are so much alike. That was exactly her reaction."

"You married?"

"No. You?"

"Not yet, but I have sort of an understanding with a woman. I'm hoping we'll get married. But I'll tell you something: We won't have thirteen kids! Just handling this with Les has about done me in."

Once the sun set, the night turned chilly. They moved closer to the fire. Wade stirred the coals and added a large log.

He shook his head. "I never thought it would take so long to find her."

"What will happen when you do?"

"I've wondered about that. I'm pretty sure she won't be going to Rosemount. My dad realizes he was pretty heavy-handed about that. He didn't give Les much of a say."

Cyrus rolled out his sleeping bag near the fire and sprawled on top of it. "It must be tough, being a parent. Sounds to me like your dad wants what's best for Leslie. She's a pretty special kid."

Wade rubbed his jaw, thinking. "She is. She's so different from Dad and me. I guess that's something Dad has seen all along. With her, it seems school and music are what's important. He doesn't expect the same of her as he did of me at that age."

"And you? What did you want when you were sixteen?"

"Oh hell, I never wanted to be anything but a rancher, just like my dad. He tried to talk me into going to college. I've taken a few classes, agricultural stuff mostly, but to me it seemed a waste of time."

"You don't think ranching is Leslie's bag?"

"Not really. She's good with horses, though, and she worked with me this summer. Most of the time her heart really isn't in it."

"It doesn't make sense then, does it? Why she would leave a nice school like Rosemount, her music, everything?"

Wade shrugged. "I guess she felt she had everything at home. She's a damned good student--better than I ever was-- and was doing good with her music. And she worked so hard." He was silent. Night noises settled in around them. A log shifted in the fire, sending a flurry of sparks into the darkness. "I think Les scared my dad."

"Scared him?"

"Yeah, the responsibility of raising a teenage girl, especially since our mom died. He was afraid for her, afraid she would get hurt. It scared him. I think that's what really made him so intent on her going to that girls school."

"At one time or another, a kid's got to grow up. It's tough for a parent to let go."

Wade nodded. "I think he's looking at it different now."

"Well, tomorrow's Sunday. Let's see what we can do to help him out." Cyrus crawled into his sleeping bag and zipped it up to his chin. "This is sure rough country. Hot as hell in the daytime and freezing at night."

"Yeah. It isn't Leslie's kind of place at all."

## TWENTY-FOUR

On Saturday morning Leslie ached to get away from Tanya and Arnie, from the camp. Away.

"What's for breakfast?" Arnie, again. What nerve.

"We don't have any food left."

"You have eggs."

"It would take too long to build a fire and cook them."

Tanya rummaged around in her pack. She pulled out a small mirror to observe her smeared makeup. "I need to clean up before we go for a job interview."

Leslie's mind whirled. "Let's stop somewhere in Burns and wash up at a gas station." Just get in town, away from this wilderness. At the gas station she could demand they leave. She should do it around people so she would have more protection.

Arnie brought the seat back up, and they climbed into the car to return to Burns.

I have to go to the bathroom so bad.

Arnie had urinated right in front of them with Tanya's mock "Arnie!" Tanya had squatted nearby. Leslie felt so put off she decided to wait until they were in town.

At a service station, she pulled off to the side of the parking lot. A big tanker truck was filling the gas station tanks; its engine idled at a roar.

From the back seat Arnie looked over her shoulder. "Why don't you get gas? You're less than half full."

"I'm going to run to the bathroom. I'll be right back."

Leslie parked, grabbed her purse, tucked her keys into her pocket and hurried out of the car and into the women's restroom. She wished she could wash up, she felt so grimy, but she was anxious to get back out there. Anyway, her pack was still in the car; she needed some things from it before washing up.

She wondered what they were doing. The din from the fuel truck's engine drowned out all other noises. She washed her hands and dabbed at her face without taking the time to dry.

Okay, this is it. This is the end of the line. They have to leave. She opened the restroom door.

Her pack and sleeping bag, propped against each other, were where her car had been. *No!*

She ran to the front of the gas station, then to the street. Her insides turned to liquid. Gone. They were gone!

Trembling, she ran to the man operating the fuel truck. "Did you see that car leave?" She shouted to be heard above the engine noise. "The station wagon? That's my car!"

"No, I didn't notice. Want me to call the police?"

She could barely choke out the words. "No. No, I'll do it."

She stood for a long time by her pack, fingers pressed to her temples, numb with shock. They did it. They stole my car. She felt for the keys, still in her pocket. She opened her purse. There was the extra set. Arnie must have hot-wired it. How could he do it so fast?

Slowly, she tied her sleeping bag and pad to the top of the pack and hefted the heavy load to her back. She took the road out of Burns. Her skin tingled; her head swam.

She turned on an unmarked dirt road. She had to get away from people. It was a tough hike, a couple of hilly miles, but she hardly noticed it.

*I can't believe they did that. They stole my car. Here I did them a favor by letting them come with me and look what they did!*

She found herself standing still. A high-pitched drilling sound rang in her head. She resumed walking, then stumbled, nearly falling. Her mind jerked back to business, she scanned the road, then resumed walking.

*They're probably laughing at how easy it was.*

A leaning sign pointed to Settler's Creek. She followed an overgrown path to a small clearing framed by a stand of pine. She shrugged out of her pack and sat heavily by the creek with her back against a tree. Absently she watched as water curled around a large rock. It seemed to hold for a moment, then ease into the mainstream again.

*I should have called the police. No, I couldn't. It wouldn't take long for them to get my story out of me, and then it would be all over.*

She drew her knees up, crossed her arms over them and dropped her head onto her arms. She was beyond tears. Her insides were cold, like stone.

*I was such an idiot to let them come with me. Maybe with just Tanya it would have been all right. No, it was their intention all along that Arnie would come. They planned it all-- how they would snooker me into letting them come along, then steal me blind. And I let them. Oh, God! I let them!*

Panic rose in her chest. *I am in such trouble now.* She stared, unseeing, into space.

Now I'm worse off than when I started. What will I do? My money! I left two hundred dollars under the front seat!

With pounding heart, she tore open her pack and found the fifty dollars in the bottom where she had stashed it.

That's it. That's all I have, fifty-some dollars.

All my food and cooking stuff are gone. My water bottle, pan, bowl, everything that was in the grocery box. She reached into her pack for her map. It wasn't there. She'd moved it to the dashboard of the car. I'll have to go back to Burns and replace that stuff.

I could call home from Burns. What would I say? That I blew it, that I couldn't even hang on to a junky car? It's as though I just threw that money away. No, I won't call. I can't.

It was so stupid, letting them join up with me. Right then, when we were getting into the car, I should have said I changed my mind, that I wanted to travel alone. But I was too chicken. It would have been embarrassing. But now look at me. Cyrus was right. I'm the original babe in the woods.

I don't think they knew about any jobs. They were just conning me. And I fell for it!

It could have been worse. They could have taken my pack and sleeping bag. I wonder why they didn't? I wonder if it was Tanya's idea, leaving my pack. But how could they do that, be so mean and take my car? I hate them! Oh God, I hate them! Waves of panic tore into her again. Her chest heaved as she took in gulps of air. She stiffly rose and began to pace the small area.

It's Saturday. If I had my car and hadn't joined up with them, I'd be in Bend now, maybe even have a job. Oh God, how could this have happened? How will I manage now?

What's the point of all this? What am I doing here? How am I going to get out of here? She drew a deep breath and tried to clear her mind.

I have to go back to Burns to get food and stuff. That's going to take a big chunk of my money. Then I'll look for a job. If I can't find a job in Burns I'll try to hitch a ride to Bend. Or, how about Frenchglen? Are there really jobs in Frenchglen or was that just another one of Tanya's lies?

She hoisted on her pack--it seemed to weigh twice as much as it did when she left home--and set out for Burns. Her queasy stomach reminded her she hadn't eaten since their skimpy meal the night before.

By the time she arrived in Burns she felt weak from thirst. She entered the first store she found and bought a 7-Up. Restored, she found a larger grocery store and partially restocked her supplies.

Hunger forced her to sit right there in the parking lot, leaning against the store to eat crackers and cheese and an apple. People stared at her. She packed the rest of her goods in her pack and began to scope out job opportunities. Her heart wasn't in it, but her dire situation forced her to try.

The old-fashioned Dairy Queen still operated as a drive-in. Several cars were parked in stalls, and a girl stood by a car taking an order. Leslie stepped into the old building and slipped off her backpack by the door. She felt a stab of envy toward the four teenage girls who worked there. They were so lucky to have jobs. Two of the girls who worked in the kitchen chatted comfortably. One of them said, "I had strawberries for breakfast this morning and they were so good!"

The other girl, continuing their disjointed conversation, said, "I have a date with Carl Lamberg tonight." The other girl laughed, but then said, "He's really nice, though."

"Can I help you?" the girl at the counter asked.

Leslie knew her awkwardness and desperation showed. "I'm looking for a job. Do you have any openings?"

The girl stared at her, and the others peeked around, wide-eyed, to see.

"No, we don't have any openings now."

She felt their stares as she picked up her pack and carried it out the door. With her back to them, she hoisted the pack on and made her way down the street. She knew that they were talking about her. She burned with humiliation.

She stopped at another store, asked for work and was again rejected. No, we only hire local kids. No, no work here. No, no, no. It was all she could do to maintain a standing position and not crumple into a ball and cry.

At the outskirts of town, after she was once again turned down, she inquired how far it was to Frenchglen.

"About sixty miles."

At least it's closer than Bend.

She trudged out to the highway. She propped her pack up by a Highway 20 sign and began thumbing a ride. After all this time, it was her first attempt to hitch a ride; all her other rides had been offers.

Truck after truck, car after car passed her by. Finally, a pick-up stopped. Three people were in front, a man, woman, and little girl, and two more kids sat in the back with what appeared to be the family's weekly purchases.

"Where're you heading?" the driver, a man wearing a beat-up cowboy hat called through the passenger window, leaning forward to look at her beyond the child and woman.

Okay, decide. South to Frenchglen or east to Bend? "Bend."

"I can give you a lift as far as Prichard, that's about half way."

"That'd be great, thanks." She hefted her pack in the back and climbed in. The kids, a girl about nine and a boy perhaps ten or eleven, scooted grocery bags over to make room for her. They sat silent and staring.

"Hi." Leslie tried to smile, but it was a weak attempt.

"Hi," they answered in unison. The man glanced over his shoulder to see that they were settled, then pulled out. Leslie could see the man and woman talking, probably about her. She was too tired to think of a plausible story of why she was out here. Maybe meeting my aunt in Bend would do it. Oh well. Who gives a shit?

The truck wasn't old, but it had seen heavy use. The springs bottomed out with every dip in the road. Even with the sun beating down, the wind whipped at her and sucked the warmth from her tired body. It was a rough ride, but better than walking.

An hour and a half later the family let Leslie out in Prichard. They talked briefly before parting. Surprisingly, they didn't ask Leslie about her situation. Dust settled around her as they drove off.

It was late now. She didn't want to hitch a ride after dark. Besides, she needed to find a camp while it was still light enough to see. She filled her water bottle at a gas station.

Her camp that night was rough. She hadn't found a stream or any source of water. She hiked back far enough from the road so that her fire couldn't be seen. As soon as the sun set, night settled in and the temperature quickly dropped.

She built a small fire in the shelter of a large rock.

She sat cross-legged, close to the fire and stared at the leaping flames. She heard a rustle close by. Probably a little animal of some kind rummaging around. A marmot or maybe a ground squirrel.

I had it so good with my car. Now I'm on foot again and nearly broke. I only have a little over twenty dollars left!

What will Tanya and that jerk Arnie do when the car runs out of gas? They'll probably just leave it somewhere.

She remembered that Arnie had suggested she buy gas before she went into the bathroom. At least they didn't get the car with a full tank of gas. A small swell of satisfaction rose in her chest. But her chest tightened again when she remembered the two hundred dollars left in the car.

What will I do if I can't find a job right away? I have to, that's all.

This whole thing has been a disaster. Maybe I should call home. No. No, I'll get a job and then call home to say I'm okay.

What would my life be like now at Rosemount? Dad was probably right--I would have made friends. Not good friends like Janelle, but friends, anyway. I wouldn't be alone, like this.

She emptied a can of stew into the new cheap pan. Within a minute or two, it stuck to the bottom.

Maureen's well prepared dinners came to mind. She stared into the fire. Are they worried about me? Are they mad?

I've been so stupid. This is dumb. *Dumb.*

As soon as she finished her dinner, she climbed into her sleeping bag, as close to the fire as she dared.

It's freezing here. I hate this.

## TWENTY-FIVE

Morning's twilight rendered Leslie's camp a chilly gray. Curled tight for warmth, she finally forced herself to get up. She slipped on her jacket and sat for a few more minutes until her body heated the coat. Each morning it seemed to take longer to warm up.

A few sticks were left over from the night before and she'd saved the grocery paper bag to start the fire. Thanks to Cyrus, she had matches in the water-proof container he'd given her. She hitched up her pants.

The fire seemed harder to start this morning. Probably because she was so tired. Her hands felt stiff and clumsy. It took two matches to light the paper. She inhaled the comforting smell of sulfur when the match flamed. The fire caught, then sparked to life with the twigs. She added a small, dry branch.

Smoked curled from the fire directly into her eyes, making her squint and blink. She moved to the other side of the fire, hitching up her pants again. Although she had brought a belt, she seldom wore it, especially since she slept in her clothes.

What's wrong with these pants? I'm just not eating enough, I guess. I was already skinny, now I must look like a skeleton.

Dad would be upset with me for losing weight. She thought of Cyrus. He'd get on her case, too. But food is expensive, and I'm running so low on money.

I dread going into town to look for work, but I have no choice. I actually feel lonelier when I'm around people than I do when I'm alone--I feel like everyone is staring at me, like they know I'm in trouble. I must look weird.

I wonder if that's why Roxanne acted so strange? She'd been in Chewack for a while, but she didn't have any friends. She probably felt strange, that no one liked her. She knew she didn't fit in. The more she felt that way, the worse she acted. Thirteen is a tough age, too. I had some rough times at thirteen, and I'd lived in the same place all my life.

She sighed.

I wish I'd tried harder with her. She probably left our place feeling awful. Her mom's okay. Anyway, I liked Lilith better than Roxanne. And she stuck up for me when she thought Dad had sent me to my room on the Fourth.

That seems so long ago. I can't even imagine the luxury of being sent to my room. A clean room, clean sheets, clean clothes. If I had that room now, they'd have to drag me out of there.

She forced her mind away from the comfort of her cozy room.

What day is this? Sunday! I don't know how much luck I'm going to have looking for a job on Sunday--most places will be closed.

Maureen will go to church today. She always invited me to go with her. I guess I went about half the time.

When Mom was alive, we always went to church, except Wade, but he went sometimes. After she died, Dad never went back. That time I asked him why, he just said, "I don't want to, but if you do, you can go with Maureen."

Maybe I can have my own little church service, right here. In a whispering voice she sang the beginning of a favorite hymn.

> "And He walks with me and He talks
> with me and He tells me I am His
> own..."

She couldn't go on. She put a handful of sticks on her small fire. Aloud, she said, "Lord, I'm sorry. I'm so sorry for all that I've done. From now on I'll try to lead a good life. Please, God, help me. Help me find a job."

Maybe I should go home. How can I? I don't even have enough money to get home. I could call. Dad or Wade would come and get me.

But then what would it be like? Dad would never trust me again. And now Rosemount wouldn't even take me back. No one would want to see me, anyway. I'd just make everyone miserable like I did before. And Lilith and Roxanne are probably there now, too. No, I'll keep trying to get a job. I'll need to pick up a few groceries in Prichard, and then I'll start looking, keep working my way to Bend.

*~*

At a small cafe in Nyssa early Sunday morning, Cyrus studied the map. "It looks like we need to cross into Idaho in order to follow U.S. Route 95. Otherwise, we'll be on little rough roads for hours before we get to Jordan Valley."

Wade glanced at the map. "On the other hand I'll bet she knows her Oregon plates will stand out in Idaho."

"Maybe, but if she follows her pattern of going south looking for work, there're no towns between here and Jordan Valley. Anyway, not on the Oregon side."

"Okay, let's follow Ninety-five through Idaho, then back to Jordan Valley in Oregon."

Several hours later, they crossed back to Oregon. Cyrus folded the map to show the southern part of the state. "Well, I guess we traveled a lot of hot miles just to know she hasn't been there."

Wade nodded grimly. "Guess so. But it made sense at the time."

They followed Ninety-five, leaving it briefly to check out tiny scattered towns. They crossed the Owyhee River, then drove through Rome with it's towering, castle-like rocks. They stopped at Burns Junction to gas up. Not much there--a weigh station and a gas-restaurant-grocery store combination. Steens Mountain loomed in the background.

They headed toward Burns on State 78 traveling northwest on the flat, sage-covered plains. At one point they came to a complete stop while cattle meandered across the highway. Dutch went into a fury of incensed barking.

Cyrus looked at the dog, puzzled. "What's the matter with her?"

"Hey, this is her line of work. If I let her out of the truck, she'd have this highway cleared of cattle in about two seconds."

"She seems so little for that."

Wade chuckled. "Size makes no difference. It's grit and determination that matter."

Cyrus finished jotting down their last location and tossed the yellow pad onto the dashboard. "I'm sorry to say it, Wade, but today I have to make some kind of arrangements to get back up to Portland. My car's there at my brother's place."

"Sure. You've been a big help, Cyrus."

"Well, I really haven't done much, but at least I kept you company for awhile."

"How do you plan to get to Portland? I wish I could run you up --"

"Oh no. You've got your own stuff to do. I just need to get up to Bend to catch a Greyhound."

"Bend? Why, that's only hundred-fifty, two hundred miles from here. I can sure run you up there. I'll need to check it out sometime anyway."

"Well, let's see what I can work out."

They ate dinner at the Nite Owl Cafe in Burns.

A big rig pulled in. Cyrus waited until the driver ordered his meal and had been served his coffee.

"I'll be right back," he said to Wade.

He returned with a big grin. "Got a ride all the way to Portland."

"Hey, that's great. I'm going to miss you, Cyrus. I've been thinking, if you're ever out our way, we have about ten thousand acres you could hike over, and beyond our place is the Okanogan."

"Yeah, I know that part of the country. I love it there. I just might take you up on that. Maybe you could teach me cowboyin'."

"It's a deal. Let me give you my phone number and address. Give me yours, too. I'd like to keep in touch."

"I want to at least hear from you when you find Leslie."

They studied each other's eyes, not mentioning the unmentionable.

"I'll call you or have that little twerp call you herself."

They had brought the yellow tablet, its pages bent and wrinkled, into the restaurant to plan the next move. Wade shoved it over to Cyrus. Cyrus took the pen and wrote his name, address, and phone number. Wade took out of his wallet one of the ranch business cards and scrawled his name at the bottom.

After seeing Cyrus off, Wade and Dutch resumed their search. At a grocery store the dog sniffed at a spot just inside the door for a long time, her tail thumping. Leslie had been to Burns all right.

Wade took the dog to the truck and returned. He questioned the woman working the cash register.

"Ma'am, I'm looking for my sister. Have you seen this girl?" He held up Leslie's picture. "She has short hair now and looks a little different."

"Yes, I have seen her. Yesterday."

"What was she doing?" His heart pounded.

"She asked if we had any job openings, but we don't. She bought a few groceries and left. Oh, she asked how far is it to Frenchglen."

"How did she seem? Was she okay?"

"Well...actually, I thought she looked miserable. I have a girl that age, and she made me think of my daughter. I'm sorry, I guess I was glad my daughter wasn't doing that."

Wade nodded. He wished Leslie wasn't, either. "What's at Frenchglen?"

The woman shook her head. "Not much."

He climbed back into his truck and glanced at his map.

It's a straight shot south to Frenchglen on 206. I should be there in an hour, hour and a half, tops.

*~*

In Prichard, Leslie picked up a small package of cheese, three apples and a pint of milk. She already had crackers in her pack.

Now I only have about eight dollars left.

As she crammed her food supplies into her pack, she overheard the checker's conversation with a customer.

"Ellie Mae, been to church? You look nice. How is your back now?" The checker's fingers flew over the cash register.

"Oh, I try not to complain but, actually, it's terrible. It couldn't have come at a worse time. Buck is about at his wits' end, what with me out of commission, Tony's broken leg, and fall round up."

"Well! Isn't his sister in the hospital?"

"Oh yes, that too. And Sara is seven months pregnant. She sure can't help."

"How old is her little one now?"

"Two. And acts it. This grandma can't be much help with a handful like him, not now anyway. I'm just hoping my back is well by the time the baby comes."

The teller shook her head. "When it rains, it pours."

"Well, I'm just trying to take it day by day. The main problem is that I just can't stand for any period of time, and I certainly can't ride a horse. And you know what else? After all that work, that tent Buck made for me, I can't even get to my tomatoes!"

"You poor thing. Here you go, honey. Shall I have Marcos take your bags out for you? He's in the back. I'll call him."

"Oh no, thanks. I can manage with the cart."

Leslie followed the woman out of the store and to her car. The woman unlocked the trunk and turned to reach for a bag of groceries.

"Ma'am?"

Startled, the woman looked up. She was a bland-looking woman, gray hair pulled back into a bun from a plain, open face. Her only makeup was a faint tinge of pink lipstick. Her faded blue eyes widened at the sight of Leslie.

"Yes?"

"I...I heard you talking in the grocery store. Ma'am, I'm looking for work. I could help you around the house. I haven't done much cooking but I can peel potatoes, make a salad, stuff like that. I can vacuum, do your cleaning. I've worked in gardens, I could help with your tomatoes." She knew she was talking fast, but couldn't seem to slow down. "I've worked stock, I could help with round up. Ma'am, I really need a job." Her voice cracked and she stopped.

The woman shifted her position, and pain flashed across her face.

"Here, let me put those bags in the car for you."

"What is your name?"

"Linda, Linda Carpenter." Leslie put the two sacks of groceries in the car.

"Linda, let's go across the street to the cafe and talk. I can't stand up any longer. My back is killing me."

Leslie turned to pick up her pack.

"Oh, don't haul that over there. Here, just put it in my trunk. For now, anyway."

A glimmer of hope sprang in Leslie's heart. "Yes, ma'am. I'll just run this cart back to the store."

They slowly made their way across the street.

"I'm really not such an old lady. But when my back goes out, I feel like it. I surely do."

They settled into a booth. "What would you like, Linda? Have you had breakfast?" She placed her elbows on the table and sat forward, making traction for her back.

"Oh yes, I've had breakfast. I'll just have a 7-Up."

"Well, let's have something to eat, at least. Betty," she called to the waitress, "bring us each some French toast. And I'll have a cup of coffee." She turned to Leslie. "Do you want coffee or would you rather have hot chocolate or milk?"

233

Leslie hesitated. She didn't have enough money for this sort of thing. *How much does French toast cost?*

"It's my treat, Linda. Hot chocolate?"

"Fine. That would be great."

"And hot chocolate, Betty." She turned to Leslie. "Linda, how old are you?"

She was sick of lying. *What difference does it make, anyway? So far, the only advantage of having I.D. for an eighteen year old was buying the car, and she couldn't even hang on to that.* "Sixteen."

"Have you run away from home?"

"No, not really."

"Then what?"

"Ma'am, I can't talk about it. I've looked for work but haven't been able to find a job. I'm a good worker. I know I could help...."

"My name is Ellie Mae VanAlmkerk. Please call me Ellie Mae. Linda, relax. I'm sure we can work something out. But we need to talk to my husband before we make any firm decisions."

Their food came. It was all Leslie could do to eat at a decent pace. She could feel the woman's eyes on her. *How would she handle her questions? The I'm-meeting-my-aunt story isn't going to work here.*

After their meal Ellie Mae's pale eyes looked directly at Leslie, through to her soul, it seemed. "Linda, tell you what. Let's go home, to the ranch. Buck will be working until late, but in the meantime, I could give you some work, Lord knows. I can't promise you anything until I talk to him, but I could use your help today. How does that sound?"

"Wonderful! Great! I know I can be a big help to you." *Slow down. Don't scare the poor lady.*

As they returned to the car, Leslie had to restrain herself from dancing across the street. Her spirits lifted as relief surged through her body.

## *TWENTY-SIX*

Wade missed Cyrus's company. It had been good to bounce ideas off him and Cyrus had come up with ideas of his own. Then, too, Wade really liked the guy, he was good to travel with. Worries seem worse when you have to carry them alone. And right now Wade was worried.

Where the hell is Les? Is she all right? She must be running out of money.

He went into the only store in the small hamlet of Frenchglen. No one had seen Leslie. There really weren't any job opportunities that Wade could see. The only business, except for an inn, was the small store.

From Frenchglen he turned south toward Lakeview. This was high desert country, lots of sage, even some pronghorn antelope. No real trees, just scraggly brush. Although the road was graveled, it was smooth and he made good time.

He wound around Hart Mountain. Suddenly, from a bluff, a magnificent scene opened up before him and he pulled over and stopped. To get a better view, he climbed out, Dutch scampering after him. From below and for miles around, dozens of blue lakes dotted the otherwise brown landscape. He could see for fifty miles but there wasn't another person or car in sight. An occasional bird's trill split the air; otherwise, nothing but silence reigned.

This is Sunday. My God, I've been looking for Les for a whole week. Oh Lord, please watch over her. Keep her well and safe.

He remained at the cliff's edge, his mind a jumble of thoughts. Finally, out loud he said, "Please, God, help me find her."

The dog trotted to him and looked up at him expectantly.

"I wasn't talking to you. Come on, let's find Les."

*~*

As Ellie May and Leslie drove to the ranch, Leslie again marveled at the speed a car offered and she felt renewed sorrow for having lost her car. In a car you could see so much more. Flat, reddish-brown rocky land streamed by, covered with dusty, pale green sage. In the distance reddish hills rose, dotted with twisted juniper trees. Between hills a canyon gaped.

"Where are you from, Linda?"

"Washington."

"Where have you been staying, just lately?"

"I've been camping out while I looked for work."

"All alone?"

"Mostly."

"Well, let me tell you a little bit about us. We--my husband Buck and I--have a ranch. We run cattle and grow wheat. Our daughter and son-in-law live on the place, too, but...well I guess you heard all about that. Tony broke his leg-- his horse rolled on him. Our daughter, that's Sara, is pregnant, expecting in about two months."

It was such a relief to hear other people's stories, to hear a friendly voice. She realized there was silence. It was her turn to talk. "Is it just the two families that run the ranch?"

"No, we have a hired hand, an older man, Clem. He was on the ranch when we got it thirty-two years ago."

"Wow. He must be old."

Ellie Mae laughed.

"How many kids do you have?" *This woman is so nice, it's going to be hard to lie to her.*

"Just the one. Sara. How about your family?"

"I have a brother, eleven years older than me."

Ellie Mae turned to look at Leslie, apparently expecting more, but Leslie had stopped talking and intently gazed out the window.

Ellie Mae took up the slack. "Every once in a while my back goes out on me and wouldn't you know it would happen now. I almost didn't go to church today--it bothered me so much this morning--but I decided that's one thing I could do."

Leslie smiled. *I'm glad you did.*

They rode in silence for miles. Rough, ridged hills, sage and juniper passed in a blur. From her side mirror, Leslie watched clouds of dust rising behind them.

They turned up a narrow dirt road. A hand-painted sign said, *THE BUCK STOPS HERE.* They passed a large, nearly full hay shed.

"Well, here we are. That's Tony and Sara's place, the double-wide mobile. The house is ours. You'll have to excuse the mess. I'm not the world's greatest housekeeper at best and now with this back...."

The house was a weathered, two-story structure, a washed-out white, with a shaded front porch. Ellie Mae parked the car and they entered the house from the back door into a laundry room which led into the kitchen.

Leslie tried not to stare. It *was* a mess.

"Here," Ellie May pushed dishes out of the way, "put the groceries on the table."

"I'll go out and get the other bag." Leslie hurried out to the car.

Maureen would *die* if she saw that messy kitchen.

Leslie put the remaining grocery bag on the kitchen table. "Do you want me to do these dishes and clean up the kitchen?"

"Good idea. Let's start right here. I'll help put the groceries away, and then I have to lie down for awhile. Darn this back."

Leslie delighted in such obvious work. She gathered dirty dishes from every corner of the kitchen.

"I'm sorry to say, Linda, our dishwasher isn't working. Buck says he'll take a look at it when he gets a chance, but naturally that hasn't happened yet. The dishes have to be done by hand. There's a dish pan buried in the sink."

"Okay. You go ahead and lie down. I'll take care of this."

Ellie Mae paused a moment, sighed, then turned and left the kitchen.

Oh, the luxury of having warm water run over her hands. She stood still, her eyes closed, soaking her hands in the heavenly steaming water.

Leslie rinsed the dishes first, then began washing them. It took many refills of the dish pan to do them all. She found a clean dish towel in the first drawer she looked. After washing and drying the dishes she put them away, figuring out as best she could where they all went. She wiped the counters clean, then the stove top. It needed a good cleaning, too, but other things seemed more urgent.

The floor was dirt-tracked, even sticky in places. She found a broom hanging near the back door. Looking around, she found a bucket and mop.

Later, when Ellie Mae entered the kitchen, her pale eyes lit up. "Oh my. Oh my! How nice!"

Leslie smiled at Ellie Mae's approval. "What should I do next?"

"I've been able to keep up with the washing, but the laundry room's a mess. We call it the 'mud room' for good reason."

"Okay. I'll do that. Then shall I do that back bathroom?"

"My back's feeling better already. Yes, dear, that will be just fine."

So it went for the rest of the day, until late afternoon. By then Leslie was exhausted. It felt good to be working, but she was so tired. Apparently, Ellie Mae could tell.

"Linda, rest for awhile. This doesn't all have to be done today. Here, sit down at the table, the *clean* table, and have some milk and cookies. Sara brought them over last night, bless her."

"After this, do you want me to start dinner? Like I said - -"

"We can do it together. Just rest awhile, Linda."

"Ma'am, do you think I could take a shower?"

"Of course. Anytime. Finish your snack. Have you lost weight or are you always this thin?"

"I guess I've lost weight. I noticed my jeans are sort of baggy. Um, another thing...do you have laundry for me to do? I need to wash my clothes. I've washed a few things by hand, but... I could do your laundry, too."

"Linda, for heaven's sake, do your laundry. We'll do ours later."

Leslie jumped up from her chair. "If you don't mind I'll get my pack and start a load now. Then I'll have something clean to wear after I shower."

Ellie Mae looked at Leslie in astonishment. "How long have you been on the go?"

"A week. But most of my clothes are dirty. Excuse me. I'll be right back." Leslie ran to the yard and retrieved her pack. As she sorted her clothes into two piles of laundry, she grimaced when dirt sprinkled on the just-scrubbed floor.

While she loaded her clothes and figured out how to use the washer, she heard Ellie Mae on the phone. She stiffened. Who would she be calling? No. It was all right. It seemed like a friendly call, like talking to family.

Leslie had again joined Ellie Mae at the kitchen table when the back door opened. A young woman entered, awkward with pregnancy, leading a little boy by the hand. She carried a bag and set it on the table.

"Mom said you could use some clothes while yours are being washed. These may be a little big for you, but I sure won't be using them for awhile." She slowly lowered herself into a chair. The little boy immediately opened a kitchen drawer.

"Linda, this is my daughter, Sara, and her son Craig."

"Hi. Thanks a lot. I'll get them back to you as soon as I can."

"No hurry. You're from Washington? Where?"

"Near Yakima." Nervousness forced Leslie to stand. "If you don't mind, I'll take my shower now."

"Linda, before you do...I'd love to have some tomatoes from my garden. Our nights are so cold here we can't grow soft vegetables, so my husband built me a sort of green house. Just a plastic tent, really. Anyway, with my back now I can't bend over to work out there."

Sara laughed as she lifted her little boy and slung him aside on her hip. "And with my big stomach, I can't either. See you guys later."

"Sure, I'll do it. Here, I'll use the dish pan and pick any ripe ones I find."

Leslie had to stoop to enter the improvised greenhouse. Inside, the smell of loamy earth and tangy tomato plants reminded her of working with Maureen in their garden. Crawling along, she picked a half-dozen ripe tomatoes. She glanced around and found a zucchini ready to pick and added that to the dish pan. She backed out of the tent and found Ellie Mae at the top of the steps, beaming.

"Did you see the peppers at the very end?"

"No. Do you want some of those too?"

"That would be lovely. We'll have a nice stew for dinner."

During her shower, Leslie was appalled when streams of dirty water drained from her body. *I was so dirty! What must I have looked like to them?* She scrubbed the tub, again.

She slipped into the clean jeans and cotton shirt Sara had brought over. She needed her belt to cinch up the jeans, but she reveled in the feel of her clean body wearing clean clothes.

*Ellie Mae's husband will be home for supper. Getting this job depends on him. Hope he's as nice as she is.*

She picked up her tennis shoes and began to put one on, frowned, then set them aside. She dug her riding boots out of her pack, dusted them off with a wad of toilet paper, and pulled them on.

*~*

Leslie heard Buck enter through the back door. He stood at the laundry tub, washing his hands and splashing water on his face. She strained to hear what he and Ellie Mae said.

He reached for the towel. "We're bringing stock down from the eastern slope. Clem's still up there, flushing 'em out. When I get back he'll come down. I told him to come here for dinner. By the time he gets in he'll be too tired to fix himself something."

"Of course, we'll have something ready for him. Buck, before you go in..."

But he had already stepped to the kitchen door. Sharp blue eyes scanned the clean kitchen, then settled on Leslie.

Leslie stood, wide-eyed. He filled up the doorway. He was a huge man, not fat, just wide, probably about as tall as her father, but not as tall as Wade. He was fair skinned and although mostly gray now, his hair had obviously been blond.

"Hello," Leslie said, trying to force her stiff face into a smile.

He nodded once. "Hello."

"Buck, this is Linda Carpenter. I met her in town this morning after church. She needs a job so I've put her to work today cleaning the house. You can see what a wonderful job she's done so far. And with my back --"

"How old are you?"

"Sixteen." Why does everyone have to ask me that?

"Where're you from?"

"Washington."

"Where in Washington? Where's your family?"

Leslie didn't answer, she couldn't lie again. She cast her eyes down, then raised her eyes to meet his, her chin rising with determination. "I'd rather not say. But I'm a good worker. I could help in the house, or help you...I can ride... whatever you need." She swallowed hard and took a deep breath.

"Are you in trouble with the law?"

She exhaled. "No, sir."

"Isn't anyone looking for you?" His blue eyes bored into hers. His bushy, blond eyebrows lifted when she failed to answer.

"I don't know," she whispered.

"What have you done before, what kind of work? Do you know anything about stock, about ranching?"

"Yes, sir."

"You do?" He showed surprise. "You've worked with stock? Cattle?"

"Yes, sir, I have. I can gather and sort 'em. I've worked round up and branding. I can vaccinate." It was certainly true, but she didn't want to come off sounding like some kind of expert, either.

"When?" He turned to his wife. "Did you know this?" She nodded.

"Mostly in the spring and summer, whenever they needed me."

"Who's 'they'?"

"My dad and brother."

His eyes swept over her, then rested on her boots.

"Well, God knows I could use some help." He nodded. "Okay, let's try it out. Finish up today helping Ellie Mae. Get some sleep tonight--you look wore out. We'll get at it first thing in the morning."

He glanced at his wife's shining eyes. "She can sleep in the bunk house. That place is a pig sty. Have her clean it up."

"This child is not going to sleep in the bunk house! She'll sleep upstairs in Sara's room."

"But I can still clean up the bunk house," Leslie put in, not wanting to cause trouble between them.

Buck looked at Leslie; his eyes shifted back to his wife. A trace of a smile twitched his lower lip. "Okay, Ellie, I'll leave that up to you. Now let's eat. I've gotta get back."

Buck finished two large helpings of stew, laid his fork on his plate, and rose from the table. "Clem will be here shortly." From a hook by the back door he reached for his hat and left.

Ellie Mae looked at Leslie and smiled. "Well, it looks like you have a job, at least for a few days. Dear, hold that stew for Clem and dish it up for him, will you? Just introduce yourself. I need to lie down."

Leslie washed the dishes they had used and soon heard a 'tap, tap' at the back door. Before she could get to the door, it opened.

"Hi, I'm Linda. You're Clem?"

"I'm Clem."

"Dinner's all ready for you, Clem. We have beef stew with dumplings."

Clem took off a beat-up hat and set it on the washer, and then, as Buck had done earlier, washed his hands and face at the laundry tub.

Leslie sat at the table with another glass of milk and one of Sara's cookies. Clem ate quickly and with a "Mighty fine. Thank you," he left.

After washing the remaining dishes, Leslie finished folding her laundry. Clean clothes! She laid them carefully on top of the washer.

She went in search of Ellie Mae. Although tired, Leslie didn't know what was expected of her. So far the only rooms she had entered were the kitchen, laundry room and back bathroom. She peeked around the corner into the living room. Big, green leaves from a laurel outside diffused light through the single, narrow window giving the room the illusion of being cool. Dinner aromas had settled in with no other place to go. She found Ellie Mae lying on an old, worn sofa, her eyes closed, an open book balanced on her stomach. Leslie tiptoed into the room and stood stock-still. There, along one wall, was a piano, an old upright. Leslie went over to it and tenderly ran her hand along the dark mahogany wood.

"Do you play the piano?"

Leslie jumped. "Oh, I'm sorry. I hope I didn't wake you."

"I was just resting my eyes. Do you play?"

"Yes, but I haven't played for awhile now. What would you like me to do next?"

"Let's call it a day. You could use the rest. I wish I could have your help for one more day, but Buck needs you more than I do. You'll sleep in the room upstairs, to the left. You'd better set the alarm for about four-thirty. Buck's storming around by then, raring to go. I'll be so glad when fall round up is over...." She closed her eyes again.

"Ellie Mae? I wouldn't mind sleeping in the bunkhouse. I could clean..."

Ellie Mae opened her eyes again and smiled. "Linda, he wasn't serious. That was Buck's idea of a joke. You'll sleep in the house, of course. Go ahead and put your things in any empty drawers you find."

Wow! Tonight I get to sleep in a real bed.

She hauled her pack and clean clothes upstairs.

She looked around the bedroom. The room had been closed and smelled stale. She opened the window making the thin, pink-checkered curtains ruffle in the breeze. It was a large room with old, faded wallpaper and a small pink shag rug alongside the bed. Several boxes lined the closet wall.

Leslie sat on the small, single bed. A mattress spring pinged. She thought of her room at home. Now I wished I hadn't packed up all my stuff and put it in boxes. I wonder what they thought when they saw that? It probably looked how I wanted it to look, then. Like I'd gone for good. She sighed. I guess that's what I did. I left for good.

She found two empty drawers in the small dresser and carefully placed her clothes in them.

An ancient alarm clock sat on the night stand by the bed. Turning it around, she figured out how to set it. Four-thirty! Yuk. She slipped into bed. The sheets felt smooth and clean. Feeling the safest she'd felt since leaving home, she slept.

\*~\*

Wade found his Sunday search frustrating. He'd checked out Plush and dropped down to Adel on his way to Lakeview. Lakeview looked promising, it was an industrial town with a lot of stores. Most of the town was closed up, but he'd inquired where he could. Two old men sat on a bench, like permanent fixtures. They hadn't seen Leslie. No one had.

Wade consulted his map.

I could spend the night around here and check this out more in the morning. Dutch hasn't shown any sign of finding a scent here though. Maybe I should use this dead time to drive to Klamath Falls. That's a fairly likely town for Les to find work. If she isn't there I can take Ninety-seven up to Bend, then check out all the stuff between south of Bend and Burns. That's a lot of driving. Well, better get to it.

It was a few minutes past six when he called home.

"Cahill. Wade?"

"Yeah, Dad. I'm a little late in calling."

"How are you doing? Where are you? Any clues?"

"I'm in Lakeview. Leslie had asked a store clerk in Burns about Frenchglen, so I headed down here but I'm sure she hasn't been in any of these towns. I haven't had a clue since Burns. I guess she could have been here and just drove through."

"I don't think so. The Sheriff's Department called. They found her car." John's voice caught. Wade could hear heavy breathing, his dad trying to control himself.

"Where, Dad? Could they tell anything..."

"They found it a few miles from Baker City. It had been hot-wired. They said there was no evidence of a struggle. From what they could tell, the car was okay, just out of gas. They found two hundred dollars under the front seat."

"I wonder if this was before or after she was in Burns. Maybe while she was there. She bought the car in Baker City, then later was seen in Burns."

"So you think she's okay, son?"

"I think so. The lady in Burns said she looked miserable. Maybe because her car was stolen. She must be getting low on cash. My guess is that she's okay, just back to hiking or hitching. Damn that kid. Why doesn't she call?"

"I don't know. I've wondered a million times. What's next, Wade?"

"I'm this far south, I might as well check out Klamath Falls. It's pretty big. Then I'll head up to Bend.

"Okay, son. Keep me posted."

On the way he checked out a few small towns but by the time he got to Klamath Falls it was too late to look for Leslie. He drove to nearby John Boyle Campground and, exhausted, fell asleep in the back of the truck with Dutch curled up beside him.

## *TWENTY-SEVEN*

Leslie awakened with a start. What was that terrible sound? Blurry eyes settled on the ancient clock on the night stand. She reached out and silenced the rasping alarm.

Four-thirty. Darkness was just beginning to fade. Her heart skipped a beat. Clatter from the kitchen drifted up, mingled with a low voice, probably Buck's.

Will I be able to do this? What if I screw up? Did I say I can do more than I really can? Pay attention. Read the cows, like Wade says. Will I work alone? Will they give me some old plug to ride that I can't make do anything? Or how about if they give me a crazy horse? Some people think that's funny. I don't think Buck would think it's funny.

She jumped at the sound of pounding on her door. "Let's get at it." Buck.

"Okay, I'll be right down." *Geez*. She slipped into jeans, long-sleeve shirt and riding boots and, with pounding heart, went downstairs to the kitchen.

"Good morning, Linda," Ellie Mae greeted cheerfully. "Sit down and have some breakfast."

Buck spooned jam onto a piece of toast. "When you're through eating, pack some lunches and bring 'em out with you."

"Yes, sir." Her heart thudded.

Ellie Mae filled Buck's coffee cup. "How many lunches, Buck?"

"Five. Strands are coming. We'll take two thermoses, too."

"All right, dear. Linda, eat up now or you won't last out there." Ellie Mae, still in an old, pink chenille bathrobe, took her seat at the table.

Leslie, so nervous she could hardly swallow, gave her breakfast another attempt.

Buck rose from the table and leaned over to gently kiss his wife's forehead. "See ya tonight. I'll send the girl back early to help you with supper."

The girl. That must be me.

Buck glanced at Leslie. "Shake a leg." At the back door he reached for his hat and opened the door with a jerk. He clumped down the stairs.

"Linda, relax. You'll do fine."

Leslie swallowed around the huge lump in her throat. "What will I fix for lunch?"

"I bought some lunch meat at the store yesterday. We'll put together meat and cheese sandwiches."

Leslie found meat and cheese in the refrigerator and took a loaf of bread out of the bread box. "How many sandwiches should I fix?"

"Ten should do it. I'll make another pot of coffee, too."

Together they packed sandwiches, apples and cookies into paper sacks. Leslie filled the two thermoses Ellie Mae had set out.

As Leslie headed out the door, Ellie Mae stopped her. "Wait, you need a hat. And what about gloves?"

"I didn't bring any with me."

"Here, use mine." Ellie took an old straw, wide-brimmed hat off a wall hook and leather gloves off the window sill and handed them to Leslie.

"Thank you." Leslie's voice quavered. She made her way to the barn on uncertain legs.

This is your first real job, Leslie. Don't blow it. Pay attention.

Buck nodded as she entered the barn. "Tom, Bobby, this is Linda. Strands' place is just north of here."

Leslie said hello to what appeared to be father and son. The son was older than she, maybe eighteen or so.

"This day is looking better all the time," Bobby grinned while his eyes looked her up and down.

"The horse you'll use is out there," Clem jerked his head in the direction where a horse waited tied to a fence rail. Clem held feed bags in his old, leathery hands.

"Okay. Where should I put these lunches?"

Buck took one of them. "Give Tom two, you keep two."

Leslie gave Tom Strand their sack lunches. Bobby's eyes followed her every move. She spotted a curry-comb hanging on a nail, picked it up, and hurried out to groom and saddle her horse.

The horse, a bay mare, stood still as Leslie brushed her. A blanket and saddle lay on the corral fence nearby.

Clem looped a feed bag over the horse's ears.

"Clem, is that the saddle I should use?"

"Yep."

"What's her name?"

"Ginny."

"Okay, Ginny. We'll get you saddled." Concentrating, making every move count, Leslie saddled the mare. The mare's gentle eyes followed the movements of this new girl.

Leslie could feel Clem watching her, too. He returned to the barn and brought out a saddle bag. "You can pack the lunches in this 'ere bag."

Bobby led two horses from around the side of the barn, looped the reins from one horse over a rail and stood with the other, grinning.

"Yes sir, the day's getting brighter and brighter."

Leslie pointedly ignored him. She stood next to her mare, loving the sound of teeth grinding grain and the mare's strong horsy smell. She ran her fingers through the horse's mane and began to relax.

Clem removed the feed bags and put them in the barn. Bobby quickly strode over to tighten the cinch on Leslie's saddle, his arm brushing her breast as he did so.

"It's fine," Leslie snapped, instantly on guard again.

Clem returned, mounted his old gray and rode over to Buck, looking more at home in the saddle than on foot. "Boss, I'll take the girl with me."

"Clem, you dirty old man..." Bobby began. His father gave him a sharp look.

"Well..."

"Shut up."

Buck nodded to Clem. "Okay." He glanced around to the others. "Listen up, now. Tom and Bobby, how about you working up at the butte? I'll join up with you later and help you bring 'em down. I'll take the dog with me." His dog, Mike, a black and white border collie, paced around the horses.

This was the first time Leslie had seen the dog. *I wish Dutch could come with me.*

"Clem, you and Linda finish flushing 'em off that east slope. Last night I saw a small bunch north of the spring, too."

Leslie had never worked land that wasn't hers. Nothing sounded familiar. She was glad to be working with Clem.

Bobby made her nervous. She wouldn't want to worry about him and learn the job, all at once.

Clem laced the reins in the fingers of his left hand and leaned sideways over the saddle horn to look at her. "Ready?"

"You bet," Leslie answered, trying to sound confident. She mounted lightly.

As they approached the first gate, Leslie said, "I'll get it." She opened and closed five gates--sometimes having to dismount--before they were on open range.

*~*

Wade broke camp to begin another day's search. Klamath Falls' business district was on flat land; the residents all seemed to live on steep hills. The dog sniffed her way around town but never showed any sign of excitement.

Nothing. Zero. I'm on the wrong track. Now I wish to hell I hadn't come all the way down here.

*~*

Clem wasn't bad to work with. He didn't talk much, but when he told Leslie to do something, he was civil. She had decided keeping quiet was the best tactic to take. She sensed Clem didn't like chatter, and she didn't want to annoy him. Also, she still felt the less they knew about her, the better.

They had gathered perhaps fifty head now, flushing them out of the brush. It was a noisy, dusty business, trying to marshal the cattle along. At least cows are the same all over. No surprises here. I've done it all with Wade.

Leslie swung a coil of rope, occasionally snapping it at the cattle to keep them in line.

Clem came alongside."Can you throw a rope?"

"No, not really. I've never taken the time to practice."

"It does take practice." Clem seemed to warm up to her as the day progressed.

"Hyaah, hyaah," he thundered past her now to catch up to a stray. She nudged her mount to move alongside the greater bunch to keep them from scattering.

They dismounted for lunch and sat on a log. Two lizards lounged in the sun on a big, flat rock near them, their quick tongues flicking in small insects. Leslie passed the thermos and a sack lunch to Clem. "There're three sandwiches, if you can eat that many."

"Looks like two for you, two for me."

"I can't eat two whole sandwiches."

"You need to put some meat on yer bones. You rattle around in them pants like a cat in a burlap sack."

Leslie laughed.

Clem regarded her. Life's wrinkles lined his face. "Why aren't you in school?"

Leslie shrugged. "I plan to go back when I can."

"Plannin' ain't doin'."

"Ellie Mae tells me you've worked here a long time."

His eyes sparkled. She wasn't fooling him, changing the subject. "I ain't circlin' the drain yet." He tried again. "You're too young to be away from yer family."

I could invent some story about being an orphan. Except I'm sick of lying. "What makes you think I have a family?"

"I can tell, is all."

Their horses pulled grass from a clearing nearby. Ginny stomped a leg, probably trying to shake off a deer fly.

Clem automatically glanced at the grazing horses. "That horse, Ginny, she had a mule colt last spring."

"Did she! I'd like to see him when we get back. I like Ginny. She's one of the best cutting horses I've ever ridden." Like I've ridden so many.

"Yeah, she could do this job without us, but she likes the company. Well girl, let's get at it, push them beeves home."

Leslie put the lunch remains back into the saddle bag. Clem had gone behind a bush to relieve himself, and she did the same.

I wonder if I'll ever feel normal again. Right now I feel like I'm full of holes and I can't plug them up. I have to worry about everything I say. I can't be myself.

As they gathered stock and pushed toward home, Leslie began to take some initiative, not just follow orders.

Think of Wade. Imitate him. Do what he'd do.

She saw some cows bunched at the bottom of a draw. "I'll get 'em."

She let her horse pick her way down the draw. The shade of trees offered sweet relief from the heat. Once there, she circled around two calves, encouraging them to go toward their mothers. Once they were together, two cows and their calves, she got behind them to push them up the draw toward Clem.

A young steer bolted to circle back. Without her urging, her horse swerved to block him.

Leslie took off her hat and waved it at the steer. "Hyah! Hyah! Get along now!"

Clem sat calmly in his saddle, watching.

The small bunch joined the larger bunch, and they slowly made their way back. Leslie kept her mind on her work, constantly watching for signs of a rebellious cow or calf.

At one point both a cow and her calf bolted. "I'll do it," Leslie said as she pulled away from the herd. The escapees had been on the far side of the bunch, and it took Leslie awhile to get herself into a position to chase them. Once she did, she threw herself into the chase.

I don't think I ever did this when I worked with Wade, put everything into it. For some reason, I held back.

At one point Clem said, "Take it easy now, slow 'em down."

Leslie backed off to slow them down. "When will we start working them?"

"Two, three days. Depends on how we do t'day and t'morrow."

Leslie's horse skittered sideways as she nickered alarm, reared slightly, and threw her head back. Leslie spotted a snake, saw it slither into the brush along the trail just ahead. Above the noise of the cattle Leslie heard the faint sound of a rattle. "Whoa, now." She patted her mare's neck. "It's all right, Ginny." The horse snorted her displeasure and jerked her head to add emphasis, her ears plastered back. "Steady, now," Leslie reassured her.

Clem observed, but said nothing.

By the time they returned to the ranch, Leslie was hot, dusty, tired, and muscle-sore.

Don't let them see how tired you are. Look alive.

"Take 'em to that far pen."

Leslie rode alongside to prevent the cattle from turning too soon.

"Run ahead and open the gate. Make sure the back gate's closed."

Leslie did as ordered.

The last of the herd filed in as Buck rode in leading the bunch he and Strands were bringing in. Mike's sharp bark turned a wayward calf back to the herd.

Leslie, on the far side of the pen, saw Buck trot over to where Clem stood near the gate. Buck signaled her.

She slowly made her way toward him through the crowded pen, careful to not disturb the jittery cattle.

Just as she arrived she heard Clem say, "Top hand, Boss. She knows how to listen." Leslie swelled with pride but tried to show no outward sign she had heard, though she suspected Clem had waited to say it within her hearing.

"Good," Buck answered. "Linda, go up to the house now and see what you can do for Ellie."

"Yes, sir."

At the house she brushed herself off and stepped into the laundry room.

"How did it go?" Ellie Mae stood in the doorway, pastry cutter in hand.

"Good. I worked with Clem and we got along fine."

"I knew you would. Before you get washed up, I need more tomatoes."

"All right. Anything else?"

"No, just tomatoes. Some that will slice good for dinner."

Stooping into the tent greenhouse, Leslie realized how tired she was. She squatted and eased her sore back by stretching her arms forward. She'd seen her dad do that.

And I may have hours to go before this day is over. I wonder how much I'll get paid. We never discussed pay. At least I'm eating and have a roof over my head.

She stepped into the kitchen with several ripe tomatoes in Ellie's dish pan. "I'm really dirty, Ellie Mae. Maybe I should take a shower before I help with supper."

"You do that, dear. I've got a nice roast beef in the oven."

That night, as the four of them ate--Strands had returned to their own ranch for supper--Buck turned his attention to Leslie.

"Clem here says you did a good job today."

"Thank you." It was all she could do to remain outwardly calm. Her insides felt like corn popping.

Buck nodded. "We'll be gathering again tomorrow, then start working them the next day, Wednesday. You say you can vaccinate?"

"Yes, sir."

"We'll have a few, those we missed in the spring. After supper we'll start sort --"

"Buck, dear, I'm sorry, but we have to go into town tonight to see your sister."

"Not tonight, Ellie."

"Tonight, dear. The hospital called and they need your written permission to move your sister to the convalescent home."

"Can't you take care of it?"

"I would if I could. They need your okay, in person. The floor supervisor needs to discuss it with you. It's time we visited her anyway. Poor thing."

Buck shook his head wearily. "It's one damn thing after another, isn't it?"

"I'll go ahead and start sorting, Boss." Clem's thin hair lay plastered against his scalp where he'd run wet hands over it, cleaning up for supper.

"I'll help, too," Leslie added, though she wasn't sure just where she would get the steam to do it.

Buck shook his head. "No, don't. We'll do it tomorrow. We'll get to it first thing in the morning. Clem, after your evening chores, that's it for today. Linda, give Ellie Mae a hand in the kitchen, and then the same goes for you."

Out of the corner of her eye, Leslie saw Ellie Mae's smile of satisfaction.

Buck rose from the table. "I'll take a shower and then we'll go."

Clem sat for a few more minutes to finish his coffee. "Mighty fine. Thank you." He left to do his evening chores.

Leslie started to gather dishes but Ellie Mae put her hand on Leslie's arm. "Linda, hold off for a minute. I'd like to talk to you."

Leslie's heart sank as she settled back onto her chair.

"Dear, did you run away from an abusive situation?"

Leslie stared at her, open mouthed. "No."

"I'm worried about you, Linda. You should be with your family."

"I wasn't with them when I left."

"Then where were you?" Ellie Mae's pale eyes were kind, but determined.

"Ellie Mae, I can't talk about it."

"Your parents must be frantic with worry."

Leslie dropped her eyes to her lap.

"Linda, think of your mother, what she must be going through."

"I don't have a mother."

"Well, your father and brother, then. You'd have to be a parent to appreciate it, but honey, I can tell you for a fact that they are beside themselves with worry."

"I don't think so."

"Why?"

She shrugged her thin shoulders, as if in slow motion.

"Have you called them since you left?"

"No."

"Would you call them? Tonight? You could use our phone."

"Maybe I'll call them sometime soon." There was so much more she wanted to say to this kind woman. Can't I just stay here? I could live here, help out, go to school. I wouldn't cause you any trouble. Please, please let me stay. Her eyes filled and she lowered them to her hands, twisting in her lap. She swallowed painfully.

"You're welcome to stay here, Linda. I'm sure you know that. But I'd like to help you work this out, if you'd let me. Whatever it is, you'll have to face it sometime, honey."

Leslie looked up briefly, then again lowered her eyes. It's too late. I've messed up so bad, it's just too late.

"No matter what you've done, dear, it can be worked out. I'm sure of that."

"Ready?" Buck's voice boomed out.

Ellie Mae looked up at her husband and sighed. "Yes, I'm ready. Just let me get my purse."

As soon as Buck and Ellie Mae left, Leslie sprang into action. She put a load of clothes into the washer, hers and theirs, then tackled the kitchen. Ellie Mae was a wonderful person, but what a messy cook! She forced her mind away from her and Ellie's conversation.

She hurried through her work, knowing exactly what she was going to do while Buck and Ellie Mae were gone.

Wiping her hands on the damp towel, she stepped into the living room. As she approached the piano, she realized what a treasure she'd always had and how much she'd taken for granted.

I can't imagine the rest of my life without a piano. I've missed it.

She sat down and began warming up with chords, then other routine finger exercises. Her fingers felt stiff after not playing for so many days. She clasped her hands together, holding them to her chest, waiting for the ache to subside.

Though it could have used a good tuning, the piano had a lovely tone, quite different from her piano, but nice nevertheless. She began to play the pieces she had mentally practiced since leaving home.

She relaxed, leaned into her music and surrendered herself completely. Other than changing loads of laundry, she continued to play until she saw the flicker of the truck's headlights coming up the drive. She reluctantly left the piano then and climbed the stairs to her room.

*~*

After coming up empty in Klamath Falls, Wade methodically made his way north, following Ninety-seven. It was slow going. He stopped at Algoma, Modoc Point, then at the dusty little town of Chiloquin and across the flats to Beaver Marsh. He pulled into Bend long after the sidewalks had rolled up for the night.

Bend. Now this is more like it. Leslie might find something here.

Still, on his preliminary search he found nothing. I'll check it out again tomorrow, when more places are open.

After a quick meal at a diner, he camped at Tumalo State Park, road weary and discouraged.

## *TWENTY-EIGHT*

Getting up was tougher this morning. Leslie reached for the alarm to silence its irritating clamor. She didn't want Buck to think he had to get her up every morning so, with supreme effort, she climbed out of bed before he pounded on her door.

At the breakfast table she tried to eat a decent breakfast. Ellie Mae served scrambled eggs, bacon and toast. It was good- -her appetite was coming back.

She looked at Buck through the steam of his coffee cup. "Do you want me to fix lunches for five, like yesterday?"

"Make 'em for six. I've got another man coming."

"Will I work with Clem again today?"

"That what you want to do?"

"Yes, sir."

"Okay." His sharp blue eyes slid over to Ellie Mae. There was a moment of tension. Then, apparently, he decided not to say what had been on his mind. Leslie suspected they had been talking about her.

As Buck left, he turned to her. "We'll sort first thing, then we'll go get the rest of 'em. Get out there as soon as you can."

"Yes, sir."

Leslie took bread out of the freezer. "Should I fix the same kind of sandwiches as yesterday, Ellie Mae?"

"Let's do tuna sandwiches and a few meat and cheese. We can pack one of each kind for everyone."

At least things were falling into some sort of routine. Leslie wished she could feel more permanent, more at ease with her surroundings. And with herself. Maybe that will come with time.

She put on her hat--Ellie Mae's hat--and grabbed the stiff, old gloves. "Ellie Mae, is it all right if I take a carrot for Ginny?"

Ellie Mae smiled. "Of course. Take one for Clem's old gray, too."

Leslie walked toward the barn deep in thought. School started yesterday, Monday, in Chewack. I wonder when it started here. Will I even be able to go this year? Maybe I'll have to work a year to get ahead enough to go to school. Clem's 'plannin' ain't doin' ran through her head, repeating itself with each step she took. *Plannin' ain't doin'. Plannin' ain't doin'.*

*~*

His empty breakfast plate pushed aside, Wade spread his map out on the table. The waitress filled his coffee cup.

I'll check out Bend this morning, or however long it takes. It's big--population almost thirty thousand. Les just might be there. If I don't find any sign of her, I'll take a run up north, as far as Madras, then work my way back down and head east, catch the towns between Bend and Burns.

He folded the map to the area he planned to cover that day. On Mrs. Holmes' yellow tablet he noted Tuesday, the date, and where he was now.

He sat back and looked out the window.

A week and two days she's been gone. What is she going through? She hasn't even called. Does she think she's in so much trouble she can't? Oh, Les, that isn't true. Just let me find you, we'll work it out.

*~*

A deafening racket rose as Leslie and Clem sorted cows from their calves. Clouds of dust hung at rider level, making it difficult to get a clean breath.

I'm so glad they let me use Ginny. She's such a good cutter. All I have to do is zero in on a calf, and she knows just what to do.

It was tough work, lots of starts and sudden stops. She had to keep her wits about her. Falling off a horse in the midst of this mess of flying hooves wouldn't be pretty.

After sorting, the three teams returned to the far summer pastures to finish gathering the last of the cattle. Clem and Leslie worked a section of land full of small canyons covered with seafoam-green sage.

Clem rode alongside Leslie. "Keep a sharp eye out, now. A good hider cow can get in here and be almost invisible. You can be just a few feet away and not see her. There, look at that."

A cow stood behind a small bush. She was so still there was no doubt she was hiding. "Watch it now," Clem warned, "when she knows she's caught she'll come out like a freight train."

Sure enough, when cornered, the cow came bellowing out, rushing past Leslie with amazing speed. Her mount skittered sideways to avoid being struck and in the process a juniper branch swiped Leslie's face, knocking off her hat.

Leslie yelped with the force of the branch. Her hand flew to her face.

Clem turned his mount and rode up to her. "You all right?"

"I'm fine," she answered quickly. Her face stung. She turned her horse to pick up her hat.

"Let's see."

"I'm fine, Clem." She continued toward her hat.

"Girl, I said 'let's see.' Now come here and let me take a look at you."

The tone in his voice stopped her. She turned to look at him. He sat perfectly still, waiting for her to come to him.

She urged Ginny to a trot to where he waited. She drew alongside.

He lifted her chin to get a better look. "Yer eye okay? The eyelid's scratched. Cover yer good eye to make sure you can see out of this'n."

Leslie covered her uninjured eye. "It's okay. I must have blinked in time."

"You're bleedin' in a couple of places there."

Leslie reached up with her sleeve and blotted the raw spots.

"When you get back to the house have Ellie Mae put something on that."

"All right."

"Okay, get your hat and let's get at it."

They stopped for lunch near a spring. Leslie washed her hands and face in the clear, cold water. The water stung where the branch had broken the skin. She sat on the ground, wearily easing her back against a log.

"Your face looks like you've been in a fight."

"It feels like it, too."

Clem took a sandwich and handed the bag to Leslie. "This what you want to do for the rest of your life?"

"No."

"If you don't do something about it, it's just what you will be doing."

Leslie looked up at him, sitting on the log. Clem had probably worked cattle for fifty years. "I need a job and I'm doing it now, but this isn't what I call a career."

"Your career right now should be going to school."

"I know, Clem."

"All right, then."

She took a bite of sandwich. "Clem, don't you have a dog? We could sure use one on this job."

"I had a dog 'til last year. He got too old. It was a race between us, but he gave out first."

"Oh, Clem, you're not that old."

"You've worked with a dog, have you?"

"Some, a blue heeler."

"That's a good dog."

"She is good. She can almost read your mind. She sure lets the cows know who's boss." Her heart felt heavy, remembering Dutch, her soft ears, how sweet she could be to people and how mean to cows.

Leslie leaned back and closed her eyes. I would come along at the busiest time of the year. Oh well. If they hadn't been busy, I might not have gotten the job.

"Well, girl, let's go. We'll have time to sort this bunch before the end of the day."

\*~\*

Wade struck out in Bend. With all the stores on the eight or so downtown streets and mini-malls on the outskirts of town, he'd held hope that Leslie would be there, but no luck. Discouraged and fighting panic, he jumped back on Twenty, the main highway between Bend and Burns.

He stopped briefly at Millican, then Brothers. Some of these places couldn't even be called one-horse towns and what was there often was boarded up. It had been a long time since he'd had a lead. Not since Burns. She'd been there Saturday. And here it was, Tuesday and he'd covered over twelve hundred miles.

Prichard. It's not very big, but bigger than the last two. He pulled into a grocery store parking lot and stepped into the store.

"Ma'am, have you seen this girl?"

The clerk studied the photograph.

"Yes, I have. But her hair's cut short." The woman looked up at him and studied his face. "She your little sister?"

"Yes, she is. When did you see her?"

"Sunday, I believe. Yes, it was Sunday."

His heart leapt. "Did you happen to notice where she went after here?"

"Another customer was in here about the same time. I saw them talking in the parking lot. I think they went across the street to the cafe. Later, they got in Ellie Mae's car and left."

"Ellie Mae? She live near here?" His tried to keep his voice calm.

"Sure. Ellie Mae VanAlmkerk. She and her husband have the old Elsworth place, Bear Creek Ranch.

"Can you tell me how to get there? Bear Creek Ranch?"

"Yes, I can. Go west on Twenty, about fifteen miles, then north on Elsworth. It's the first gravel road, then another twenty miles or so. You'll see their gate. You can't miss it."

If she's still there, it will be some kind of a record. Two days. But at least I'll talk to someone who has spent some time with her.

He retraced his way back on Twenty, then turned north on Elsworth. As he passed under an arch made of logs bedecked with deer and elk antlers, he could make out buildings in the distance, nestled in the shadow of a butte. The drive from Prichard took about forty minutes, but it seemed like hours to Wade.

He glanced at his watch as he pulled up to what appeared to be the main house. Three o'clock. Please God, let her be here.

He knocked at the front door. No answer. He walked to the back door and tried again. He heard the volume being turned down on a radio talk show. A woman came to the door.

Her pale blue eyes lit up. "Yes?"

Wade took off his hat. "Ellie Mae VanAlmkerk?"

"Yes, that's right."

"My name's Wade Cahill. I'm looking for my sister, Leslie Cahill. I understand she was seen with you on Sunday."

"We have a girl here. But that isn't her name."

Wade nodded, hope banging against his chest. He showed her Leslie's picture. "Linda Carpenter? That's the name she's been using. Is she here?"

Ellie Mae stood back and studied his face. "Yes, that's it. Well, I can certainly see the family resemblance. Come in, won't you?"

"Can you tell me where she is, Ma'am?"

"She's here, but right now she's on the range someplace. We're in the middle of fall round up. Please, come in."

Wade stepped into the house reluctantly. "Leslie's working here?"

"Yes. She approached me Sunday in Brown's parking lot saying she needed a job. Sit down, let me pour us coffee, and I'll tell you all about it."

"Excuse me, Ma'am, would you mind if I go back to the truck to get my dog? She's been with me the whole time. I'd like her to pick up Les's scent again, see what she'll do." Before Ellie Mae answered, he left to get Dutch.

His feet felt like he was walking on springs. His mind raced. Dutch popped out of the truck and took off, nose to the ground. At first she headed toward the barn, but Wade called her back.

He opened the back screen. "Ma'am? Would you mind if I bring her in?"

"Please call me Ellie Mae. No, of course I don't mind."

Dutch was all over the house, sniffing, wagging her tail, occasionally barking. She climbed the stairs and before Wade could catch up with her she barked sharply and thudded her tail against a bedroom floor and doorway. She stood on her hind legs and smelled the bed, side-stepping the length of it. The dog went to the gray pack that stood in the corner and gave it a once over, then back again to the bed. She looked up at Wade and he could have sworn he saw a smile on her face. A joyous bark cut the air.

"Good girl. Good girl." He knelt to pet the wiggling dog.

*I've found her. We've found her.*

Still kneeling, he looked around the room. It was tidy, just like Leslie's room at home. He could feel her presence here. With finger and thumb he squeezed the bridge of his nose and the corners of his eyes where tears hovered.

By God, we've done it. He breathed deeply, as though he'd been running. He returned to the kitchen.

"Sit down, Wade. Let's talk."

"All right. Would you mind if I kept the dog here with me. I'm afraid if I let her out she'll take off after Les."

"The dog's fine. I'm sure you have a lot of questions, Wade. So do I."

They talked steadily for two hours. Wade told her how it all began, and Leslie's reasons, what they'd been able to piece together anyway. He told her of his long search, of his father's worry and burden of guilt.

Ellie Mae told Wade of how she and Linda--Leslie-- met, of the girl's desperation. "With all that's happened, we sure needed the help around here. Besides that though, she looked so thin and troubled. I just wanted to give her a safe place to stay for awhile until she could get things worked out.

"But she was determined to pay her way, and that girl can certainly work. We've had a string of bad luck around here. Our foreman, our son-in-law, is laid up with a broken leg, my daughter can't help this year because she's pregnant and already has a two-year-old, my back's been giving me grief....

"Your sister cleaned this kitchen up slick as a whistle. Lord knows it needed it. When Buck found out she's worked cattle I lost my girl to him. He was surprised with her ability.

"She's a wonderful girl. It bothered us though, knowing someone must be frantic for her. I tried to talk to her, but she wouldn't talk about home, wouldn't tell us where her family was. The only thing she said, really, was that she hadn't run away from home. We decided to give it a few days and then try to talk to her again. Maybe by then she would trust us enough to let us help her."

Wade had been leaning forward, taking in every word. He sat back, more relaxed now. "I can't tell you how grateful I am. It seems I would get close and then she would slip through my fingers. I needed her to stay in one place long enough for me to catch up to her."

Wade remembered his father. He pointed to the wall phone. "Would you mind if I use your phone to call home? I have a calling card."

"You go right ahead. I'll just step into the next room, give you some privacy."

With unsteady fingers Wade dialed the phone.

"Cahill."

"Dad, I found her."

"Oh, thank God. Where? She is okay? When did --"

"Hold on, now. Let me tell you." Wade gave his father a quick run-down. "I haven't seen her yet, but she's staying here. They should be coming in pretty soon."

"Okay. Call me back as soon as you actually see her and talk to her."

"I will. Take it easy now, Dad."

"All right, son. Call me back as soon as you can."

Wade stood at the back door. Hundreds of cattle were in large holding pens. He could see they'd begun sorting. From beyond the corrals a cloud of dust rolled toward the pens. He heard a man's voice shouting, but couldn't make out the words.

His heart beat faster.

Ellie Mae returned to the kitchen and cocked her head. "They're coming in now."

Wade stepped out into the yard. He glanced around to see if his truck was visible; it wasn't, it was parked in front of the house.

Two people were coming in with a large bunch of cattle. It was hard to tell with all the dust, but he didn't think either was Les. Right after them, just a short distance away, was another bunch with two more people. There was some disturbance at the second bunch. A dog barked and a lot of dust swirled around.

"Don't let that bull out!" he heard someone yell from the first, closer bunch. Now the person riding in front took off after the bull, a huge animal, heading for an open gate. The rider rode like hell, trying to get to the gate before the bull did. My God, that's Les--he could tell by the way she sat in the saddle. She must be wearing someone else's hat.

Dutch took off, barking her orders before she even reached the pens. This was all happening in seconds but for Wade it appeared to be slow motion. Les gained on the bull, trying to block it from going through the gate. She leaned forward, determination showing in her every fiber. "Hyah! Hyah!"

Les, my God, be careful. Let the damn thing go. I've never seen her ride like that. Dad would have a stroke if he saw this.

Dutch flew under the wooden fence like she'd lived there all her life, barking ferociously. She jumped and bit the bull on the flank. The bull swerved away and Leslie rode through the open gate, leaning over to swing it shut.

She dismounted in a flash, latched the gate, and jumped back on her horse. She urged her horse on a few steps, then reined in and looked down. Dutch tore toward her, barking and wagging her tail so hard her whole body moved with the motion.

"Linda! Open the damn inside gate!"

Leslie looked up with a start and rode the length of the pen, then made her way through the midst of confused, milling cattle and, still on horseback, leaned over to open the gate.

Some cattle had strayed by this time and Dutch, who had followed Leslie, barked and snarled them back into place.

The other person, an older man, Wade could see by this time, urged the reluctant cattle into the pen, swinging his rope and whistling. Leslie had circled to the back of the herd to push them in. She deftly blocked the cattle's every attempt to escape.

She's a pro. The kid's really good.

The last of them in, Clem approached Leslie. "That the blue heeler you was talking about? Who is that guy?" Clem jabbed his thumb past his shoulder.

Leslie followed Clem's thumb. Wade. She sat immobile. Dutch. Wade. They're here. I've gotta get out of here. That's stupid. Why would I run? Wade stood still as a fence post, his legs spread, his arms relaxed by his side. His hat shaded his eyes, but she knew he looked steadily at her.

Clem reached down to gather her reins. "Go ahead."

She climbed down. This is so unreal, like a dream. Dutch ran circles around her, then shot forward to Wade, then returned to Leslie and circled her again, all the time barking. Leslie began to walk toward her brother, slowly at first. Then, like a train, she picked up speed and by the time she reached him they had a real collision as she flew into his arms.

"Wade! How did you get here? How did you know where I was?"

"It wasn't easy."

### TWENTY-NINE

Wade had barely allowed himself to dream of the time he'd find Leslie. Now he hugged his little sister, hard. Then he held her away so he could look at her. One side of her face was scratched and swollen. Dirt caked on her neck and ears. Her sweat-stained tee-shirt hung on her thin body. But she was all right. Thank God.

"What happened to your face?"

"My horse shied and a branch swiped it."

"Les, what are you doing here?"

"Working. It took me a long time to find work, but I finally got this job."

"Why?"

"Why? What do you mean? Because I need the money. So much has happened, Wade. I can't think of how to even begin --"

"Wait, Les. Let's go into the house. I need to call Dad. Then we'll talk."

"Dad?"

He'd already begun to walk toward the house but stopped to look at her. "Yes. Dad. I told him I'd call as soon as I saw you."

"Does he know where I am?"

"Yes, but he needs to know you're all right. Come on." He tugged at her arm, and she walked into the house with him.

"Oh, Ellie Mae. This is my brother, Wade." Leslie sat at the kitchen table.

"Yes, dear. We've met."

"Oh. Sure."

Wade sat down at the kitchen table, near the telephone. "If you don't mind, we'd like to use the phone again, Ellie Mae."

"Of course. You go right ahead." She discreetly left the kitchen.

The phone barely ticked. "Cahill."

"Dad, guess who I've got here." He held the phone out to Leslie. She shrank back. Surprised at her hesitancy, Wade glared at her, and impatiently motioned her to take the phone. She left the table and retreated further.

"Well, Dad, I guess she's not quite ready for this. No. No, Dad, she's fine. I'll call you back after awhile."

Wade stood as he hung up the phone. In two steps he grabbed Leslie, his big hand completely encircling her thin arm, and led her out the door. Her feet touched the floor about every third step.

At the bottom of the steps he roughly turned her to face him. His face was red with anger as he spoke through clenched teeth. "It would give me great pleasure to give you the whipping Dad never did. Leslie, do you have any idea what Dad has gone through, how worried he's been?" She glared at him. He shook her. "Do you?"

Her eyes blazed with anger. She jerked her arms free, punching him in the chest with her sharp elbows with the effort. "Let me go! No, I don't know what Dad's gone through. Do you have any idea what *I've* gone through? It was Dad's idea to send me away. I just did him one better and went farther than he had in mind. What difference does it make anyway? He --"

Wade held up his hands in surrender. "All right. All right. Hold on, Les. Let's calm down."

Leslie took a half step towards him and wagged her finger an inch from his nose. "You calm down. You're the one dragging people around!"

Wade's eyebrows shot up in surprise.

"Are Lilith and Roxanne living there yet?"

"What?"

"Are Lilith and --"

"I heard you the first time. What kind of a question is that? Of course not."

She showed genuine surprise. "I thought they would be."

"Les, Dad's been out of his mind worrying about you."

"I don't know why. I wouldn't have been home, anyway. I was out of his hair once he left me at Rosemount. He could go on with his life with Lilith and Roxanne. I expected Roxanne to have my room by now."

Wade shook his head, trying to clear it. "Let's start at the beginning." He put his hand on his sister's shoulder and led her over to a picnic table in the shade of the side yard. They sat facing one another.

"Les, why did you run away?"

"Because I didn't want to go to Rosemount. I know Dad sent me there to get rid of me so he and Lilith --"

"Les, that isn't true. Why didn't you talk to him about that, about what you thought his reasons were?"

"He wouldn't have changed his mind. You know I tried."

"But did you talk to him about Lilith?

"No."

"Why?"

"I couldn't. But his reasons for sending me were so phony. I knew the real reason."

"You're wrong, Les. Lilith had no part in his decision."

"When did you start looking for me? Did Dad send you? I thought you'd be busy with fall round up."

"Whoa. One question at a time. In the first place, finding you was a lot more important than the round up. I left home as soon as the school called, even before Dad got back from taking you to Spokane."

"The school called? Do you know what time?"

"Monday afternoon. I took off right away. You'd been planning this for some time, hadn't you?"

Leslie nodded. And so it went, each answering the other's questions and asking one in return. "I was so surprised to see Dutch. At first I thought it was someone else's Blue Heeler, except she was so glad to see me. How come you brought her?"

"To help me find you. Why didn't you at least call home?"

"What would I say? At first I was so mad. Then I decided I had just screwed up so bad and Dad would be mad. And what good would calling do? Nothing had changed." She looked off into the distance, remembering. "Sometimes I did think of calling, but I didn't know if my calls could be traced. And I was so homesick, I was afraid if I called, all I would do is cry." Her eyes filled.

Wade covered her tightly clenched hands with his big, warm ones. "You've had a rough time, haven't you?"

She nodded. "Wade, I bought a car, but it got stolen."

"I know."

"You know?

"Not the details. But they found the car near Baker City. The Sheriff called Dad. What happened?"

The story came out in starts and stops. She ended with, "I was such a chump. I stashed two-hundred dollars under the front seat. I wonder if those scums found it."

"No, the police did. Well, Sis, we can get caught up more on the way home. We need to call Dad back. Will you talk to him now?"

"Home? Wade, I can't go home. I've got a job here. I've been looking for work since almost the first day and it took me all this time to --"

"Les, for once in your life will you think of someone besides yourself?"

Her eyes flared. "What do you mean?"

"I mean Dad has probably aged twenty years over this deal, and you need to get home so you guys can get this straightened out."

"But I've told them I would help here. I'm going to vaccinate tomorrow and --"

"Les! Listen to me. It's over. It's time to go home now."

"It may be over for you, but it isn't for me. These people have been good to me, Wade. They gave me a job and a place to stay when I really needed it. And they need me."

"Les, Dad needs you."

"Dad sent me away."

Wade looked up at the cloudless, blue sky, then down at the grooved, sun-bleached table, and finally trained his eyes steadily on Leslie. "I've talked to Dad at least once a day, every day, since this all began and I can tell you that he feels differently now."

"But I told Buck and Ellie Mae I would help." Yelling and whistling reached their ears, above the din of bawling, anxious cattle. "I should get back to work now."

Wade leveled his finger at Leslie. "Leslie, you're sixteen years old. Your place is home with us, your family. These are nice people and I will be forever grateful for their kindness, but you belong at home."

"But I told them I would help!"

"They'll understand."

"Wade, I'm not ready to go home. What if it all happens again?

"Like I said, Dad feels different now."

"Why? How do you know?"

"Because he's had a chance to think it over. Les, you and Dad need to talk this over."

"We did. And guess who won."

"I can guarantee that won't happen again."

"Did he say that?"

"He told me he'd made a mistake. Les, let him tell you for himself."

"Well, I can't go home now anyway. I have work to do here. I can't let them down after all they've done for me."

Wade took off his hat and ran his fingers through his hair. He sighed. "Okay, how about this. I'll help out tomorrow, too, then we'll leave the next day."

"You would help? Great! I know Buck could sure use you. Your help would be like two extra men."

"On one condition."

She looked at him warily. "What?"

"That we go in the house right now and call Dad and you talk to him."

She looked into the distance toward the sound of agitated cattle. In a tiny voice, she said, "What will I say?"

"Don't worry about what to say, it'll come."

"Is he mad?"

"He's more worried than mad. Les, he takes a lot of the blame for this himself."

Her eyes swam through tears. "He does?"

"Let's go in and call. I'll talk to him first, let him know our plans and then you talk to him. Okay?"

After a moment, she nodded, her eyes troubled. They entered the empty kitchen. Dinner simmered on the stove. Pans, bowls, and mixing spoons cluttered the counters. Wade dialed the series of numbers, using his telephone card. Leslie stood frozen to the floor, her hands slippery with sweat.

Her father must have been waiting by the phone. Wade had barely finished dialing when he started talking.

"Dad? Tell you what we're going to do. Leslie has been staying at an outfit near Prichard, working on fall round up and... Dad, wait a minute. Let me finish. I'm going to give them a hand tomorrow, along with Les here, and then we'll head out first thing Thursday morning."

Leslie heard a crackle over the line, her father sputtering an objection.

"Les wants to talk to you, Dad." He held the phone out to her, and she stepped forward slowly and took the phone in both hands.

"Dad?"

"Oh, Leslie, honey. Are you all right?"

"I'm fine. How are you?"

"I'm better now that I know you're safe." His voice caught. "I'll be even better when you get home."

"Dad, will I have to go back to Rosemount?"

"No, Honey. I want you here, with us."

Tears streamed down her face. "Dad, I'm...I'm sorry."

"So am I, honey. Leslie, everything will be fine. We'll see you Thursday?"

"Okay."

After the call, Leslie blew her nose on a paper towel, then stepped into the laundry room to wash her hands and face.

"Why don't you introduce me to your boss? I could get in a few hours today. Was that the guy you were working with?"

"No, that was their hired man, Clem."

They walked out together.

As soon as they approached the pens Buck rode over to them and dismounted.

"Buck, this is my brother, Wade."

Buck's sharp blue eyes sparkled as he extended his hand. Wade took it firmly and nodded to Buck.

Leslie took a deep breath. "Buck, Wade said he would be glad to give us a hand for the rest of today and tomorrow." She hesitated, then continued. "On Thursday we have to leave, for home."

"I never turn down good help. Can you spare the time?"

Wade looked over the herd with an experienced eye. "Sure. I'd be glad to."

Buck turned to Leslie. "Why don't you go up to the house now and give Ellie Mae a hand with supper. Have her patch up your face, too."

"Yes, sir."

Leslie turned to take care of her horse but Clem stopped her. "That's okay. Your brother can use 'er."

In the kitchen she found a beaming Ellie Mae. "Linda-- Leslie--I'm so happy for you."

Leslie sat down at the kitchen table. "Everything is happening so fast."

Ellie Mae joined her at the table. "Everything is happening as it should. Are you happy to see your brother?"

"Yes, I am. And surprised!"

"Did you feel better after your talk? Are things straightened out in your mind now?"

"Pretty much. Wade seems to think everything will be all right at home. I guess a lot of the things I was worrying about never happened. And when we called my dad, he said I don't have to go back to that school."

She looked out the window and saw Wade riding Ginny. He was sorting cow and calf pairs with Clem. "My brother has been looking for me since about four hours after I left Rosemount. For a week and two days."

"Your family must love you very much."

Leslie regarded this kind woman whose pale blue eyes were shining now. "They do. You were right, Ellie Mae, they've been worried.

"Ellie Mae, Wade is going to take me home, on Thursday. I'm sorry, I thought I could --"

"Leslie, don't give it another thought. I'm just happy that you and I found each other when we did, and I appreciate all the help you've given us. You should go home, dear. It's where you belong."

"I'll be able to go to school. I've only missed about a week."

"I'm glad."

Leslie set the table for five. It seemed so strange to have Wade there. During the meal Buck and Wade compared ranching in Oregon and Washington, their voices soothing Leslie's soul.

After the meal the men trooped out to finish the day's work and Leslie remained inside to help Ellie Mae. Later, Buck, Clem and Wade returned to the house. They gathered in the living room for coffee. Ellie Mae and Leslie joined them. Leslie sat on the floor by Wade's chair.

Wade noticed the piano and nudged Leslie. "Have you played the piano since you've been here?"

"Yes, I did, last night." She looked over to Ellie Mae. "When you and Buck went to see his sister."

Ellie Mae perked up. "Will you play for us now? I'd love to hear something come out of that old piano. Nobody plays it anymore."

"Don't you play, Ellie Mae?"

"Not for years and I never was any good. Sara took music lessons, but she never plays now. Please play for us, Leslie."

Leslie stepped up to the piano and sat on the old adjustable wooden stool. She played a few chords, then began with Chopin's "Polonaise," feeling these people would enjoy something lively and spirited. Once she had told Mr. Baxter she liked to play "Polonaise" because she was "all over the keyboard" and he laughed.

She finished with a flourish and glanced at Wade. He was sitting forward in his chair, elbows braced on knees, intently watching her.

At the final note Buck said, "Damn, girl, you should be on a concert stage."

Wade nodded. "That's right."

"Right after she finishes school," Clem put in.

Leslie, surprised at Wade's comment, said, "You've always thought my playing was some kind of hobby."

"I was wrong about that."

Ellie Mae looked at Leslie with pride as if the girl were her personal discovery. "Leslie, you play beautifully. Play something else, please."

Leslie chose another of her favorites. "This is by an American composer, John Stewart, called 'The Gathering'." The piece started out simply and gathered momentum in complexity and volume as it went along. High notes sprinkled down like a soft spring rain, then low notes rumbled with a waiting storm. Her fingers leapt over the intricately layered composition. This was one of the pieces which she had concentrated on when trying to get to sleep this past week. One part had always eluded her, but once at the piano, it came easily. When she finished, the room reverberated with the final notes.

"Leslie, that was lovely," Ellie Mae beamed at her, then at the rest of them.

Clem rubbed his old-leather hands together. "Can you play 'Shenandoah'?"

"I'm sorry, Clem, I don't know that one. Most of my training has been classical, but I keep trying to get my teacher to work with me on other kinds of music, too. Here's one exception to classical that I've worked on."

She went into a lively rendition of Joplin's "The Entertainer." Heads nodded and toes tapped in time to the music. The few notes she missed were barely noticeable.

Leslie could have gone on for much longer, but didn't want to overdo it. Three pieces were enough. After playing the final number she lowered the key cover.

"My, that was wonderful."

Leslie smiled shyly. "Thank you." This was such a different role than she had been playing. Now she felt more like a guest, rather than a "hired hand."

Buck stood and rotated his big shoulders. "Well, if we're going to get an early start tomorrow, we'd better turn in. Ellie, have you told Wade where he can sleep?"

"Oh, I'll just sleep in the back of my truck."

Ellie Mae stiffened. "You'll do no such thing. There's an empty bedroom right next to Leslie's. She can show you."

Upstairs, as Leslie showed Wade where he would sleep, he turned and looked deep into her eyes. "I'm so glad you're all right."

"Now that you're here, I'm feeling more like myself."

"But you could have ended it any time. Why didn't you?"

"I just couldn't see how it would work out."

"Can you now?"

"I think so. I guess it depends on how it goes with Dad, but I think so."

## *THIRTY*

The day's work began in morning's coolness, just before full light.

Buck faced his waiting crew--seven of them this morning. "How about a couple of you going over with a pickup and getting Tony? He can tally from the back of a truck. It's killing him, missing out."

Clem and Wade tossed a couple bales of hay into a truck and drove to the mobile to get the foreman. They lifted him into the bed of the truck and onto the hay bales, sliding a wooden box under the man's heavy leg cast.

*~*

Clem prodded the calves down the alley and into the chute. Tom Strand worked the V-gate, holding the calf's head in its grip, then compacted the sides of the chute to hold the calf fast while it received treatment.

As planned, Leslie vaccinated the late spring calves. Buck had arranged the serum for her and set it up on a makeshift table in the branding pen. Buck watched the first time

Leslie slipped the needle under the loose skin on the calf's shoulder. Satisfied, he turned to his own work.

As Tom punched the numbered identification tag on the calf's ear, he called out the number to Tony. He then seared the calf's horn nubs with an iron to prevent the horns from growing. Wade branded. If the calf was a bull they turned the chute on its side so that Buck could castrate. "Brain surgery," he called it.

After working the calves they allowed the bawling, frightened youngsters to return to their mothers. Later the pairs would be taken to the lower winter pastures.

Together they kept Tony busy, registering new calves and noting the vaccines each received. Later, he kept tallies on heifers to be shipped, heifers they would keep, counts of dry cows and steers going to market.

After a large noon meal, they returned to sorting and driving cattle to winter pastures. For Leslie, the day flew by.

They worked late into the evening. Weary heads nodded as they gathered for final cups of coffee after supper.

*~*

Right after breakfast the next morning, Wade and Leslie stood in the yard to say their good-byes.

"Oh, oh, here come the waterworks," Buck said when he saw Ellie Mae's tears, then Leslie's.

Buck extended his hand to Wade. "Sure appreciate your help."

"Glad to do it. Thanks for being so good to Leslie."

"Oh, Leslie, I owe you something." Buck reached into his shirt pocket for an envelope. "Here's your pay for the days you worked."

287

Leslie face colored in embarrassment. They had done much more for her than she for them. But she had done a good job and felt pride in that.

"By the way," he turned to Wade, "your sister earned every penny of this." He placed the envelope in her hand. "You ever come back our way, I'll hire you in a minute."

"Thank you," she said, her voice barely audible.

Ellie Mae stepped forward and took Leslie in her arms. "Please let us hear from you. You have our address, now, so write or call, won't you?"

"I will. I want to keep in touch."

As they drove out Leslie turned to watch the diminishing figures. "They were so nice to me."

"Yes, they were. But it sounds to me like you were able to help them out, too."

Leslie took a deep, ragged breath. "I never worked so hard in my life."

Wade looked affectionately at his little sister. "I'm proud of you, Les. I could tell you made a good impression."

She turned to look for them once more, but they were out of sight.

As the truck sped down the highway, Leslie remained quiet, pensive. Dutch's head rested in her lap and she rubbed the dog's soft ears.

Wade watched his sister. He realized her need to get caught up and then to face her uncertain future. She seemed remote, almost sad.

She noticed the yellow tablet on the dash. Absently, she reached for it.

Wade grinned. "Know who gave me that tablet?"
"Who?"

"Mrs. Holmes. I went to Rosemount first thing. She and I went to the bus depot together. Later, she gave me that so I could keep track of things. She's a nice lady."

Leslie studied her brother, then sighed. "I guess she probably is." She glanced at the first page, then reached for the map and followed Wade's scrawl with the map.

"Pilot Rock? Ukiah? I didn't go to those places."

Wade smiled ruefully. "I wish I'd known that."

Leslie again regarded him for a long moment, then returned to the tablet. "Oh, there. La Grande. You got on track again."

Wade shook his head. This must seem strange to her, piecing it all together. "Where did you go after La Grande?"

"To the Wallowas. I got off the beaten path for awhile there. It took me a couple of days to sort things out and decide how to go about getting a job...." Her voice faded and she stared out the window.

"Wade, do you think Dad will marry Lilith?"

"I think you've built this up to more than it is. But I do think it'd be good for Dad to have someone. Before you know it, you'll be going off to college and have a life of your own. I'd like to see Dad marry again, not be alone. But I don't know if it will be with Lilith."

"Well, they seemed serious to me. I can't stand the thought of sharing my room with Roxanne though."

"What makes you think you'd have to?"

"What other room is there?"

"Who knows? Maybe the room across the hall will be available."

"Your room? Why? Where are you going?" Concern filled her voice.

"Les, it's about time I had a place of my own."

"Just you? All alone?"

"Well...."

"Teresa! You're going to marry Teresa! Where will you live?"

"Slow down, now. I haven't even asked her."

"Oh, she'll say yes. She'd be crazy not to."

"I wish I could be so sure."

"Where will you live?"

"We'll probably build a house on the ranch, on the other side of the old orchard."

Relief flooded through her. "Wade, that's great."

"Les, things have a way of working out. Don't borrow trouble before it happens."

Leslie nodded. "Actually, I don't mind Lilith. She's okay. And maybe I could get used to Roxanne, especially if I didn't have to share my room with her. Maybe she just feels weird in Chewack, out of place. I know how that feels. Now."

Wade nodded. "I'd like to know Dad wasn't going to be lonely when we're gone. Wouldn't you?"

Leslie nodded. "It'll seem strange, though, having other people around." She thought of something else with a start. "Maureen! What about Maureen?"

"Sis, Dad isn't going to turn his back on Maureen after all she's done for us. Lilith has a career. She won't have time to do all that Maureen does around there. This is what I mean. Don't borrow..."

"...trouble before it happens. Okay."

She directed her attention back to Wade's tablet. "Baker City. That's where I bought my car." Then she frowned. "Who's handwriting is this?"

Wade glanced at the tablet. "Oh, I met up with a guy in Baker City."

"A guy? A hitchhiker?"

"Sort of. He had some time and joined me for a couple of days."

They were traveling fast, heading west across the flat, desert country on Highway Twenty. Traffic was light; miles stretched by before they saw another car or, more likely, a rancher's pick-up.

Leslie turned the page of the yellow tablet. Her eyes caught a break in the systematic recording of places with the accompanying comments.

"'Cyrus Daniels'! Cyrus! That's your passenger? This is his handwriting?" She pointed to the tablet where Cyrus had written his name, address and telephone number.

"Yep."

"Well...how did that happen?"

Wade told her of his encounter with Cyrus and how they had joined forces. "He was concerned about you."

Leslie sighed deeply. "He's a nice guy. He helped me a lot."

"I just remembered--we need to call him. I promised him that one of us would call as soon as I found you."

Wade could see Leslie thinking about that, about talking to Cyrus. She traced her finger along his signature.

At Bend they turned north on Ninety-seven. Miles churned by. Finally, Wade spoke again. "Let's stop for lunch and gas up in Goldendale. It'd feel good to stretch our legs."

Leslie agreed but not very enthusiastically. "Okay."

They crossed over to Washington at Biggs, then climbed the long hill into Goldendale. "We'll go to a place where Dad and I have eaten, Washburn's."

"You've eaten here? When?"

"Oh, a couple of years ago. Dad and I came over here to buy that Red Angus bull."

They parked in the street close to the plain, stucco building. Heat shimmered off the black top at the hottest time of the day.

Wade let the dog out, gave her some water and commanded her to stay in the shade of the truck.

Wade motioned Leslie to choose their table and they sat opposite one another. He laid his hat beside him on the bench seat. Leslie noticed anew his two-toned forehead, the smooth upper light part where his hat protected the skin from sun and wind, the lower part tanned and creased with weather. They were quiet while they waited for their meal.

Their burgers and fries came in plastic baskets and they began to eat, Wade with his usual gusto, Leslie slower, obviously contemplating something other than her lunch.

Wade regarded her. *Something's wrong. She's not herself. Maybe she's getting cold feet. Her eyes look so dull.* "What is it, sis?"

She shrugged.

"What?"

"I don't know. I feel...like I've made such a mess of things. I don't know if Dad will ever be able to forgive me, or trust me again. And I don't know how it will be at school. Will the kids think I'm weird?" She put her half-finished hamburger down. "I'm afraid my life will never be normal again."

Wade reached over to help himself to her neglected French fries.

He wiped his hand on the paper napkin and sat back. "I can tell you for a fact that Dad forgives you. Like I said, he takes part of the blame for this, too. When you talk to him, Les, level with him. Tell him just what you've told me, about Lilith and Roxanne."

"Oh, Wade, I can't talk about that."

"Yes, you can. You need to bring it out in the open. That's the only way to get to the bottom of this thing. For your sake, and for Dad's. Okay?"

She sighed. "Okay."

Suddenly Wade leaned forward and hit the table with the edge of his big fist. "By God, Les, you did it!"

She jumped. "What?"

"You did it! I'm sorry you felt you had to run--it's been hard on everybody--but you did what you felt you had to do. The point is, Les, you made it.

"You struck out, all alone, and found your way. You even stayed in the wilderness, all alone. Not many people could do that, adult or kid. You didn't have to do like a lot of kids do, sell their bodies to survive. You used your skills and knowledge and found a real job, real work."

"But look how long it took me. I was down to about eight dollars and a hundred pounds. I was so skinny. I think Ellie Mae just felt sorry for me."

"No way, Les. You found yourself somebody that could use help and you filled the bill. Looking for work for a week isn't that long, though it must have seemed like it to you. But look how you worked. Both Ellie Mae and Buck told me what a hard worker you are. They weren't giving you charity, Les. Room and board is payment too, you know, and you got cash besides."

"But my car, I couldn't even hang on to a car. I just let those creeps take advantage of me!"

"Okay, you ran into some rotten people and had some bad luck. You think you're the only one who's had a car stolen? Next time you'll know to listen to your gut and follow your hunches. Everyone has to learn that."

"Wade, I was scared all the time."

"Of course you were scared. But look at you, Les, you survived. You didn't call it quits when things got tough--you found more strength and just kept going."

He looked straight into her eyes. "I'm proud of you, Leslie. Not many people could do what you've done. You're tough and you're a survivor. I'm proud you're my sister."

Her face lit up. The sparkle returned to her eyes. Then a slight frown gathered again. "What will I say to the kids at school?"

"Just keep it simple. Say you didn't like the school, so you took off and got a job on a ranch in Oregon." He smiled. "They'll be jealous as hell."

Leslie laughed.

"Les, it won't come together all at once, but you'll get there. Be patient. You've had an experience not many people have, ever. It's caused a lot of pain and more worry than I ever care to go through again but you reacted to events as you saw them and what's more, you had the strength to survive it. It's enough, Les, knowing that."

Leslie sat back. Her shoulders relaxed. She looked out the window, back to her brother, and then out the window again. "Let's go home."

## END

# *About The Author*

Mary E. Trimble, a Northwest writer, draws on personal experience including purser and ship's diver aboard the tall ship Explorer; Peace Corps in West Africa; sailing 13,000 miles throughout the South Pacific; extensive overland RV trips and with her involvement locally and nationally with the American Red Cross. Her 350-plus articles have appeared in national and local publications. Her first novel, Rosemount, a young adult contemporary western, has received high acclaim. Rosemount's sequel, McClellan's Bluff, will be released in coming months.

Made in the USA
Charleston, SC
17 August 2010